Elusive Identities

ELUSIVE IDENTITIES

The Cowboy Justice Association:
Serials and Stalkers
Book One

BY OLIVIA JAYMES

www.OliviaJaymes.com

CHAPTER ONE

C HRIS MARKS EASED into one of the leather chairs that surrounded the conference room table, setting his coffee in front of him along with the paper and pen he'd brought to take notes. It was his first day at a new job. He was nervous; he would readily admit to that, although it might not be the manliest of confessions. He wasn't sweating through his brand-new shirt nervous, but his heart was beating faster than normal and the bagel he'd eaten on the way to the office wasn't sitting well in his stomach.

He wanted to do well. He wanted to impress. After all, he had a hell of a lot to live up to. His father, Sheriff Tanner Marks of Springwood, Montana was practically a legend. Even at the height of his father's alcohol issues, he'd been one of the best lawmen around. Now that Tanner Marks was sober – and had been for many years – he might just be the best. Period.

Running a close second and third to his dad were the two men sitting at the head of the table – Logan Wright and Reed Mitchell. They were former small town sheriffs themselves but now worked for Jason Anderson's law enforcement consulting

1

firm. So many small towns didn't have the manpower or experience to deal with crimes such as stalking and serial killers. That's where this group came in. A town could hire them to help with a case and get it solved without having to hire permanent staff that wanted things like medical insurance and vacation days.

Jason's firm had recently moved into a new office just outside of Seattle and the smell of fresh paint and sawdust still permeated the air. The table and chairs were obviously brandnew and the carpet didn't have any coffee or mud stains. It probably wouldn't stay that way for long, however.

In addition to himself, Reed, and Logan there were two other men sitting at the table. Chris knew a little bit about each of them from his conversations with Reed. One was named Luke Brewster and the other Ryan Beck but he didn't know which was which. Both men looked about his age and they didn't look nervous at all.

The door to the conference room swung open and another man strode in, slapping his coffee cup on the table and sitting across from Chris.

Christ on a unicycle. Knox Owens.

Knox had taken the sheriff's job when Jared Monroe had moved on to work with Logan and Jason. Chris had been a deputy for Knox for about a year and they'd butted heads constantly until the day Chris walked out. He didn't get time to glower at his former boss, however, because Logan began to speak.

"Looks like everyone is here so we're going to get started. As you were informed in the interview process this is a tryout, so to speak. There are four of you and two positions to be filled. We're planning to take the two best performers, so this is a sort of competition. But...we're looking for people that can work together and mesh into a team. There are no lone wolves here and we're not looking to hire any."

Work with Knox? Fuck no.

His expression must have told the story because Reed was staring directly at Chris, his brows raised in question. Shit.

Logan was still speaking and Chris had missed some of it. "Each one of you is going to receive a cold case to work on but you'll also be helping the other team members with theirs. While we hope that some of these cases can be closed that's not going to be the final criteria. We want to see the steps you take, what your ideas are, and how you work together and have each other's backs. Any questions?"

Everyone was quiet.

"Great. Chris, you're meeting with me in my office. Knox, you're with Reed. Brew, you're with Jason, and Ryan, you're with Jared. Good luck."

Chris was going to need all the luck he could get. This was a huge opportunity and he didn't want to screw it up.

He wouldn't let Knox Owens get to him. He'd just act like the guy didn't exist.

THE COLD CASE that had been chosen for Chris was a murder from thirty years ago. The victim – a female – had never been identified. Her hands had been removed and by the time they'd found the body it had been badly decomposed.

Chris flipped through the grisly photos from the crime scene. "They were never able to identify her? Not even a possible list of missing persons?"

Logan shook his head, sitting back in his leather chair. "It was 1989 and they didn't have the tools that we have now. Without fingerprints all they could do was ask the public for help so they set up a hotline. They got some leads but nothing panned out. The state, local, and federal databases weren't linked together the way they are now, either. I'm hoping that if we can't find her killer that we can at least find her identity and bring some peace to a family out there."

"There's not much to go on here." Chris perused the autopsy report. "Age eighteen to forty. Cause of death is believed to be blunt force trauma to the skull. Body found in a scrub of trees by the highway about thirty miles south of Seattle."

"Turn to the last page," Logan suggested. "A new development."

A rendering of a young woman with long dark hair. Petite features. Full lips. Big eyes. Pretty.

"It's a forensic reconstruction," Logan explained. "Technology has come a long way since 1989 and I hope we can use some of it to finally give this woman a name."

"This is what they think she looked like?"

In his classes, Chris had seen how the facial reconstruction was put together. It took an expert to do work like this.

"Yes, right down to what she was wearing that day. Her clothes were found at the dump site."

If her identity could be found, Chris would do whatever he could to make that happen. Logan was right, somewhere out there a family was in limbo and grieving. They needed closure.

He couldn't wait to get going.

"Where do you want me to start?"

Logan chuckled and grinned. "That's not for me to say, Chris. That's your call."

"That's very…trusting."

"We're hoping that you have what it takes to be a part of this elite team. Of course, worst case scenario, you don't make it and you end up working the regular cases. But frankly, Chris, If I thought you couldn't do this, you wouldn't be here."

Because of what I've accomplished or because of my dad?

Chris didn't ask the question out loud. He wasn't too damn sure he wanted the answer.

"I have a few ideas about the case," he said instead. He was filled with excitement and adrenaline. This was his chance to make a difference and show what he was capable of. "I'll get right on it."

Logan stood so Chris did as well. "I had a feeling you'd say that."

Chris was already itching to start doing research on missing persons that matched this new description. The firm had a state of the art computer system and he couldn't wait to conquer it.

"You won't regret giving me this chance."

"I know that." Logan placed his hand on the doorknob and then paused. "I saw something pass between you and Owens. I know you worked together for a little while… Is this going to be a problem? Because I need you two to be able to work together. He's your wingman for want of a better term and you're his. He's getting his case particulars right now and I want you to help each other."

Working with Knox was the last thing Chris wanted to do. He didn't trust the other man to have his back. That was the honest truth. But even more true was that he wanted this job and if he had to team up with the devil himself Chris would make it work.

"It will be fine," he assured Logan. "We have history but I can keep it professional."

Logan slapped him on the back and grinned. "Excellent. Let me know if you need anything. Good luck and welcome to the team."

Chris wasn't going to let them – or himself – down.

CHRIS STARED AT the rendering of the victim's face again, taking in every detail. He was amazed yet again how far they'd come in forensic technology to be able to do this. He wanted to put a name to this face and give her family some peace. But a thirty-year-old murder case wasn't going to be easy.

Hazy memories. Deceased witnesses. Time changed all and nothing would be the same. It was going to be the challenge of his career and one that he relished taking on.

"What are you looking at?" Annie plopped down on the couch next to her father and peered over his shoulder. "Who is that?"

Carefully slipping the crime scene photos behind the boring police reports so his young daughter wouldn't see them, Chris tapped the computer drawing. "It's a case I'm working on. I told you about my new job."

The job that would keep him close to Annie. No. Wait. Annalise. She didn't want to be called Annie anymore. She was now a sophisticated nine years old. Nine going on twenty-nine. Heaven help him. She was also far too intelligent for her own good. Sometimes it was like talking to another adult. He was going to have his hands full in a few years.

Who was he kidding? He had his hands full now.

"Do you miss home?"

"Do you?" he countered. "You seem to like your new school."

Stacey had moved herself and Annie here two years ago after the divorce so she could marry her high school sweetheart Ben. They'd been reunited and were madly in love.

Ben seemed like a pretty decent guy. Hardworking and he clearly adored Stacey and Annie. The move had meant that Chris didn't see his daughter nearly enough, although he could have shown up at Ben and Stacey's front door unplanned and unannounced and they would have welcomed him inside and let him take Annie for the weekend. He and Stacey had worked hard to make their divorce friendly and amicable if only for the sake of their child.

"I like it but I miss Grandpa and Maddie. Grandma, too."

Ah yes, Chris's strained relationship with his own mother. She'd settled down and married a nice widower a few years ago but he'd never regained that closeness with her. It was almost as if she preferred it when he was drunk.

"They miss you, pumpkin. We'll go visit them in the summer."

"That's a long way away," Annie complained, her mouth a perfect "O" as she was overtaken by a gigantic yawn. "Can we call them?"

"Yes, but not tonight. You need to get some sleep. You have dance class in the morning."

That was one of the more annoying things Stacey had done. She'd loaded up Annie with a bunch of extracurricular activities so the kid barely had any free time.

Annie twisted Chris's wrist so she could look at his watch. "Just fifteen more minutes?"

What was it about kids and bedtime? Chris would love to go to bed early and maybe even be forced to nap. That sounded like nirvana.

"You can have two. To brush your teeth."

Rolling her eyes, Annie hopped off the couch but paused, her brows pinching together. "What happened to her?"

"Who?"

She pointed to the picture of the victim. "Her. What happened to her?"

Annie didn't need the grisly details. She'd have nightmares for the rest of her life. As it was, Chris was concerned about the effect his job might have on his daughter.

So he tiptoed around the particulars. Annie was aware that bad things happened in this world. He was always harping about safety.

"We haven't been able to find out who she is for thirty years. I'm going to give it a try."

He should have known she'd catch his omission.

"She was killed?"

"Yes," he replied reluctantly, and only because Annie really already knew the answer. "I'd love to give her family some peace."

Her expression eased into a smile. "You'll do it."

His chest didn't seem large enough for his heart. What had he done to deserve such confidence? He couldn't think of one thing.

"Your belief in me is strong. What makes you think I can do it?"

"Because you won't give up until you do."

Annie was absolutely right.

CHAPTER TWO

ELLA SHRUGGED INTO her trench coat and slung her purse over her shoulder. It had been a damn long day and she was looking forward to relaxing on her couch with some takeout and the remote control.

"Night, Ella," Don the evening producer called. "Too bad about today. It came out okay though, so don't worry about it."

Mumbling under her breath about the unfairness of the universe, Ella mustered a smile for Don. It wasn't his fault that her day had gone to hell in a hand basket. She'd been assigned to cover a bridal show at the local mall. Just one in a long line of boring as shit assignments. It should have been a no brainer – film a little, interview a gushing bride, talk to a few vendors.

At least that's what her boss Galen Winters had expected.

Ella had wanted the story to go in a different direction. She wanted to talk about the commercialization of the wedding industry and to a few brides who were going into debt over their special day. When she'd come back with the footage, Galen had hit the ceiling, telling her that she'd been assigned to do a local human interest piece, not an expose. Then he'd personally edited the shit out of the interviews until it was what he'd wanted. All her excellent reporting had been deleted. She was pretty sure that her boss hated her guts.

"Thank you. It could have been a lot better," she grumbled, palming the keys to her car. "I think Galen hates me."

Galen had been hired about a year ago from another station in Miami and since then she hadn't had a decent assignment.

Don shook his head. "Galen's an old school reporter and a stickler for what he wants, and he's usually right. He's one of the best station managers in this market. We were lucky to get him. I heard he used to live here and wanted to move back."

The producer was exaggerating. They worked at a small twenty-four-hour cable news station that served a good chunk of Washington State. They were what people watched when they wanted to know the traffic or the weather, and as Galen had pointed out, they didn't care about the commercialization of the wedding industry. They just wanted to know how long their commute was going to take.

"I'm sure he is," Ella sighed. "I was just hoping for an assignment that had more meat to it. Something interesting that sparks conversation. Not big white wedding dresses and doves."

"Everyone has to pay their dues in this business," Don reminded her with a gentle smile. "You'll get your shot."

By that time I'll be too old to care.

"Thank you, Don. I don't suppose you'd show the original story at eleven?" she asked with hope in her tone. It was worth a shot.

She'd done the story for the daytime audience but that was for a different producer. Don had the authority to run anything he wanted to at night when Galen gave him almost free rein.

Grimacing, Don rubbed his stubbly chin. "About that, I may have to cut fifteen seconds from it. I'm running a little long."

And he couldn't cut headlines, weather, or sports. Fluff was the first to get cut.

"I understand. It's okay. Goodnight, Don."

"Night. Drive careful. There's a lot of crazies out there."

Don said that to everyone but then he'd been in this business for over thirty years so he would know.

"I will."

It didn't take long for Ella to drive home. Up until about three months ago, she'd had two roommates but then her parents had told her about a terrific opportunity house sitting for a professor friend of theirs on sabbatical in China for a year. Now she lived in a large loft apartment in a safe part of the city. It was fantastic not to have to share a bathroom vanity with two other females.

She pushed the front door open and flipped on a few lights, dumping her purse and keys on the kitchen island before slipping off her jacket and hanging it over a barstool. As usual in Seattle, it had been misting rain outside but the weatherman at her station was predicting sun tomorrow. Too bad he was usually wrong.

Mercutio, a half-tabby half-something else, jumped up on the counter purring loudly for his welcome home pet. He belonged to the owner of the home but he had luckily taken a liking to Ella. The first few days had been a little rocky as he'd hid under the bed until his appetite had finally forced him out.

"You should have been a dog," Ella laughed, stroking the cat's silky fur. "Or is this just about dinner?"

At the *dinner* word, Merc purred even more loudly and Ella quickly filled his dish with dry food and a spoonful of canned. The feline was rather persnickety about its food and he liked it with the wet on the side, not mixed in.

"Now that I've fed you, what am I going to have?"

Having never been much of a cook, Ella had a wide variety of takeout menus by the phone. She perused the offerings while Merc daintily ate his dinner, and finally settled on Chinese. She loved the honey chicken. With forty minutes before it would arrive, she had plenty of time for a long, hot shower.

The master bedroom had huge windows that overlooked the city, an amazing view that never ceased to catch her attention, especially at night. Maybe it was the journalist inside of her that wondered what was going on behind those lighted windows. Were the inhabitants happy? Sad? Angry? What were they hiding? She'd learned as a reporter that people had secrets. Painful and dangerous ones to go along with the simple and innocuous. Secrets ate away like termites in the darkness. Eventually the structure of a human's life was weakened and it would all collapse on itself. Sadly, she'd seen it happen too many times.

Mom would say that I'm nosy.

Mom would be right.

Shedding her clothes on the way to the ensuite bathroom, she showered and pulled on a pair of ratty sweats and sweatshirt, piling her hair on top of her head to get it out of the way. The humidity always made her hair curl and most of the time she didn't care but she was already annoyed tonight.

She liked the news station, but perhaps she might do better to look for another job? A different station might give her more responsibility.

Right. Because journalism is flourishing and jobs grow on trees. Not.

A knock on the door announced her dinner and she greeted the familiar delivery guy, making sure to give him a generous tip. It was kind of embarrassing that he knew her by her first name and even asked about her job and the cat. When she was dating she often tried to cook but it never turned out well. Her last relationship had been over a year ago. Mark had been frustrated with all the hours she worked and he'd also been vocal that she wasn't more...domestic. She didn't like to cook or clean and that was a major issue for him. They'd parted less than amicably. After that she'd decided to concentrate on her career for awhile.

It meant some long lonely nights but she consoled herself with the fact that it was better to be alone than with the wrong person.

"At least that's what I'd say if anyone asked me," Ella said to Merc when he jumped up on the couch next to her. She was lounging and watching television, an activity that she did far too often these days. She needed to get her ass in gear and go to the gym, get outside and do something instead of sitting like a bump on a log. "I'm just taking a breather from dating. I'll get back into it before long. I'm just fine the way I am. Right, Merc?"

The cat meowed loudly as if to agree, rubbing his head against her shoulder. She didn't need anything more than this. Great takeout, a borrowed cat, and comfy clothes. Life was good and peaceful.

★   ★   ★

CHRIS HAD A bad habit of falling asleep on the couch in front of the television. He had a perfectly decent bed in the other room but for some reason he fell asleep more quickly out here in the living room. Perhaps because there were voices and it gave the illusion that he wasn't alone? Or maybe because he was simply too fucking tired most nights to get his ass up off the couch and go to bed. Either way he'd done it again tonight.

Stretching and yawning, he swung his legs onto the floor so he could crawl into the bedroom and spend what was left of the night in bed. He reached for the remote to turn off the television but his hand froze in midair. There on the news was a pretty young reporter with big eyes and long dark hair.

The spitting image of the forensic rendering he'd studied earlier tonight.

Shaking his head a few times and blinking back the fatigue, he rubbed his eyes but the woman on the television didn't disappear. She was standing there speaking into a microphone but she couldn't have anything to do with his victim.

His sluggish brain didn't do math well but even he couldn't mess this simple calculation up. The reporter couldn't be over thirty – if that – and his victim had been gone that long. No, this was simply a coincidence, possibly fueled by his exhaustion.

He clicked the off button and the television went dark, along with the lovely reporter. He wanted so much to find his Jane Doe that he was now superimposing her face onto other women.

That was surely a sign that he wasn't getting enough sleep. Time to go to bed.

CHAPTER THREE

THE NEXT MORNING – after getting a decent amount of sleep – Chris took Annie to her dance lessons, trying to put his cold case out of his mind. Since he didn't get to spend as much time with his daughter as he liked, he wanted to enjoy when he was, and that didn't include brooding about work.

Or reporters, either. This morning he'd decided that he'd been imagining things. But just in case, he'd check out the television station's website later on when he had the time.

"I get to wear a purple sparkly outfit," Annie gushed right after class. Stacey and Ben were at the dance studio to pick her up as she was attending a birthday party in the afternoon. There was going to be a bouncy castle and lots of cake. Annie had been talking about it all morning. "Purple is my favorite color."

Last month it had been green but Chris appreciated that Annie didn't feel the need to be held to only one favorite. Everyone should have as many as they wanted.

"That's wonderful, sweetheart," Stacey said, giving their daughter a hug. "Why don't you get your water bottle from Ben, okay? I need to talk to your dad."

Shit. This couldn't be good. The last time Stacey had wanted to speak to him privately she'd told him she was moving and getting married.

Annie skipped off happily, leaving Chris with his ex-wife. More and more this was becoming awkward as hell. Because he hadn't remarried, Stacey had taken to giving him pitying looks and heaped less than subtle hints about getting out more and meeting people.

Yes, they had that weird of a divorce. They didn't hate each other. They'd simply married far too young. His drinking and subsequent sobriety hadn't been the issue that had eventually broken them up. They'd grown apart until they were almost strangers. No more, no less. Chris would have stuck it out and tried to repair the relationship but by then Stacey had reconnected with her old boyfriend online. They'd ended things as friendly as possible for Annie. So far, they'd done an okay job.

He checked his watch, hoping she'd take the hint. "I have to meet Knox at a crime scene. Will this take long?"

Stacey sighed and glanced over her shoulder to where Annie was speaking animatedly to her stepfather.

"It won't take long but it is important. Why are you working on a Saturday, anyway?"

"Cops work seven days a week. You should know that."

Stacey hadn't been a fan of the crazy hours demanded of an officer. She'd taken after his mother like that.

"You're not a cop anymore."

"You're right. I'm a law enforcement consultant so I really

can't sit around. I have a case that I need to work on."

He'd made it sound urgent even though his victim had been waiting thirty years. He didn't want her to wait a moment more than necessary.

"Then I'll make this quick." She hesitated, her fingers rubbing her chin. A sure sign that she was nervous. "I'm not sure how to tell you this."

"Jesus, are you moving again? I'll fight it this time, Stacey."

He hadn't raised a fuss the last time because she'd promised him visitation whenever he'd wanted it and she'd stuck to that. But he'd just taken this new job to be closer to his daughter and he wasn't going to be jerked around about it.

She quickly shook her head. "No. No, not at all."

"Then spit it out."

She'd always done things in her own time.

Another sigh. "I didn't want you to hear it from Annalise so I need to tell you now. I'm pregnant."

He blinked a few times, his brain playing the words over in his head until he was sure there was no mistake in his comprehension. Stacey was pregnant.

"That's great," he finally said, the shock wearing off. He shouldn't have been surprised. Stacey had always wanted more children. "I'm really happy for you. Congratulations to you both."

"Thank you." She was eyeing him up and down like he was a live grenade. "Are you sure you're okay with this?"

Her question made him laugh. "Would it matter if I wasn't?

I'm okay with it. Seriously. I'm happy for you."

"It's just that you have no one—"

"I'm happy," he cut in. "For real. I'm concentrating on my career right now. I don't have time for a relationship. Maybe when I get settled in."

"You wouldn't have trouble finding someone. You're not bad to look at and all."

"Thank you. I think. My goal in life has always been to be not too hideous."

She rolled her eyes just like Annie did. "You're not hideous and you know it. The fact is you are far too good-looking. I just didn't want your ego to get too big."

"Because I'm an arrogant SOB?"

"Yes."

She'd know.

He nodded toward Annie. "Has she heard the good news?"

"We're going to tell her tonight. We had a scan yesterday and everything looks good."

"She'll be happy. I think she'd like a little brother or sister."

Stacey smiled and patted her stomach. "She'll have to wait six more months but I agree. She'll be a terrific big sister."

Annie joined them, her pink backpack slung over her shoulder. "Mom, can we have pizza tonight?"

"We sure can," Stacey agreed. "Lots of extra cheese."

Ben nodded and Chris nodded back. That was about the extent of their relationship and it seemed to work fine so far. He would have congratulated him and shaken his hand but Annie hadn't heard the news yet.

Chris knelt down and gave her a hug. She was growing so fast. "I'll see you on Tuesday. Be good for your mom. Love you, baby girl."

Annie hugged him back and dropped a peck on his cheek. "Love you, Dad. Good luck on your new job."

He was going to need it. Working with Knox Owens was going to be a real pain in the ass.

★　★　★

"DO YOU HAVE the weekend off?" Dana Scott asked. Ella had stopped in to say hello to her parents and had ended up staying for lunch. "We should go shopping today. I've been needing a new handbag and we haven't spent a Saturday together in forever."

Ella had to smother a chuckle at her mother's declaration. Dana Scott had a closet full of purses, shoes, and clothes. She didn't need to buy anything else for the rest of her life. She had garments and accessories for every occasion and then some.

As for how long it had been since they'd hung out together, it hadn't quite been forever but it had been too long. As an only child, Ella was close to her parents and liked spending time with them.

"You just want to try that new little bistro, Mom. Admit it."

"I wouldn't mind but what we really need to do is get you some new clothes. Those jeans have holes in them."

Ella grinned wickedly. "And I paid extra for that, I'll have you know. Besides, I love these jeans. They're my favorite."

Her mother sniffed but gave in gracefully.

"I saw your story last night. You did a good job."

Dana would have said that even if Ella had dropped her microphone, peed her pants, and cried in front of the camera.

"It was just a lousy story about a bridal show," Ella groused. "Nothing important. Tomorrow I'm covering a dog show."

"You love dogs."

"That doesn't mean I want to spend all day interviewing them. I need something important, a story that can change lives."

"Be careful what you wish for, sweetheart."

"You always say that," Ella sighed, taking a sip of iced tea. "But seriously, what bad thing can happen if I get a great story to cover?"

Her mother's brows rose almost to her hairline. "You could be killed or even just injured. That's been known to happen, you know. Journalists who find out the wrong things about the wrong person. I don't want you in any danger."

"The vast majority of reporters don't have death threats, Mom. They live completely quiet and uneventful lives reporting on the exciting events that happen to other people."

"When you say it like that, it makes me think that you picked the wrong profession," Dana laughed. "You could have gone to law school, for example."

"I could have but then I'd have to gouge my eyes out because I hated myself."

"Always so dramatic," Dana chided. "You've been like that since you were a toddler. Everything was an emergency, even getting a cup of juice."

"I don't think I'm that dramatic."

"I'm sure you don't but you are. You like being in the thick of things. No shame in that – it just makes a mother worry about her little girl."

"I haven't been a little girl in a long time. I'm thirty-two, remember?"

Dana pushed the small plate of cookies toward Ella. "How could I forget? I'm your mother. Now have a cookie. I baked them yesterday. The secret is a little orange peel in the batter."

Ella's mother had taken up baking after watching that British baking show. So far she'd perfected cakes and cookies but bread was still a work in progress.

Ella bit into the chocolate cookie. Her mother was right. They were delicious.

"These are amazing. I really should learn to cook something."

Someday.

"You could do it if you really wanted to. I think you like ordering takeout."

"It makes the cleanup easier."

It wasn't as great for her waistline.

Dana Scott went quiet, simply sipping her own iced tea. Ella was familiar with this tactic, though.

"Was there something you wanted to say, Mom?"

"Well…since you asked," Dana said with a growing smile. "Your father is getting an award from a local charity. They're going to have a party to honor him and a few others as well. I was hoping you'd be there."

"Of course I'll be there. Why wouldn't I be?"

Looking down at her hands, Dana chewed on her lower lip. "I know that your career is important to you and we want to support that, but the party is on a Saturday night. Your dad knows that you work most weekends–"

"I'll be there," Ella interrupted. "You couldn't keep me away. I'll just talk to Galen. He's not going to be sending me to any important breaking news anyway so he won't care."

The last part was muttered under her breath but Dana seemed to get the gist.

"That's wonderful, sweetheart. Your father is going to be so thrilled to see you there. He's always telling our friends about his daughter the reporter. He's going to want to show you off a little bit."

Dad had been doing that for as long as Ella could remember. It was embarrassing as hell but so sweet.

"Just send me the date and the dress code. I'm there," Ella vowed, biting into another cookie. These were really good. "There isn't anything I wouldn't do for you and Dad."

"We couldn't have picked a better daughter." Tears sparkled in Dana's eyes, making Ella's throat close up with emotion. "We're so proud of you and all that you've accomplished."

"I couldn't have picked better parents, either."

"Then we're both lucky," Dana laughed.

Yes, Ella was a lucky woman to have Dana and Will Scott as parents, and she'd never take that for granted.

CHAPTER FOUR

"**Y**OU'RE LATE."

Those were the two words that greeted Chris when he arrived at the dump site for his Jane Doe. Located on the side of a busy highway, it didn't appear to be the ideal spot to place a dead body.

Chris checked his watch and then glared at his former and new co-worker Knox Owens. "Two minutes. The traffic was bad. How long have you been here?"

"Two minutes."

"Next time I'll just interrupt my daughter in the middle of a sentence so you're not put out for even a second."

And fuck you and the horse you rode in on.

"How is Annie?"

What did Knox care? They were there to do a job and they were being forced to do it together.

"Fine," he replied shortly. "Growing up."

"How old is she now?"

"Nine."

Knox grinned and chuckled. "I remember when you brought

her into the station house. She was…maybe three? She wanted to take those old cats that lived in the back room home."

Chris had vivid memories of that day and he couldn't suppress a smile, either. Those two cats had shown up one day and Jared had taken them in, giving them a place to sleep out of the elements and feeding them top shelf cat food. The two felines had grown fat and lazy.

"Crockett and Tubbs. Jared gave them their names. Shit, I don't even think they were male. Annie threw a fit when I wouldn't let her take them home. I tried to explain that they belonged to all the guys that worked there but she wouldn't listen. She cried all the way home and until bedtime. She called me mean."

"If you're a decent father it won't be the last time she's pissed at you."

Still irritated, Chris shrugged. "This little trip down memory lane has been fun but we're here to work."

Knox's smile didn't waver. "Then let's get to it. Do you have the file?"

Chris almost bit out that he did, indeed, have the file because he wasn't a fucking idiot who would come to a crime scene without it…but then he remembered that they were being evaluated as to how well they could work as a team. He'd told Logan that this wouldn't be an issue and he didn't want that statement to be a lie.

Chris held up the file, far too thin for a murder investigation, and handed it to Knox. "I have it. This was the dump site, apparently. They don't think she was murdered here."

Knox paged through the file, his smile gone and replaced with an ever-deepening scowl.

"Fuck, they don't know shit about this murder. There's nothing here."

That was true. The file contained little information. A diagram of the dump site, a pathology report from the coroner, a police report from the investigator, photos, and a statement from the man who had found the body. The only thing new was the forensic rendering of the victim's face.

"We have the drawing to help now. I can try matching it to missing person reports."

Knox looked up from the file, his brows raised. "Reed and Logan must have it out for you. This is pathetic. What did you do to piss them off? Aren't they best friends with your old man? You'd think they would have given you an easy one. Everyone knows that you're a shoo-in for this elite team."

Stiffening at the mention of his dad, Chris's jaw tightened with anger. That little voice inside of him was saying to shut up but he'd never liked that inner voice. He was a real pain in the ass.

"Fuck you, Knox. Every one of us have the exact same chances. I'm not getting any special treatment."

This time. Throughout most of Chris's life though, he'd been treated differently than others because of who his father was. People had wanted to curry favor with the local lawman through his son. Sometimes it was overt but more often than not it was subtle, like when the principal would overlook some high school hijinks Chris had pulled.

"You're certainly not by the looks of this case," Knox jeered, handing the file back. "They must think you're Superman to be able to solve this. Your only clue is a drawing that may or may not be correct. It's only as good as the person who made it."

"Maybe they gave it to me because they knew you couldn't handle it."

Knox just laughed and shook his head. "You keep telling yourself that, Chris. In the meantime, I'll be solving my cold case and making this team."

Chris nodded toward the shoulder of the highway where Knox had parked his truck. "You're welcome to leave. I don't need you here."

"We're supposed to work together."

"I'm not the one being an asshole. I told Logan this wasn't a problem but I'd forgotten what a prick you can be."

Knox shook a finger under Chris's nose. "And you're an impetuous brat. You think you know better because your daddy's a legendary lawman. You don't know shit, little boy. You wouldn't even be here if it weren't for Sheriff Tanner Marks. You'd still be a junior deputy in some chicken shit little town in the middle of nowhere. Just admit it."

The whole time that Knox had been speaking Chris had felt the red tide of anger rise inside of him, making the back of his neck hot. His fists clenched at his sides and he desperately wanted to take a swing at the man standing in front of him.

He wasn't going to do that.

Because if he did, he wouldn't get the job that he wanted so much. He also wouldn't be proving anything other than that he couldn't control himself, which was what Knox was hoping.

Chris had learned quite a bit since getting sober and one of the most important things was how to fucking keep himself out of trouble. He'd found it far too often when he was younger and hell of a lot more stupid.

The silence had stretched on between them and eventually Chris turned on his heel and walked halfway up the hill to scan the highway.

"He would be seen from here," Chris said, keeping his voice even. He was going to act as if Knox hadn't said anything. "So why pick this place to dump Jane Doe? Does it have any significance? Was it just convenience?"

At first, Chris didn't think Knox was going to acknowledge that he'd spoken but then the other man walked closer, pointing a finger at the overpass. "You should check and see how much of this was here thirty years ago. I think a lot of this construction is new. Did you check out the businesses and houses on the way? They all look like they'd been built in the last fifteen years or less. This may have been a hell of lot more secluded in 1989."

Chris looked back at where Jane would have been left. "It's still a risky business. Those trees would have been smaller and less cover for him. So why here?"

"It was on his way home. Or on the way to work. But it was familiar. He knew when there wouldn't be people watching, probably in the middle of the night or early morning."

Chris nodded in agreement; they were slowly building their profile. "So he felt comfortable here. Maybe he lived in the area or in the surrounding areas, not more than twenty miles each way I'd guess. He knew this route well."

"Because he drove it all the time."

Chris studied the landscape and then opened the file folder to the few photos that were taken the day Jane was found. "She was discovered because a driver pulled over with a flat tire and then walked behind those bushes to take a leak. So he didn't necessarily want her found."

"He wanted her found," Knox contradicted. "But not right away. He wanted to drive by all the time knowing that she was there. He liked having the secret. He got off on it. Smug bastard."

Chris walked back down the embankment closer to where the drawing said that Jane was wrapped in a black tarp and partially covered with dirt and leaves. "Guys like that need the adrenaline rush, the thrill."

"That's a good point. How much did he plan and how much was improvised?" Knox asked, his eyes squinting against the weak sunlight peeking through the clouds. It was beginning to rain again, a metaphor for this case if Chris had ever seen one. "Was your Jane a victim of opportunity or did he choose and stalk her?"

"I have a better question. Did he know her? Was he someone she trusted?" Chris rubbed at his aching temples. He had the headache from hell after dealing with Stacey, Knox, and this case. "Sometimes it scares the shit out of me…having a daughter. I look at Annie and want to tell her that she shouldn't trust anyone but then I think that's a shitty way to live."

Chris didn't know why he'd said that out loud, to Knox especially, but the other man didn't crack one of his usual jokes. His own expression was somber as well.

"You do what you need to do to protect that little girl, Chris. If people saw what we've seen, fuck, they'd never leave their house." Knox pulled a camera out of a small leather bag that he'd had slung over his shoulder. Chris hadn't even noticed it until now, he'd been too distracted. "You want me to take some pictures? I brought this just in case. Camera phones just don't do the job."

Knox was almost being nice. This wouldn't last. Chris assumed that he'd been given orders from Reed that they had to learn to work together.

"That would be good. Thanks."

See? I can be nice, too.

Knox snapped several pictures and then tucked the camera away. "I'll email them to you. So what are the next steps?"

"The obvious ones. Re-interview the guy that found her, use the new forensic rendering to look through missing person cases. I was also thinking of looking for similar crimes. My gut is telling me that this is not an isolated incident. I'm not feeling the whole crime of passion thing here with Jane, but it's really too early to know."

Chris didn't mention the woman he'd seen on the television last night. Her resemblance was probably just his imagination. He'd been thinking about this case too much and it had spilled over into his visual entertainment.

Knox's lips twisted. "Looks like I'll be staring at file folders for the foreseeable future."

"You don't have to help if you don't want to."

It came out sounding more aggressive than Chris had planned but Knox had a way of pissing him off without really trying all that hard.

"Hey, relax. You're really wound up today." Knox's phone chirped, interrupting their conversation. Or argument, depending on how one looked at it. He thumbed the screen and grinned, tapping out a reply. "Brew and Ryan are at the office but are getting ready to go for a beer. They want to know if we want to join them. I told them yes."

Chris didn't drink beer anymore.

"I'll take a raincheck–"

"The hell you will," Knox said, slapping Chris on the back and pushing him toward their vehicles. "We're supposed to bond as a fucking team and that's what we're going to do. No one cares if you drink a soda. Let me repeat that. No one cares and if anyone gives you shit just deck 'em. You don't have to take anybody's shit about not drinking."

That was one thing that was cool about Knox. When they'd worked together, he'd been a supporter of Chris's sobriety.

"Jesus, Knox. You kiss your mama with that mouth?"

"I've never had any complaints from the ladies about my mouth."

"TMI, man. Keep that shit to yourself," Chris complained, unlocking his SUV as the cars whizzed by on the freeway. "No one wants to hear that."

Knox gave him a mock salute. "See you back at the office. Last one there buys the first round."

This might not be so bad. He and Knox could tolerate each other. In small doses. He'd spend some time with the other guys, too... Then he could size up the competition.

Chris was determined to solve this case, get the job, and make a good life for himself and Annie. He was going to show everyone that he wasn't just Tanner Marks' son.

Knox Owens could go fuck himself.

CHAPTER FIVE

C HRIS DIDN'T HANG out in bars anymore and honestly, he didn't miss it much. If there was anything that he regretted leaving behind it was the camaraderie that he felt with a bunch of guy friends, playing pool or darts, or watching a game while eating greasy food that would eventually kill him in thirty years or so.

The alcohol-fueled evenings? The fights? No, he didn't miss that at all.

Even the sour smell of beer turned his stomach these days and luckily this bar didn't reek of it. Mostly he smelled pizza and nachos, his stomach growling in appreciation and letting him know that it had been hours since he'd last ate.

The place was crowded and loud, but it had a casual sports bar sort of vibe. There were several women in the place as well, which usually meant that it wouldn't be too rowdy. At least until later tonight.

Logan was at the head of the table drinking a beer and munching on an order of cheese fries. When he looked up and saw Chris and Knox approaching he waved them over, pushing out a chair with his boot.

"Chris, Knox, I don't think you've been introduced to the team." Logan nodded toward the man on his right. Tall and muscular, he looked like a walking wall. He was fucking huge, dwarfing the chair he was sitting in. "This is Luke Brewster."

Brew swallowed the bite of hamburger he was chewing and held out his hand. "Nice to meet you. Call me Brew. Everyone does."

Logan clapped a hand on the shoulder of the man to his left. "And this is Ryan Beck."

Ryan wasn't quite as massive as Brew but he wasn't tiny, either. Dressed in faded denims, black leather jacket and boots, along with a silver hoop in one ear he looked more like a biker than a lawman. He'd been dressed more conservatively yesterday. He stood and reached over the table to shake their hands.

"Nice to meet you. Have a seat. I'll get the waitress to get your order."

The table was round so the way the chairs were situated meant that Chris was sandwiched between Brew and Knox. Brew and Ryan were having a friendly debate about a local sports team and every now and then Logan would chime in when his mouth wasn't full. The waitress took their orders and headed back to the kitchen after bringing their drinks.

No one said anything about Chris's soft drink.

Logan stuffed a few fries into his mouth and turned his attention to Chris and Knox. "So what are you guys up to today? Any progress?"

Since Knox didn't speak up, Chris replied. "We went to see the dump site for my Jane Doe."

Brew and Ryan immediately stopped speaking, their entire focus on Chris.

Shifting his large frame in the small chair, Brew leaned forward so he could be heard over the din.

"So what did you think?"

"We need to learn more about how the surroundings looked back in 1989," Chris replied, taking a sip of his soda. "But we do think that the guy was familiar with the place. We think that he may have worked or lived nearby, maybe even drove by the site every day."

Brew nodded, rubbing his chin. "It's also interesting that he made sure to dump the body out of the city and county where a smaller police force with less resources would have jurisdiction. It might mean that he planned it all carefully or that this wasn't his first go."

Confused, Chris frowned, staring at Brew. "Are you familiar with the case?"

Brew's cheeks reddened. "I may have looked through all the files. I was the first one into the office yesterday."

Logan just laughed, elbowing his new recruit. "Brew has a masters degree in psychology so if any of you are having trouble with your profile, he's your guy."

"That's great," Chris said to Brew. "Seriously, I'd love to hear any ideas that you may have."

"That's what I love to hear," Logan said, pushing away his

empty plate and rising to his feet. "Working together. That's how we're going to succeed. Now enjoy yourselves. I'm heading home to my family. See you all on Monday morning. We'll have a status meeting at nine."

Everyone nodded and bid him goodbye. They all respected the hell out of Logan Wright. He'd brought in serial killer Wade Bryson not just once but twice. Of course, he simply said that the team did it. He was modest like that.

"So what are your next steps?" Ryan asked as more food was placed on the table. "Review statements and forensics?"

Brew laughed and shook his head. "He's got nothing, dude. Nada. No witnesses. No statements. No forensics. Thirty-year-old murder and they don't even know the name of the victim."

Ryan's brows shot up and he blew out a slow breath. "And I thought they gave me a tough one. Shit, that's a challenge."

Chris opened his mouth to say that he relished a challenge but Knox beat him to it. "He can handle it. His old man is Sheriff Tanner Marks from Springwood, Montana. He helped Logan and Reed bring in Wade Bryson."

They'd all heard the stories. That's what made them want to work for Jason Anderson and his partners.

Chris had put his anger with Knox away earlier but it came back fast and with force, his neck growing hot. "Fuck off, Knox. My dad doesn't have anything to do with this."

Holding up his hand, Ryan gave Knox a dirty look. "I don't think our parental units should come into play here. We're either up to the job or we aren't. End of story."

Knox shrugged. "That's what I think, too. I was just saying–"

"Too damned much," Chris broke in. "It might be better to keep your mouth shut for once."

Clearing his throat, Knox stood. "On that friendly note, I'm going to take a leak. Order me another beer if the waitress comes by."

Pushing back his chair, the legs scraped the tile floor loudly. He strode away without a backward glance, leaving Chris with Brew and Ryan.

"I kind of get the feeling you and Knox have some history. Am I right?" Brew asked, taking a long draw from his beer.

"We do," Chris confirmed. "It's not a good one, to be honest."

Ryan grinned and shook his head. "That's why Logan and Reed paired you to together. To see how you'd handle it. They're such assholes sometimes, but geniuses, too."

Chris had already figured that out for himself. "We'll be fine. I won't kill him even if he deserves it."

"He's just trying to get a rise out of you," Ryan said. "Just busting your balls. The less you react the less fun for him it will be."

That sounded like advice Chris's dad had given him in grade school.

"He wants this job," Ryan went on. "He's trying to get an advantage by knocking you off your game."

"He's not."

"That's good," Brew said. "Seriously, how is it going?"

"That's a hell of a good question. I'm starting to build my profile after seeing the dump site today but I have long way to go. Now that we have a picture of Jane I'm going to look through the missing persons from that time, talk to the guy that found her, and also look for similar crimes." Chris hesitated but then went ahead. "I actually thought I saw a woman on the news last night that looked just like my Jane. Couldn't be, of course. She probably wasn't over thirty. I think I'd just stared at the drawing too long."

Ryan pulled out his phone and thumbed the screen. "What was the channel you were watching? She could be a relative. It's a long shot but you never know."

It was a long shot. A remote chance at best.

"I was really tired but I think it was channel thirty-six. I'm honestly not sure."

Holding his phone screen where Chris could see it, Ryan scrolled through some photos. "Any of these look familiar?"

At first no, but then one caught Chris's eye. "That one. That's her."

Brew leaned across the table and whistled softly. "Nice-looking woman."

"Gabriella Scott," Ryan read off the screen. "Can't hurt to talk to her. Maybe your Jane is a long lost relative or something."

Chris had to follow every path no matter how faint. On Monday morning, he'd go talk to Ms. Scott. He couldn't afford to overlook any potential clue.

CHAPTER SIX

T HE RECEPTIONIST STUCK her head around the wall of the cubicle. "Ella, there's someone here to see you."

Ella didn't turn around, her focus on the document she was currently creating for Galen. It was a story proposal regarding a soon to be built luxury condominium community and the environmental impacts of the construction. He was going to hate it.

"Can you tell them I'm busy?"

"This will only take a second, ma'am."

A deep voice. Definitely not Ellen's.

Hitting the save button, Ella swiveled in her office chair only to find herself looking up. Way up. This man was tall. Maybe six-two or six-three. Handsome, too.

"How can I help you?"

He held out a hand for her to shake. His grip was warm and firm, not limp like so many people's.

"My name is Chris Marks and I work for a law enforcement consulting firm. I'm looking into a murder that occurred in this area thirty years ago. A Jane Doe that was never identified and her killer never found."

Ella didn't have a clue as to what murder that was but she was already intrigued. He'd come to see her about it? Not the crime reporter three cubicles down?

This better be worth my time.

Quickly standing, Ella grabbed a chair from another cubicle and waved her guest into it. "It's nice to meet you, Mr. Marks. What can I do for you?"

The man sat down, an accordion file on his lap. "Please call me Chris. As I said I'm looking into this cold case from thirty years ago. The victim is a Jane Doe that has never been identified. With up-to-date forensic technology, a drawing of the woman has been created and I hope to be able to find out who she is."

Pulling a sheet out paper out of the folder, Chris then handed it to her. The woman was pretty with long dark hair and delicate features.

"Are you wanting the station to show her picture during the news? See what leads might come in?"

Ella was sure that Galen would do that.

"That would be great but that's not the important reason that I'm here."

"What is the important reason?"

Chris appeared to be having trouble finding the words for what he wanted to say. He opened his mouth and then closed it a few times before finally speaking.

"Because you look just like her, Ms. Scott, and frankly, I was hoping you might be a relative."

CHRIS MARKS EXPLAINED it to Ella but she still had questions. Several of them, as a matter of fact. She wasn't sure exactly where to start. Since she was extremely interested in the murder, she'd begin there.

"This murder took place in late 1989?"

"Not exactly," he answered patiently. He'd already said it but he didn't seem perturbed that she'd made him say it again. "That's when her body was found, or more precisely her skeletal remains. The coroner could only estimate how long Jane had been out there."

"And they couldn't identify her because…"

She didn't really want to say it.

"Because her hands were cut off," Chris said somberly. "We're assuming that was deliberate to keep authorities from making any identification."

"What about dental records?"

"That really only works when you have a possible match. They did compare her to several missing persons but nothing came of it."

This was the big question.

"And you think that I look like her?"

"I do," he replied with a nod, his expression still sober. "I think you look very much like Jane. So much so that I sought you out. Perhaps you have a missing member of your family?"

Ella shook her head, her thoughts already racing. "I can't think of anyone. They're all accounted for. It's probably just a coincidence. I mean…this drawing looks like a lot of women if you think about it. Not just me."

A corner of his mouth lifted in a half smile. "It was worth a try. I don't suppose you could speak with your family? Ask them if anyone of your extended family has gone missing? Maybe there was someone before you were born?"

She'd already silently decided to do that but she didn't want to raise this man's hopes. Her family was small and tight-knit. The chances of there being a missing woman in her family tree that her parents hadn't talked about all these years was remote.

"I'm having dinner with them tonight. I'll ask them. But I don't think they're going to have a different answer than I will."

"I appreciate you doing it then."

"No problem."

Standing, he hesitated as if unsure as to what to say next. "And thank you for talking to your boss about showing the drawing on the news. I'm hoping someone might recognize her or come forward with any details they might know."

Hoping the same thing, Ella stood as well, still holding the drawing. "I really hope that we can help you with this. This case is so intriguing. I'll be honest with you, Chris, I'd like to cover this for the station if I can get my boss to okay it. Have you talked to any other reporters?"

Chris shook his head. "I just started investigating this a few days ago and you're the first person I've spoken to."

A rush of adrenaline ran through Ella. She was finally getting a chance to be first up at the plate.

Placing the drawing on her desk, she pointed to the accordion file he'd tucked under his arm. "I don't suppose I could get a copy of that file?"

So much for being optimistic. Chris Marks frowned, his gaze going to the file folder and then back to her. "I don't think so."

"I need the story so we can report it when we show her picture."

"I gave you the pertinent details and you wrote them down."

Yes, she had but she'd bet money there was more in that file.

"Listen, I can help you with this case. Reporters can get into places that other people can't, plus we have a great computer research team."

His smile slowly widened, showing off a dimple in his right cheek. He found her amusing. "I don't think I need any help."

"Everyone can use help."

He regarded her steadily. "Have you ever investigated a murder, Ella?"

"Well...no."

"Have you ever covered a murder story?"

Shit.

"No."

This time her reply came out short and terse. She was getting nowhere with him.

"Then I'm not sure how you could help me other than publicizing Jane's picture."

She wanted to cover this murder. Hell, she needed this.

"I'd really like to do a story about this case, Chris."

"I'm not stopping you," he said. "When I identify Jane, you can report on it."

Ella's gaze turned back to the drawing, the soft brown eyes looking right back at her.

Maybe we look alike. Sort of. Either way, I want to help this woman find a name. And maybe some justice.

"This case could make you famous, Chris. You'd be a hero."

She didn't know which part of her statement pissed him off but he went stiff, his smile disappearing and turning into a grim line.

"That's not why I do this job. Now if you'll excuse me, I have other appointments."

Turning on his heel, he strode toward the newsroom door. Dammit. He was leaving.

"Wait," she called, running to keep up with his long legs. "Listen, I'm sorry. Whatever I said that upset you, I'm really sorry. I'm just excited about this case. It's the most interesting thing I've heard about in a long time."

She was about out of breath when he finally stopped in the hallway.

Damn, I need to start working out again.

"I'm grateful that you're going to run Jane's picture but I'm not looking to make a name for myself or get any sort of publicity in that way. I just want to identify her and find the person that did this."

Fine. If Ella wanted to pursue any sort of investigation it looked like she was on her own.

"Okay, is there anywhere I can get a hold of you and let you know when we're going to run the picture?"

Reaching into the breast pocket of his light blue button down shirt, he handed her a plain white business card with black lettering.

Chris Marks
Law Enforcement Consultant
JLJ Consulting, Inc.
Serials and Stalkers Division

"You can use that phone number twenty-four hours a day. Thank you, Ella. Now I really do need to go."

Without another word, he turned and walked briskly down the hall before turning the corner and disappearing out of sight. She lifted the card and read it again. JLJ Consulting? Who were they? What were they?

Time to be a reporter and get some answers.

CHRIS WAS COMBING through missing persons reports when Knox plopped himself down on a chair, sliding two cans of soda on the desk.

"I brought you a drink. You've had your head down all day."

Biting back a caustic retort, Chris instead reminded himself that they were supposed to be working together. They didn't have to be friends but they did have to get along.

"Missing persons reports from 1989." Chris reached for a soda and popped it open. "What have you been working on?"

"Jared and I were researching crimes with the same MO as my serial."

"You don't know for sure that it's a serial."

"True, but there's something about the case. What about you? Do you think Jane was killed by a serial?"

Did he? It was a possibility but he didn't want to make that call yet.

"After looking through the file again, I think it's more likely it was personal," he said. "But honestly, it's too early to tell."

"So did you meet her?" Knox asked, changing the subject. "Is she a lead in the case?"

It took a second for Chris to realize who *she* was. Gabriella Scott.

"I don't think so. She says she doesn't have any missing relatives. She's going to get the station manager to show the picture on television, though. That might bring in some leads worth following."

"Too bad. It would have been sweet if she'd been the clue to crack the case. After all these years and you just watch the news and solve it."

Tensing, Chris waited for a remark about his father's prowess as a lawman but Knox didn't go there. This time. He would, though. Eventually.

"That would have been nice but it's not going to happen like that. I'll have to actually work to solve this one."

Knox grinned. "And I'll be there to help you."

An image of Gabriella Scott floated through Chris's brain. She'd been eager, but he didn't need a rookie's help with this investigation.

"The reporter wanted to cover the case. Follow us around, I guess, and see what we do, then do a story on it."

"What did you tell her?"

"I told her no, of course. She's never even covered a murder." Chris chuckled softly. "She said that she could get into places that I couldn't. She even touted their computer research team as something we needed."

Knox threw back his head and laughed. "The little lady doesn't realize that we have our very own hacker. We could have her panty size and credit score in less than a minute."

"I didn't say that to her. I just told her no thanks."

"Technically, you can't stop her from covering this story. She can do whatever she wants."

Chris had a feeling that Ella Scott wasn't going to give up, either. She'd had a determined glint in her eye this morning. There was something about her... She was gutsy, but it was more than that. Maybe it was the curiosity he saw when he'd explained the case. It was the same inside of himself. The need for answers.

"That's true but she might not know that."

But he had a funny feeling that she did. He hadn't seen the

last of Ella Scott.

★　★　★

LUJACK, THE STATION'S research guru, handed her a small stack of paper. "There's not much out there on the consulting firm. It was when I dug into the owners that make up JLJ that's when it got really damn interesting. These guys are the real deal. The L stands for Logan Wright. You may remember his name in the newspapers not long ago. He was the one that shot and killed Wade Bryson."

"Wade Bryson?" Ella repeated, remembering back to that story. It had been big and dramatic with lots of coverage. Of course, she'd been covering a fishing tournament that weekend. "The cold-blooded serial killer? Wait…the man that shot him was the one that put him behind bars in the first place."

If Ella remembered correctly, Bryson had tried to kill Wright a few times.

"The two Js in the name stand for Jason Anderson and Jared Monroe. Anderson is former DEA. He was held prisoner by a drug cartel for months and managed to escape. That's no small feat. He also broke open a double murder cold case. Jared Monroe is no slouch, either. He's put some major bad guys behind bars but keeps a low profile. They all do, actually. I had to really dig for all of this information."

"That's…impressive."

She'd had no idea.

Lujack was grinning and nodding. "It gets better. That guy

that came to see you this morning? He's the son of Tanner Marks, who put a different drug syndicate out of business about eight years ago and was also involved in the apprehension of Bryson. He worked with Anderson on that drug bust. He also helped put a major weapons dealer behind bars. I could go on and on about these guys. Every one of them has a long record of being a total badass."

Chris hadn't looked big and scary but he'd certainly been serious about his job.

"So what's a law enforcement consulting company? What do they do?"

"According to the website, they can be hired out by small communities who may not have the resources or expertise for murder investigations and the like."

Chris worked in the serials and stalkers division. Had Jane been killed by a serial or a stalker?

"Thanks, Lujack. I wanted to make sure that he was who he said he was."

"If whatever he's working on doesn't pan out, Ella, you might want to interview him and his employers. I bet they've got some great stories."

They probably did but right now there was only one story Ella was interested in.

Jane Doe.

CHAPTER SEVEN

ELLA COULDN'T WAIT to tell her parents all about the case she was working on. It was official now. She'd had a short, terse conversation with Galen next to the coffeemaker where she'd had to corner him. She wanted him to say that he was okay with her spending time on the case but she'd told him she would do it anyway if he said no. She'd take some of the gazillion vacation days she had saved up to do it. He'd looked like he'd wanted to argue with her but he'd simply shrugged and said fine.

"Keep me in the loop."

Those were the words he'd thrown over his shoulder as he and his full coffee cup walked back into his office. That meant an email every couple of days, right? That sounded reasonable. Covering dog shows and charity bake sales didn't require keeping Galen updated. He usually acted like he didn't want to talk to her anyway.

Once a week Ella made sure to have dinner with her parents, Will and Dana Scott. She wished it could be more but work was always crazy and she never seemed to have enough free time. Her parents, both real estate lawyers, weren't exactly sitting around doing nothing either, although Dana constantly said that they needed to slow down now that they were over fifty-five. Will, on the other hand, was a bonafide workaholic and he frequently said he wanted to work until he dropped.

Dropping her handbag onto the foyer table, Ella rushed into the kitchen where her mom and dad were preparing dinner – spaghetti and meatballs. The smell of tomatoes and garlic hung in the air and Ella sniffed the aroma with appreciation.

Yum. One of my favorites.

"How's my little girl?" Will asked, looking up from a huge pot of sauce he was stirring. "Did you have a good day, honey?"

Dana had been spreading garlic butter on thick slices of bread but she immediately stopped to pour Ella a glass of merlot. "Let the poor girl sit down and take a breath before you pepper her with questions. She probably came straight from work."

"Weren't you covering a dog show this week?" Ella's father asked. "I saw some pictures in the paper."

Laughing, Dana handed Ella the glass of wine. "She hasn't answered the first two questions yet."

Everyone knew that Will Scott loved to talk and he loved asking questions even more.

Taking a sip of her red wine, Ella sat down at the kitchen island. "I'll get to all three. I'm fine. I did have a good day. And yes, I was covering the dog show but now I have a brand-new story I'm very excited about."

Dana slipped the tray of garlic bread under the broiler. "Let's dish up this meal and you can tell us all about it."

When it was just the three of them they didn't eat in the dining room. They sat around the large island in the center of the kitchen with the food plopped in the middle where they could all reach it if they wanted seconds.

"So tell us about your new story," Will urged. "What's it about?"

Ella's smile widened and she placed her fork on the edge of her plate. "A cold case murder."

Dana's eyes widened. "A murder? Since when do you cover crime?"

"Since now," Ella replied smugly. "I convinced Galen to let me investigate this story. It's fascinating."

"How did you even find out about it, honey?" Will asked. "Was this in the news recently?"

"It will be tonight, I believe. They have an artist's rendering of the Jane Doe and they're trying to get leads."

"Jane Doe?" Dana repeated. "I'm not following. Do they not know who the victim is?"

"I think I got ahead of myself. Let me start at the beginning."

Starting from Chris's visit, Ella explained all about the murder and Jane, what Chris was going to do to try and identify Jane, and then hopefully find the killer. By the time she was done, Dana and Will were pale and they'd abandoned their meal. They exchanged a worried glance that Ella didn't know how to interpret.

This wasn't a bad thing, it was good. She was finally getting a story that she could sink her teeth into. Work she could be proud of. It wasn't that she was ashamed to cover small local human interest stories but that wasn't the kind of journalism she'd dreamed of doing back in college. She'd wanted to be Woodward and Bernstein, or something close.

"So tomorrow I'm going to interview the detective that worked the case," Ella finished, picking up her fork again. Frankly, she'd hoped for more enthusiasm from her parents. "I'm also trying to get in touch with the man that found Jane."

"You can't do this," her mother said, her voice choked. "You can't."

Ah, I get it now. They're worried for me.

"Mom, you don't need to be worried about me. It's all fine. It's not dangerous. The murder was thirty years ago."

Dana raised a visibly shaking hand to her cheek. "You can't do this. Will, tell her she can't do this."

Her husband, however, had taken to hanging his head, his eyes closed. Ella watched as her usually smiling and jovial father whispered something that she couldn't hear, then raised his head and reached for his wife's hand.

"We have to tell her, sweetheart. It's long past time."

Beginning to understand that there was far more going on here than she was aware, a shiver ran down Ella's spine and her heart shifted into a higher gear.

Fear. She felt afraid and it was because her parents looked absolutely *terrified*. Like they'd seen the boogeyman or a machete-toting killer from the movies. She'd never seen her parents look like this before and it scared her.

"What do you need to tell me?"

The Adam's apple in Will's throat bobbed and he glanced at Dana once more before he spoke.

"This Jane Doe," he said, his voice low and strained. "She–she could be a relative, Gabriella. It's possible."

THEY'D LIED. DANA and Will Scott had been lying to Ella her entire life. They'd sworn up and down it was to protect her but that was just bullshit. Right now, all she could see was that they'd done it to make life easier for themselves. So Ella would never ask them any of the hard questions.

Now she wanted answers. All of them.

"You said that you adopted me from your sister," Ella said accusingly to her father. Angry and confused, she'd walked out of the kitchen for a time after they'd told her the story but now she was back and wanting to know details. "That she was sick and dying and you adopted me when I was just a few months old. You lied to me."

Both of her parents were crying and a part of Ella was crying with them. They were close and always had been and normally she would have thrown her arms around them to offer comfort, but right now she couldn't even fathom that act. She was livid and she didn't even have the words to express how hurt and upset she was.

They'd lied.

"Laney was sick and dying," Will replied, his arm around Dana's shoulder. They looked far older than they had only thirty minutes ago. "That part is true. We just told you that she was your mother so you wouldn't have to live with the doubt and wonder why your parents gave you away. We didn't want you to hurt and think that you weren't wanted. Because *we* wanted you so very much. We were desperate for a child and then you came into our lives. We didn't ever want you to think that you weren't wanted."

Ella reached up to her hot cheeks and found that they were wet. She was crying and she didn't even realize it. That's how angry and turned around she was.

"So you lied to me," she repeated, scrubbing at her face but the tears kept on falling. "You led me to believe that I was biologically connected to you. That I was family."

Will jumped up from his chair, his once pale cheeks now red. "You are family. You're our child and it doesn't matter whether we share DNA. You're our daughter and we love you more than anything in this world, Gabriella. You're everything to us."

Ella didn't doubt their love. It was plainly written across their face along with fear and regret. But at the moment she couldn't summon the forgiveness that her mother and father sought. Inside she felt...cold. Frozen. Not because she didn't love Dana and Will Scott. If anything she loved them too much and their betrayal sliced far too deeply. She simply didn't have the tools to deal with the blow they'd dealt her.

Dana held out her arms, beckoning to Ella but she couldn't move. Not now. "I'm your mother, Ella. We just didn't want you to have any doubts."

What am I supposed to say? Or do?

How am I supposed to react now?

"Well...I have them now," Ella finally said as the silence stretched on. She sat down on the bar stool and used her sleeve to rub at the tears. "If you've lied then it's time to come clean. What do you know about my mother and father? And don't leave anything out this time. Tell the truth."

Her parents exchanged a glance and then Will began to speak.

"We don't know much. We weren't given the names of your biological mother and father nor any reason as to why you had been surrendered."

Depending on the timing, Jane could be Ella's mother. It was possible. She might be a relative as well. Or she might not be any family and the resemblance was simply a coincidence.

"So my mother or father abandoned me?"

Will paced the small space between the island and the cabinets. "This. This right here is what we sought to keep from happening. We never wanted you to feel abandoned. We wanted you to feel wanted and loved."

"I do," Ella replied automatically. Because she did feel loved and wanted. She had all her life but she couldn't walk away from the fact that at one point she had been abandoned by her mother. "You've always made me feel that way. But at some point, my biological mother decided I was too much trouble or work. She bailed."

Dana wiped away a stray tear. "We always liked to think that your mother knew she couldn't give you what you needed in life so she stepped aside and let you be adopted by a family that could. We like to think that she loved you so much she wanted you to have a good life, Ella."

That did sound like a great story. It might even be true.

It could also be true that Ella's mom just got tired of being a parent or that Jane was Ella's mom. Death was a pretty decent excuse not to be a mother.

"Do you know anything about my father?"

"Nothing," Will said quietly. "We never heard anything about him."

A reasonable assumption in those circumstances.

"Did you hear anything about my mother? Age? Name? Where she was from? Anything at all?"

"No," Will replied again. "We don't know anything."

It left open several explanations. Too many of them.

"What are you going to do?" Dana asked anxiously, her lips trembling. Will reached for her mother's hand and held it tightly. "We're so sorry for not telling you, sweetheart. We were just trying to keep…this…from happening."

This. This was a clusterfuck alright. Ella didn't want to hurt her parents but the need to know if Jane was a relative, or even her mother, was strong. It burned in her gut like a lighted match.

"I don't know exactly what I'm going to do," Ella finally said, reaching out for her wine glass and taking a gulp. Alcohol wasn't the answer but then it wasn't the problem, either. "But I do know that I'm going to continue to investigate this Jane Doe. I also know that taking a DNA test is a possibility. I just haven't decided for sure if that's what I want to do. I do know one thing for sure and it's that I love you both. Very much. I'm just not happy with you right now, but I do see why you did what you did."

Another glanced exchanged by her parents, an unspoken message passed between them.

"We'll help you in any way that we can," Will said. "Whatever you need us to do."

"That's more than I could ask for."

"You were more than we ever dared hope for," Dana said, a fresh spate of tears falling down her face. "I love you so much, Ella. More than you can possibly ever believe."

"I love you, too. I just know that I need the truth."

Whatever that was.

I can handle it. I can. I'm sure of it.

WHEN ELLA LEFT her parents' home she wasn't sure where she was going but she found herself back at the station. The great thing about a twenty-four-hour news channel was that there were people around at all times and no one would think it was strange for Ella to be there. She slipped into the foyer, waving at the night guard as she headed for her desk, but then changed her mind at the last second and took a left instead of a right. Directly to the research department. What she wanted probably wasn't going to be found on the internet.

The research department was like a small, private library without any of those pesky fiction books. But they did have every Seattle newspaper going back to the turn of the century.

On microfiche.

Ella hadn't even known what that was when she'd taken the job here. Starting out as an entry level reporter, she'd often been asked to do background research for the reporters which meant that she'd spent a great deal of time right here in this dusty old room. Shelf after shelf of books. Drawers of old black and white photos each catalogued carefully with the date, time, location, and the subjects in the picture. Stacks of blueprints and maps, too. It was all there if you knew where to look.

Lujack, the head of the research department was working hard to move it all to digital but that took time and money, something there never seemed to be enough of. So for now she'd have to pretend it wasn't the twenty-first century. The nineties had been fun.

Quickly she found the microfiche she was looking for and whirled through the newspaper articles around the date that Jane was found. It wasn't long before she was reading the article written by...

No, it couldn't be. The newspaper story about finding Jane's body was written by none other than Ella's current boss. Galen

Winters. Why hadn't he said something when she'd talked to him about the case? It didn't make any sense.

Making a note to corner him tomorrow about it, she printed off the articles – there were two – and highlighted the important parts. The name of the man that had found the body. The detective in charge of the case. She'd start with them first thing tomorrow morning.

In the meantime, she'd go home and try not to think about her parents or her life. She'd deal with her personal problems later when she could wrap her head around the mess. And a mess it was. No matter what she was going to do, somehow her parents were going to be hurt. She couldn't go back in time and pretend she didn't know what she knew now. She could only go forward.

That could be the most painful path of all.

CHAPTER EIGHT

THE NEXT MORNING Chris was up before dawn to get on the road for his meeting with the detective who had headed up Jane's murder case. Now retired, Wallace Wade lived in a small town about three hours east of Seattle.

Knox was driving because he was an obnoxious pain in the ass whenever Chris tried to drive.

"You have control issues," Chris told Knox when he climbed into the truck, the cab warm despite the chilly temperatures. It was also still dark as hell but the morning traffic was already beginning to build at this ungodly hour. "You need to relax and unwind a little bit. Let someone else drive for a change."

"I like being in control. I don't think it's a bad trait," Knox laughed, pointing to the two paper cups situated between them. "I stopped to get us coffee. You're welcome."

"Thanks," Chris said, taking a small experimental sip. Delicious. Knox must have listened the last time they'd gone through a drive thru. "So you're a control freak and you pay attention to small details. A little stalkerish, don't you think?"

"That's what makes me a good cop." Knox shrugged and

then changed lanes to pass a slower vehicle. "I suppose those qualities would be helpful to a stalker as well."

"Maybe that's what it was."

"I'm not following you. What was it?"

"Jane," Chris explained. "Maybe she had a stalker. Law enforcement wasn't as sophisticated about that back in the eighties."

"It's a possibility. The most dangerous person in a woman's life is her husband or boyfriend. Statistically speaking, that is."

"Do you have another theory?"

Knox shook his head but never took his eyes from the road. "I don't have any theory. Not yet. We don't know shit about this case. I'm just glad they gave it to you and not me."

With Knox talking a mile a minute, the time flew by and soon they were pulling into the tiny town of Fern Ridge, population 2,016. The main drag through town appeared to be bustling with activity. There were several restaurants, bed and breakfasts, along with antique shops dotted in between.

"Looks touristy," Chris commented. "I didn't expect this."

He knew a hell of a lot about Montana but not so much about Washington state.

"Good fishing," Knox replied. "Hiking trails and camping. There's always something to do around here."

"GPS says to turn right at the next corner. Third house on the left."

Wallace Wade's home was a large rambling Victorian with a big porch that wrapped around half of the house. Knox parked behind a little blue Civic while Chris gathered up the file and tucked it under his arm. He had brought it in hopes that it might jog the detective's memory. Thirty years was a long time.

They both bounded up the front steps just as the door swung open. A tall, thin man with silver hair stood in the entryway, smiling and waving them inside.

"Come on in and get out of the cold," he said, closing the door behind them. "I think we might get some snow tonight. I'm Wallace Wade and you must be Chris Marks and Knox Owen."

Chris stuck out his hand. "That's right. I'm Chris and this is Knox. It's a pleasure to meet you, Detective."

The older man chuckled and shook his head. "I'm retired now, son. You can call me Wally. Everyone does."

"Wally it is, then."

"Come on in and join your partner. I've got her drinking coffee and eating a bear claw. She beat you by a good fifteen minutes. I told her we ought to wait for you. No sense going over the same information twice."

Their partner?

Knox and Chris exchanged a puzzled glance but followed the former detective into a sitting room off of the foyer. They passed a front desk of sorts with a sign that read *Mountain Breeze Bed and Breakfast*.

There was a coffee service set up on a cart when they first entered. A fireplace took up most of the far wall and two couches sat perpendicular with a low table in between.

Their *partner* was sitting on one of those couches drinking coffee.

Ella Scott, the reporter.

Dressed in an almost identical outfit to yesterday with dark blue slacks and a cream colored sweater, she appeared at ease with the retired cop. Her dark hair was pulled back into a neat ponytail and tied with some sort of fluffy scarf. She looked pretty and professional at the same time. From the look on Wally's face, she'd charmed him completely.

But what in the hell was she doing here?

Chris nodded curtly to the woman as he accepted a cup of coffee. "Ella."

"Chris," she murmured in response, her cheeks going pink. "You made good time on the drive."

Knox was watching all of this with great interest, his gaze darting back and forth between them.

"We did make good time," Knox agreed. "It's nice to see you again…Ella."

She looked up from her cup, her eyes pleading with them not to give away that she wasn't one of them. Chris decided to play along if only to see what she was trying to do. She was a reporter so she obviously wanted a story, but he wasn't sure that there was one here. There could be but it was all still very much up in the air. Still…any publicity regarding Jane would probably be a good thing. The more people heard about her the better chance they had of perhaps finding someone who knew her.

They settled onto the couches, Chris and Knox flanking Ella

while Wally sat across from them. Chris shot Ella a warning look. He wouldn't blow her cover but he was in charge. He and Knox had had that discussion on the drive here.

His case. His interview.

Chris placed the file on the table between them before reaching in and pulling out the rendering of Jane. Wally had worked this case with little information, including what his victim looked like.

"This is what the forensic artist came up with." Chris turned the drawing so Wally could see it. "This is our Jane."

The older man's eyes narrowed and he leaned forward to study it for a long time. Finally, he reached for it with shaking fingers, but at the last minute he pulled his hand back as if he'd changed his mind.

He looked up at Chris. "That's what they think she looked like?"

"They do."

Sighing, Wally rubbed his chin. "Damn, technology sure has come a long way, hasn't it? We didn't have all of that fancy CSI stuff back in my day."

"It has come a long way," Chris agreed. "Wally, I'm trying to put a name to Jane's face. Can you tell me what you remember? Do you mind Knox recording our conversation? I have a shit memory."

"Not a problem," the older man replied with a weak smile. "I'm not sure what I can tell you. It was so long ago."

Anticipating this, Chris pulled some of the other papers from the file. The diagram of the body dump site. The coroner's report. Wally's own police report. A few grisly photos.

"I know it was a long time ago but whatever you can remember might be of help. I brought these to help jog your memory."

This time Wally did reach for the photos, but instead of looking at them he turned them facedown. He did pick up his own reports and seemed to be scanning them. Chris stayed quiet as well as Knox and Ella while the man gathered his thoughts.

"I got the call during dinner," Wally finally said, his gaze somewhere far away. Maybe back there in 1989. "Jenny, my wife, wasn't happy that I didn't stay to finish my meal but she should have been used to it. A detective's hours can really suck. She hated that I was a cop. She wanted me to be anything else but that."

Chris understood that well.

"When I got there they had cordoned off the area and placed some lights so we could see when the sun went down. At that time of year we would have had good sunlight until around eight but it was already almost seven. The coroner was still doing their work so I talked to the guy that had found the body."

"Robert Trask," Chris said, pulling another piece of paper from the file. "This is his statement. There's not much to it."

Wally nodded in agreement. "Because there wasn't much to tell. He had a flat, pulled off the road to fix it, went to take a leak behind the bushes and found her. He got in his car and drove to the nearest service station and called 911. He met two patrolmen back at the site. Told them his story, and then waited to tell it to me again."

"So what did you do then?"

Wally folded his hands, one thumb tapping on the other. "We combed through missing person files and did the usual plea to the public for help. Didn't get much. We followed a few leads but they were dead ends."

"But someone did come forward," Ella said, scooting forward to the edge of the couch. "Leo Gates. He came forward and said his wife Susannah was missing."

That information wasn't anywhere in Chris's file. He didn't like not knowing all the details and what was going on. He also didn't like Ella butting into his interview.

"Gates did come forward," Wally replied, rubbing his chin again. "But we never made any headway there. When we talked to his neighbors, they claimed to have seen her load a suitcase and drive away. If you'd met Leo Gates that wouldn't surprise you. He was a drunk who couldn't hold down a job. Friends said he was abusing Susannah and the neighbors corroborated that with stories of their fights. But we couldn't find any link between her and the Jane Doe."

"What about dental records?" Knox asked.

Wally shook his head. "Susannah Gates had never been to the dentist so we had nothing to match."

"Never been to the dentist," Ella echoed. "Ever?"

"They were poor."

"And the clothes Jane was wearing?" Chris asked, finally able to get a word in. "Did they match anything that Susannah Gates had been seen wearing?"

"No, and they were one size too large, too. Jane Doe isn't Susannah Gates."

The way Wallace Wade spoke it made it sound final. But... One size didn't seem like a big deal to Chris. Maybe she'd put on a few pounds. She probably wasn't going to announce it to the world that she was buying a larger size in clothes.

"Did Susannah Gates have any children?"

Another question from Ella. Chris shot her a glare. She wasn't even supposed to be here.

"She did," Wally confirmed. "A young daughter about one and a son about three."

"Did she take her children with her when she left?"

Where in the hell was Ella going with these questions? They didn't have anything to do with connecting Jane to Gates.

"She did."

Even Wally looked confused by the turn the questioning had taken.

"Let's get back to your investigation, Wally," Chris said. "Who else did you talk to?"

"We talked to everyone that called in but as I said they didn't lead anywhere. The missing person files were also a bust."

Chris took a sip of his coffee. Too cold now. "You looked through the missing persons in King County, correct?"

"No, Pierce County. Police departments weren't connected back then like they are now. In 1989, we were just getting to the point where we were trying to do that. I suppose you can look nationwide by now. Just press a button and there it is."

"We can and we are. Knox and I have been working that list."

With no luck, however.

Wally shrugged. "That's about it. There were no other leads so we had to shelve the case. We never closed it, of course, but we couldn't waste manpower on it when there were so many other cases that needed our attention. The investigation was going nowhere."

Hiding his frustration, Chris reluctantly packed away the papers into the folder. "I do appreciate you meeting with us today, Wally. Is there anything else, anything at all that you can remember about the case?"

"It's all in my reports, son. There's nothing hidden here because there wasn't much to the case. We found a body that we couldn't identify. There were no witnesses and all leads were no help. There wasn't anything else we could do."

They all thanked Wally again. He slapped Knox and Chris on the back and invited them back to go fishing sometime. He shook Ella's hand a little too long and thanked her for stopping by. He said she brightened up the place. To her credit, she didn't outwardly act creeped out, although she probably was.

Walking out of the house and down the steps, they waved to Wally who stood in the doorway. Ella walked straight to the blue Civic.

Not so fast.

"You don't mind if I catch a ride back to Seattle with you?" Chris asked, following on her heels. "Knox has things to do. Right, Knox?"

The other man wore an evil smirk. "Yes, I do. Things. Stuff. It would be a great help to me if you could ride back with Ella. So I could do those...things."

Ella rolled her eyes and groaned. "No need for theatre, gentlemen. Yes, Chris, you can ride back with me. Just don't yell at me too loudly, okay? I'm a jumpy driver."

Chris wasn't making any promises.

CHAPTER NINE

ELLA HAD BARELY pulled out of her parking space before Chris started in.

"Are you going to explain to me what you were doing there? You could have blown this entire investigation."

She'd expected this.

"I hardly think my mere presence could have *blown* your entire investigation. That seems a tad overdramatic."

Honestly, Chris Marks wasn't nearly as mad as she'd expected him to be. He was far more Zen than she'd given him credit for.

"How about answering my first question? What were you doing there?"

"The same thing you were doing there," she replied placidly. "I wanted to ask Wallace Wade about the investigation. I was as surprised as you were when he told me that he was expecting you any moment. He jumped to the conclusion that we were together so I decided not to disabuse him of that notion. It seemed easier."

"Easier," Chris repeated. "For whom? Wait, that would be

you. It was easier for you."

Now that wasn't fair. She'd been honest and upfront.

"I told him when I got there that I was a reporter but I don't think he was listening because he immediately started talking about you."

The fact was the former detective Wallace Wade was a huge flirt. He considered himself something of a ladies' man from what she'd been able to see and his wife Jenny, bless her, appeared to let him think it. When she'd rolled in that coffee cart, she'd given Ella a big smile and a wink.

Snorting, Chris rolled his eyes. "I'm sure that was the case. He seemed to really like you."

"I think he likes most women under the age of fifty."

"Okay, let's start again," Chris sighed. "You wanted to ask Wally about the investigation. Why?"

"I told you yesterday. I want to do a story on this cold case. You told me to go ahead. So I did. Surprise. We both started at the most logical place. Wallace Wade."

"How did you even know about him?"

"I can do research, too. It was easy. I looked up the old newspaper clippings."

Blowing out a noisy breath, Chris moved restlessly in his seat. "What was all that about whether Susannah Gates had any children?"

She squirmed under Chris's direct gaze. Just how much was she willing to tell him?

Not this much.

"You said you were hoping to find a family member."

He seemed to accept her explanation, which was a relief. It was none of his business that she had personal reasons for wanting to be a part of this investigation. She did, however, feel badly about her lie by omission. He'd asked her point blank yesterday if she could be related to Jane and she'd said absolutely not. Now she knew that wasn't the case, but she hadn't enlightened him as to what had changed. She was, in fact, making it more difficult for him to solve Jane's murder.

I just can't talk to him about this. No.

He grabbed the dash of the car as the vehicle suddenly sped up. "Shit. Slow the fuck down, Ella. Are you trying to get us killed? You were about two inches from that guy's bumper."

"I had the right of way."

She slowed down and moved into the right lane, her heart racing in her chest.

"They can put that on our damn tombstone. *They had the right of way but now they're dead.* I think I should have driven."

"I'm a very good driver. You're alive, aren't you?"

"So far."

Her fingers tightened on the wheel as she worked up the courage to ask the question that had been bugging her since last night.

"Do you have a DNA sample from Jane?"

He didn't bat an eye at the question, thank goodness.

"They were able to extract some DNA from her teeth and jawbone, which is really a miracle if you think about it. Luckily we have a profile that we can compare if someone comes forward and claims that she's their sister or cousin. If they're not a relative then that's going to be trickier. I doubt dental records will still exist that we can compare with Jane's."

"You're saying that they may not be able to prove that Jane is who they say she is."

"Exactly, although we might get lucky and they have an old photo of her wearing the same clothes but that's a long shot at best." Chris scraped his fingers through his short, dark hair. "The sad fact is that finding out Jane's real name is practically an impossible task. But I have to believe that somewhere out there is a relative."

The guilt inside of Ella grew about ten times larger. She wasn't just making Chris's job harder, she might be making it impossible. Crap.

Or not. I might not even be related to Jane. It's only a remote possibility, after all.

A possibility that Ella wouldn't know unless she was willing to take a DNA test and allow it to be compared to Jane's.

Am I ready to do that?

At this moment, Ella didn't have an answer. But she had a whole bunch of questions.

ELLA PULLED INTO the parking lot of the consulting firm and put the vehicle into park. She'd been quiet for most of the drive. Chris had thought that he would prefer it that way but he found that he rather liked her sharp questions and observations about Jane. She'd fallen silent about a third of the way into the trip and he hadn't wanted to bother her, especially as what she'd said turned out to be true.

She was a jumpy driver.

She kept hopping into one lane and then back into another, muttering under her breath. Frankly, they were lucky to be alive. She really needed a defensive driving course. Chris had learned at the police academy.

"Safely home," she said with a smile. "I told you that you'd be fine."

"It was pure prayer that got us back here in one piece."

"So dramatic."

He looked out of the window at his SUV sitting in the parking lot and then back at the woman sitting next to him. Well, shit.

"What are you going to do now?" he asked, already wishing that he hadn't brought it up. This was probably a huge mistake. But...

"What do you mean? Are you asking me to a late lunch?"

Food hadn't even occurred to him.

"No," he answered. Dammit, now he was thinking about a burger. "I was asking what you're going to do now. You know, on the case."

A corner of her lips curved up in a half smile. "What are *you* going to do next?"

Seriously? Chris didn't want to play games but he would if

she insisted.

"I asked you first."

"I asked you second."

He'd had enough. He was trying to be nice.

"Fine, don't answer. I was just thinking that maybe you could tag along with me but–"

"I will, I will." She twisted around in the driver's seat so she was facing him, a look of panic on her face. "I'm sorry. I was thinking that you were going to try and discourage me again. This case is important to me."

He could see that it was, although he didn't know why. His reasons were far more obvious. He wanted a job but her? The chances were high that there would be no amazing scoop here that would end up on the front page of the newspaper – or in her case on the six o'clock news.

"If you come with me, we're going to have some rules."

That statement seemed to amuse the hell out of her.

"I'm serious, Ella. We're going to set some ground rules and you are going to stick to them."

"Do you get rules, too? Or is it only me?"

Rubbing at his temple, he could feel a headache beginning to bloom. It had her name written all over it.

"What rules do you want me to have?"

"I don't know. I just think that it should be fair."

Was Ella like this with everyone? Confusing and frustrating.

"I have no idea what you're talking about," he finally replied, deliberately keeping his tone even. "Let me ask you a question and don't answer it with another question, please. If I don't let you tag along with me are you going to go behind my back?"

To her credit, Ella didn't even hesitate to tell the truth. "Yes. You can't stop me from talking to people, Chris. I may not have all the information that you have but I have some and I'm going to look into this murder."

"Because it's important to you?"

Something passed over her features. A shadow that he couldn't quite decipher but it was gone as quickly as it had come. In its place was a steely determination that he had to admit that he admired. Her elfin chin had raised and her full lips were firm. Even her eyes sparkled with passion. There'd be no deterring her from her set path. It would be better to have her with him where he could keep her out of the way and make sure she wasn't causing any trouble. What was it that his dad used to say?

Keep your friends close and your enemies closer.

Ella wasn't his enemy but she could be trouble with a capital T.

"Yes, it's important to me. I assume it's important to you as well."

"It's my job." He pointed to his vehicle parked several feet away. "If you come, I will be driving. You're a menace on the roads. I will also be in charge. You've never done any investigative work so you are in watch mode, got it? I don't want you to go off half-cocked and get yourself hurt or killed."

Her brows rose and her eyes widened. "This is a thirty-year-old case. Do you think it's actually dangerous?"

"Probably not, but you cannot be too careful when investigating something like this. The killer got away with it, Ella, and he's not going to like us poking our noses in his business. So follow me and it will all be alright. Don't go out there on your own."

She held out her hand. "Deal."

He accepted it, noting how soft her skin was. This was such a terrible idea. He should be kicked in the ass several times for being an idiot.

"Deal. Now let's get some lunch. Then we have a lot of work to do."

"Fine, but first I have this one thing to do."

ELLA PLACED THE newspaper article she'd printed up on the desk between herself and her boss. She'd finally cornered him in his office, carefully sitting down in the lone empty chair. Most surfaces were covered with books, folders, or the plethora of memorabilia Galen had brought from his previous jobs. The walls were covered with news stories and photographs, some with famous people.

"Why didn't you tell me?"

Tapping away at his phone he finally lifted his head to look at the paper. He picked it up and read through it, then scowled and placed it back on the desk.

"I'm not sure what you're talking about, Ella. What didn't I tell you?"

"Why didn't you tell me that you investigated the Jane Doe case that I'm looking into? Why didn't you say something?"

His brows knitted together and he picked up the story, quickly perusing it.

"Because I had no idea that your Jane Doe and *this* Jane Doe were one and the same."

He could he not know?

"You heard me describe the case. You had to know that it was the same murder."

Placing his phone down, he leaned forward, his elbows resting on the scarred oak. "I didn't know. Ella, think about it. Do you know how many Jane Does we have every year in this city and county? It's been thirty years, so do the math. It's far too many, of course, but cut me some slack, okay? This was one article I wrote three decades ago when I was first starting out. I don't even remember it. It was too long ago."

"You don't remember it?"

She sounded far more scandalized than she'd planned to but the way he said it... It was like the case was nothing to him.

"No, I don't," he replied firmly, almost dismissively. He hated meetings and he didn't like to sit still in his office. "And when you're my age and a few years from retirement you won't remember every case that you covered. either."

A flush crawled up her cheeks and she nervously fidgeted in the chair. "I mean...I know I won't remember them all but this was a murder case."

"Seattle may be one of the safest cities in the country but it does still have violent crime. I didn't memorize them for the last thirty years." His gaze swept her from head to toe. "And I don't get personally involved either, advice that I hope you follow. Don't get emotionally involved with this, Ella. It was a long time ago and there isn't anything you can do for this Jane Doe."

That wasn't true.

"I can help find her identity or her killer."

"It won't help her," he repeated. "She's gone and she has been for a long time. You can't bring her back to life."

"I can give her family and friends closure."

Galen shook his head. "Perhaps, but it isn't your job to do that. Let these cops work on the case. You report on it, then you move on to the next story. That's what we do. We report and inform. If we do our job right, we report on it accurately and honestly, and with integrity."

"So don't get involved?" she said, bitterness in her tone. He didn't understand just how close to home this case might be. "Just watch from the sidelines?"

He sat back in his leather chair, his gaze still resting on her. "How else can we stay unbiased? And make no mistake, Ella, that's what we're supposed to be. Unbiased. I know that's not popular right now. Everyone has to have an opinion about everything but back when I started out in journalism we reported the news and let people make up their own minds about what they thought about it. I'd like to think we can still do that. But if you're part of the investigation, how are you going to be able to report it without your bias coloring it? That's my question back to you."

Ell had heard this mini-speech from Galen before. Sometimes to her and sometimes to other reporters. He certainly believed what he was saying and if this were any other case...

But it wasn't. He didn't need to know that, though.

He lifted the article up again, perusing it. "Damn, this was a long time ago. I was just a cub reporter back then looking to make a name for myself."

"So you do remember? I mean...now that I've reminded you?"

He shrugged. "A little bit. I worked the crime beat so this was my usual day. Talking to cops and getting the story."

"You talked to Wallace Wade then? I talked to him this morning. He's retired now."

"Wally? I've known him for years. He was nice to reporters. Not all of the cops were." Galen sighed and shook his head. "I bet he liked you. He always had an eye for a pretty girl."

Rolling her eyes, Ella stood and reached for the article, slipping it back into her messenger bag.

"He hasn't changed."

"I'm not surprised." Galen steepled his fingers and let out a long breath. "Just don't get too wrapped up in this, okay? You need to stay objective. If you're going to do stories like this you can't get emotionally involved with every one. You'll burn out before you're thirty-five if you do."

It was a good warning, but it was far too late.

CHAPTER TEN

"**S**O TELL ME something about yourself."

Ella and Chris had stopped at a local eatery for lunch. It was the usual chain restaurant with music too loud but it served decent cheeseburgers. Ella had ordered hers with ketchup only and Chris had ordered the works. They were sharing a large basket of crinkle fries.

He dipped a fry into the splotch of ketchup on his plate. "What do you want to know?"

Chris wasn't against sharing any information about himself; he simply wanted to know what she was trying to get at. As a reporter, she was probably naturally a little nosey. Which was fine as long as she didn't want to know something truly personal likes his hopes and dreams.

"Anything. For example, do you like sports? Or what's your favorite food? What's your favorite movie? I just thought it might be nice to know a little bit about each other since we're going to be spending so much time together."

That was a reasonable request, although he was still wondering if inviting her along had been a wise move. But that's how he was, a little impetuous. Knox had complained about it but then Chris thought that Knox analyzed everything to death. They were two sides of the same coin.

"I do like sports," Chris replied, wiping his hands on a paper napkin. "I played football and baseball in high school. My favorite food is steak, medium rare, and my favorite movie is *Die Hard*. Now it's your turn."

"Um…okay. That was succinct. I don't really like sports all that much. I can watch it on television but I'd rather read a book. My favorite food is sushi and my favorite movie is *Titanic*."

"Sushi," Chris echoed. "Raw fish is your favorite food?"

If he thought she'd take offense, he was way off base. She only laughed and popped a fry into her mouth. "Hey, I didn't say anything about your movie choice. *Die Hard*? I mean…really? It's so cliché."

"What's cliché? It's a great movie."

"A renegade lone wolf cop movie. That's cliché. And it's a good movie. I wouldn't say it's a great movie."

He pointed to himself, ignoring her use of the words *good* and *great*. "You think I'm a renegade lone wolf cop? You couldn't be further from the truth. I'm a team player all the way."

"Oh really? You didn't look very chummy with your partner this morning. There were definite icicles between the two of you."

Chris hadn't thought anyone would notice the tension between him and Knox. He was trying to keep his personal feelings out of his work.

"I don't know what you mean. He's not my partner, actually. We're just supposed to be helping each other if needed. Ultimately I'm responsible for this case. Not Knox."

"See? Lone wolf." She playfully shook a fry at him. "And you do know what I mean. You and Knox don't seem to get along very well. It was obvious to anyone paying attention."

He could only hope that no one at work would pay any attention then.

"Knox and I have a history," Chris admitted. "But it doesn't affect how we do our jobs."

Her eyes widened and her mouth formed a perfect "O". "I see. I didn't realize you two had been a...couple."

What in the ever-loving hell was this woman talking about?

He slapped his forehead with his hand and sighed. Loudly. "We were not a couple. We were co-workers and then he became my boss for awhile. We didn't see eye to eye so I quit. End of story. There was no coupledom or romance or anything like that."

"You worked for him?"

"I did," Chris confirmed. "We were both deputies for the Montana town of Fielding."

"Montana? Are you a cowboy?"

"No."

"Do you ride a horse?"

"Yes."

"I bet you're a cowboy. Now tell me about you and your partner."

What a strange conversation.

"We worked for Jared Monroe who now is one of the partners in the consulting firm where I work now. Then Jared left Fielding and Knox became the sheriff."

"And you were mad that you didn't get the job?"

Chris really didn't want to talk about this but here they were.

"No, not at all. I was too inexperienced at the time to take over that job. Knox has been a cop much longer than me."

"So you left because you didn't like working for him?"

She seemed to be getting it. Finally.

"That's right. I had other opportunities so I quit and moved on."

Cocking her head, she gazed at Chris for a long moment. "What happens if he gets promoted over you and you work for him again?"

Christ on a unicycle, he couldn't imagine that happening. It just couldn't happen. No. No way.

"That's not a possibility."

"You sound very sure."

"I am very sure. Can we change the subject now?"

She took a bite of her burger and nodded. "Sure we can. Why don't you tell me why you became a cop and then now a consultant?"

"I can certainly tell that you're a reporter. You like to ask questions."

"I do."

With raised brows, she waited for him to answer. He had to give it to her, she didn't mess around. She just jumped in with both feet, pummeling him with questions.

"You missed your calling. You should have been a police interrogator."

That made her smile. "I'm still young. I could change career paths."

There was silence again. He hadn't distracted her.

"I became a cop because my old man was one."

"In Montana?"

"In Montana," he replied. "In fact, he's still a working sheriff."

"That must have been a little scary growing up with a father as a cop."

"What, are you my therapist now?" He sat back and patted his full stomach. "I didn't really think about it at the time. He was just Dad and he went off to work like every other kid's dad."

"Still it had to be difficult having a cop for a dad. I bet you didn't get away with anything when you were a kid."

How wrong Ella Scott was.

"You'd lose that bet," he said with a laugh. "I was a hellion and I made my parents' lives hell for a while. Even as a child, I couldn't seem to sit still. Every summer I broke something and had to wear a cast. Every year in school I'd just scrape by with terrible grades. I raised hell in high school with my buddies, drinking and playing poker. Later, I drank too much and got into fights. My sister Emily was the sane one. She got good grades and went to art school. I got tattoos and a bad reputation."

He didn't imagine the way her gaze swept over him nor the way her cheeks turned a pretty shade of pink.

Ella Scott was wondering where his tattoos were located. She might also be wondering if he was still a bad boy. Was she attracted to those kinds of guys? He hadn't pictured her as the type. He'd have thought she'd go for more of the country club type. A guy that played golf and traded stock tips with his buddies. The kind of guy that he wasn't. He didn't know shit about the stock market and golf put him to sleep.

"What about you, Ella?"

CHRIS SEEMED GENUINELY interested in Ella's life, to her surprise. He wasn't asking to be polite or because he thought it was expected of him. Her last boyfriend – an attorney – hadn't been interested in anything much except himself. She should have figured out way sooner that he was completely self-absorbed but he was so good at *acting* like he gave a shit about her life that she'd been convinced for a long time.

Eventually she'd noticed that he never asked her any follow-up questions or that he never remembered what she'd told him the last time about a subject. It became so bad that whenever she opened her mouth, he'd get a faraway look in his eyes. She could practically see him mentally checking out to Tahiti with a bunch of scantily clad girls gathered around him. The only time he'd pay attention to her is when they talked about *him*. The latest word was that he was dating another lawyer and Ella had to wonder how that woman was dealing with a man that was so self-absorbed.

Hold the phone. Why am I comparing Chris to my last boy-friend? He's not even a friend, really.

"I'm not sure what to say," she said, taking a sip of her soda to gather her thoughts. "I had a pretty boring childhood. I didn't do anything wild like you did. No drinking or playing poker. I guess you could say I was a good student and I tried not to give my parents any trouble."

A slow smile grew on Chris's handsome face. "I bet you were a cheerleader."

Ella could feel the heat in her cheeks. "So what if I was?"

He was openly laughing now, his blue eyes sparkling. "I knew it. You were a cheerleader in high school."

"You don't like cheerleaders?"

"Not like them? I loved them. I dated most of them at one time or another. I told you I played football."

"Let me guess…you were the quarterback?"

"I was."

She should have known.

"Were you any good?"

She'd blurted out the question without thinking about its double meaning. Damn, it kind of sounded dirty when she said it in her head.

Clearly, Chris was thinking the same thing. His cheeks were red but not from embarrassment. Hell no. He was loving this line of conversation. Asshole.

"Let's just say that I got the job done."

Another double entendre. Ella cleared her throat and then took another drink of her soda, hoping to cool herself off. It was so hot in this place. They'd turned the heat on far too high.

Change the subject.

"And then I went to college. I've always wanted to be an investigative journalist."

Until this case, however, that's not how she would have described her job.

"You said you've never done a murder case before. What kind of stories have you done?"

Sighing, she slumped back in her chair. She could lie but that wasn't in her nature.

"I wish you hadn't asked me that. I've never really had a story I could sink my teeth into. Not until now. My boss keeps assigning me fluff pieces like dog shows and charity three-legged races."

"They have three-legged races for charity?"

"They do," she confirmed. "You wouldn't believe some of the stories I've covered. I would beg to be assigned to something serious but Galen always said that the public loved my human interest pieces. I'm a victim of my own success. I even get fan mail."

"That sounds...creepy. Yep, creepy. And strange. To think

about all the people that see you on television every day and then write to you."

It could be creepy. Luckily, most of the time it was fine.

"They think they know me because they see me so often."

One of his brows lifted. "Do you get some jerks writing to you?"

She had a feeling he was trying to be a gentleman about the subject.

"If you're asking if I get dick pics the answer is yes."

"I never understand why guys do that," Chris declared with a grimace. "I had a buddy that would do that to women. When I asked him why he was doing it, he couldn't explain it. I also asked him if it had ever worked with a woman and he admitted that it hadn't. I just told him that the definition of insanity was doing the same thing over and over and expecting a different outcome."

"So he stopped?"

"No. He said he didn't know what I meant. He's still single, by the way. None of us are losing any sleep wondering why."

She couldn't help but giggle at the story. She was having a good time with Chris. In fact, she was enjoying herself more with him than she had with her ex the entire last six months they'd dated.

Nope. Don't go there. You're working with him. Keep it businesslike.

"So you went to college," Chris prompted. "And became a journalist. Except that you don't get to do any stories that you want to do. Is that about right? Why do you keep doing it then? Why haven't you changed jobs?"

She didn't even have to think about her answer. Sadly, she knew it all too well.

"The state of journalism," she replied crisply. "It's not doing well if you haven't noticed. Originally I wanted to be a newspaper reporter and I was hired to work at one but then there were cutbacks. I tried to get another job but newspapers aren't hiring these days. I was lucky to get the job at the station after I was laid off. Really lucky. Some of my friends that went to journalism school are doing other things these days. I don't suppose you subscribe to a newspaper?"

"I don't," Chris admitted, rubbing his stubbled chin. "But I just moved here about a month ago and I haven't even fully unpacked. I tell you what…I promise to subscribe to a local paper, okay? Just as soon as I unpack my dishes."

Another blush – this one not as bad – crawled up her cheeks. "I wasn't pushing. I guess I do get up on a soapbox about it, though. I mean, how do people expect news when they're not willing to pay for it?"

Shit, I did it again.

"I'm sorry," Ella rushed to say before he spoke. "I'll shut up now. I swear I'm done talking. I'll be quiet. Because I know that I'm a pain in the ass about this. I just need to keep my mouth shut."

This time she did shut up, snapping her lips together and pretending to zip them closed before throwing away the key.

Chris leaned forward, a smile playing on his lips. "Ella, would it make you feel better if I walk outside and buy a paper from the machine out front? Because I will if you want me to."

She lifted her hand from where she'd placed it over her mouth.

"You don't have to. I'm done."

Them she smacked her hand back so the bottom of her face was covered. Maybe he wouldn't see the color in her cheeks.

"Maybe we should just talk about the case."

The case? Yes, that was a good idea. It would keep it all on a professional level too. She was having far too good of a time with this man.

"Yes, let's do that. Do you have a plan for the next steps?"

"I'm going to keep going through the missing person files and tomorrow morning I'm going to meet with the man that found Jane's body. Robert Trask. Did you want to come along?"

Absolutely. She had so many unanswered questions about Jane Doe.

And herself. Were they related? Did she dare take the step to find out?

CHAPTER ELEVEN

JARED HAD GIVEN Chris some background on Robert Trask but had also said that he was still digging for more. Stay tuned. What he had given described a self-made millionaire in Seattle real estate.

Basically Robert Trask had been born lucky.

His family had purchased land around the city and as Seattle had expanded the price of the land had skyrocketed. As the last remaining Trask, he'd profited big and parlayed that money into buying and selling stocks and bonds. He'd done well enough that he didn't have to work for a living if he didn't want to. From what Chris could see in the file...he didn't want to.

Chris didn't blame the guy. If he'd hit the financial jackpot he might spend a little more time fishing and camping than working.

"Fancy," he said as they drove through the gates of the community where Robert Trask lived. The neighborhood was tucked near Washington Park and every one of the homes had to be several million dollars. "I couldn't even afford the property taxes on these places."

"Neither could I," Ella laughed. "I had two roommates before I took this housesitting job. What about you? How many roommates do you have?"

"Just one, and only part of the time. My daughter Annie. She's nine."

"Oh. I didn't realize you had a child."

"I guess I didn't mention it. Sorry about that. I'm just used to living in a small town where everyone knows your business."

Apparently Ella had not pictured him as a parent because she appeared quite shocked.

"I'm divorced," he went on, trying to explain without going into personal details. "She got remarried and moved here, so I did, too. You know…to be closer to Annie, not my ex-wife."

He chuckled at the thought of moving anywhere to be closer to Stacey. That wasn't going to happen. They managed to get along fine as long as they kept their distance from one another. Too much togetherness was an issue.

Parking the car in front of a large two-story home, he pulled his phone from his pocket and thumbed through his photos. They were almost exclusively of Annie. He held up the phone for Ella's perusal.

"This is Annie."

"She's pretty." Ella accepted the cell and smiled as she paged through the photos. "She dances? That's so sweet."

"She's pretty excited about that, too. She gets to wear a purple sparkly outfit for the recital. That's her new favorite color."

Ella handed back the phone. "She looks like you."

"Nah, she looks like her mom."

"No, really she does. Around the eyes and mouth. She definitely looks like you. Of course, she could look like your ex, too." She looked up at the house. Neither of them had moved to get out of the car. "So how do you want to play this? Like a good cop, bad cop thing?"

Now it was Chris's turn to laugh. "What do you know about good cop, bad cop? Hell, no. We'll play it straight and honest. That's always the best way to go into a situation. Most of them, anyway. There are exceptions, of course. If Wade's report is to be believed, and I don't have any reason not to believe it, Robert Trask found the body and that was pretty much it. He doesn't know anything more and we're probably wasting our time here today, but that's the nature of working cold cases."

"Have you worked a lot of them?" she asked as they exited the vehicle. "Cold cases, I mean."

"A few. Every police force has a couple stuffed in dusty drawers or file cabinets. You work on them when you have time, which is almost never. That's why they rarely get solved. Time goes by. Witnesses die or their memories fade. Evidence goes missing. It's an uphill battle for sure."

"But you like it."

"I do." He reached out and pressed the doorbell. "Because it's a challenge. I wouldn't want to make a career of cold cases but I do like working them when I can."

They heard the shuffle of feet on the other side of the door and then it swung open, revealing an attractive middle-aged woman dressed in casual jeans and a sweater. Her hair was dark and long, and her face perfectly made up. On her left hand she wore a huge diamond ring and band.

"Can I help you?"

"Good morning, ma'am. I'm Chris Marks and this is my associate Gabriella Scott. We have an appointment to speak with Robert Trask."

The woman's eyes widened as she gazed at Ella. "You're that woman from television. I saw you reporting from that seafood festival a few weeks ago. Right after that I had Bobby take me out for shrimp."

"That's me." Ella gave a weak smile. "I hope you enjoyed your shrimp dinner."

"It was delicious." The woman seemed to suddenly remember why they were there. "Please come in. Bobby mentioned that you were stopping by. I'm his wife Diane, by the way. Nice to meet you."

She opened the door wider and stepped back so they could enter. The foyer was done all in marble tile and the air instantly felt cooler in that room even though it wasn't warm outside.

"I'll just take you to his study. He's finishing up his shower now."

They followed Diane Trask down a long hallway to a dark oak door. She pushed it open to reveal a matching study complete with leather chairs, heavy bookcases, and a huge desk near the windows looking out on the back lawn.

"I'll just go get him. It won't be a minute." She turned to go and then paused. "Can I get you anything? Coffee, perhaps?"

Both of them shook their heads. "Thank you, we're fine," Chris assured the woman.

The door closed behind her with a click.

"I hope you enjoyed your shrimp?" Chris teased. "Really, Ella?"

She shrugged, stepping over to the windows. "I never know what to say to people when they recognize me. It's always awkward whether they like me or hate me."

"Some people hate you? They don't even know you."

"They think they do. Sometimes people are just mad and they want someone to take it out on."

Chris nodded in understanding. "If it escalates then that's when the cops get called. That's where I come in."

"I hope it doesn't come to that."

They weren't alone for long. The door swung open again and an older man – around sixty – stepped into the room. A little under six feet tall with silver hair, he was dressed in khaki pants and a light blue button down shirt.

Chris held out his hand. "Robert Trask, I presume? I'm Chris Marks and this is Ella Scott. Thank you for taking the time to meet with us."

The two men shook and Robert Trask took a seat behind his desk, indicating that they should sit also. Chris and Ella sat down on the leather chairs opposite, which afforded them a better view of their interviewee.

Tanned. Very tan for this time of year. Chris's gaze zeroed in on a few photos on the credenza behind Trask. Golf. The man liked to golf. That would explain the golden coloring.

"Please call me Bobby. Everyone does. Whenever I hear Mr. Trask I always look around for my father." Bobby laughed and sat back against the dark leather. "You wanted to talk about that day."

That day. It was an interesting way of phrasing it but yes, that's what he'd come about.

Clearing his throat, Chris perched on the edge of his chair. "We wanted to talk about the day you found Jane Doe."

Bobby nodded, his thumb and forefinger pinching his lower lip. "Have they re-opened the case then? I hadn't heard that."

Chris wasn't sure why Bobby thought they'd let him know what was going on in the investigation. Was it a case of a rich man having friends in the right places?

"The case was actually never closed," Chris explained, sparing a quick glance in Ella's direction. She was studying the room closely so he left her to that. She'd already agreed to let him take the lead in questioning. Not that she had much choice. "I'm working on trying to identify Jane."

That was step one, anyway.

"Her hands were cut off," Bobby said, as if explaining it to a child. "They can't identify her."

"Technology and time march on," Chris said, pulling out the rendering of Jane. He slid it onto the desk in front of Bobby Trask. "This is a forensic rendering of what Jane might have looked like. It was on the news last night. You didn't see it?"

According to a text Chris had received this morning, the office was busy taking leads from the hotline they'd set up. Hopefully one of them would pan out.

"I didn't," Bobby replied slowly, his gaze riveted to the drawing in front of him. His face had gone pale and for a moment Chris thought the man might pass out. "This is her?"

"Yes, it's Jane."

Hand shaking, Bobby's hand reached for a water bottle, drinking down half in seconds.

"I guess…I don't know how to explain…"

Chris didn't interrupt and neither did Ella. They let Bobby gather his obviously scattered thoughts.

"I know this is going to sound terrible," he finally said, looking up from the picture. "But it was easier not to think of her as an actual real person. You know… She was just an idea, a concept. This…this changes things."

Ella looked appalled at Trask's explanation but Chris kind of understood. Everyone dealt with things in their own way. In the past, Chris drank to numb his emotions. Bobby had pretended that Jane Doe wasn't real. It was cold and slightly callous but people had to find a way to sleep at night and it wasn't always nice and pretty.

Not wanting to cause Bobby any more turmoil, Chris quickly slipped the drawing back into his bag. "I'm afraid you might see her face on the news or in the newspaper. We're trying to see if anyone might recognize her. We want to give her a name."

"Of course, of course. A name…" Trask took another gulp

of his water. "I don't know who she is so I don't know how I can help you."

"You can tell us about that day," Chris replied. "Anything at all that you can remember. Sometimes it's the littlest details that make the biggest difference."

"It was a long time ago," Trask said. "To be honest, I've spent the last thirty years trying to forget it."

"You were driving to work." This time it was Ella who spoke in a low, almost musical voice as if telling a story to a child. "You got a flat tire and had to pull over."

His gaze somewhere far back into the past, Trask nodded. "Yes, I was working as a night guard at a warehouse. Decent pay and lots of time to study but it was boring as hell. I wanted to grab a burger on the way because I was hungry."

Bingo. Ella had a great deal of experience getting people to talk and she'd hit it out of the park this time. Bobby Trask was firmly in 1989, reliving that morning.

"You were familiar with the route," she prompted. "You'd driven it three or four times a week for almost a year."

"Yeah, I used to joke that I could do it with my eyes closed. Sometimes I was so tired that I almost did. It was an easy route and I was driving against traffic so it wasn't too bad."

"But that day it wasn't a smooth drive."

"I got a flat. I had to pull over and change the tire."

He stopped speaking, his face turned away toward the window.

Chris didn't want to break the spell that seemed to have

fallen over their witness. Holding his breath, he stayed silent praying that Ella would, too. Trask had to work through this in his own way and time.

"I'd drank a bunch of coffee to stay awake," he finally said, his lips barely moving. "So I had to take a leak. The sun hadn't gone down yet and I didn't want to be seen so I walked down the embankment and behind some trees and bushes."

Trask was pinching his lower lip between his fingers again, still not looking them in the eye.

"I was taking care of business when I saw it. At first I thought it was some sort of Halloween decoration. I mean...I'd never seen a real skull before so I wasn't expecting it. It was covered with a bunch of leaves but since the sun was up I could see it. I don't know what made me walk over and take a closer look but I did. That's when I saw there were other bones. It dawned on me that this wasn't any Halloween prank. It might be real. So I ran up to my car and drove away. At first, I wasn't going to call anyone or say anything. I was scared, you know? And I still didn't trust what I'd seen. I kept thinking that I must have been mistaken. I must have just misunderstood."

Trask's breathing was ragged now, his shoulders rising and falling rapidly. His hands gripped the edge of the desk, the knuckles white. When he suddenly turned back to Chris, the pupils of his eyes were blown wide and his face was an ashen color.

"Whatever had happened I didn't want to get involved but something kept me from just walking away. So I pulled over at a gas station and called the cops. They said they'd check it out."

The color was coming back into Trask's face. He appeared more relaxed with each passing moment.

"What happened then, Bobby?" Chris asked. "They found Jane Doe. Did they come talk to you?"

Chris already knew the answer but he always made a point to ask those types of questions. Just to make sure that he was getting truthful answers. Trask didn't have any reason to lie though, so this was more testing what he remembered.

"They did. I came home from work and the cops were waiting for me. They asked me a bunch of questions and I answered them. They went away and a couple of new guys came back a few weeks later, asked the same damn questions again. I gave them the same answers, and that was it. The story fell out of the paper and I never really heard anything about it again. One of the detectives gave me his card and I called him some months later to ask him if they'd ever found out who she was or who did it. He said they didn't but that he'd call me if they did. I never got a call so…"

"Was it Detective Wade that gave you his card?" Ella queried. "Wallace Wade?"

"I don't remember." Trask frowned and then pulled open the top drawer of his desk, retrieving his wallet. He fished in it for a moment and then produced a small white business card. "Here it is. Detective Wallace Wade. Yeah, that was him."

The dude still has it?

Then Chris remembered that this moment in Trask's life

would have been traumatic. He'd found the remains of a murdered woman and something like that was going to haunt a person. Especially as there had been no closure in the case.

"Did you ever go back to the scene?" Ella asked, her voice soft. Chris's head whipped around at the question. It wasn't anything he would have asked normally but now that she'd asked it he wanted to know the answer.

"Hell, no." Trask shook his head vigorously. "No way. I drive out of my way not to go there. For the longest time I had these nightmares that I would drive by, get another flat, and find another body. So no. Never. I won't ever go there again. I quit my job and got a new one."

Yep, traumatic as hell. Chris hoped that at some point Robert Trask had sought counseling to deal with what he'd seen that day.

"Is there anything else you remember about that day, Mr. Trask? Anything at all? Maybe a car parked in the median or a vehicle driving by way too slow?"

"No, I don't think so. To be honest, I wasn't really looking around me. I just wanted to get to work and not be late."

After a few more questions, Chris and Ella bid Robert McKay goodbye and headed back to their car. As they drove out of the ritzy neighborhood, Ella was scowling.

"What's wrong?"

"You asked him if he'd seen anything that day?" she replied, her brows pinched together. "But we know that the murder was long before. Why would he see anything?"

"Because the murderer might be watching and waiting for someone to find the body," Chris explained. "It's a total long shot and probably not even a possibility but I had to ask."

Ella shivered and wrapped her arms more tightly around her messenger bag. "The thought of some guy sitting there day after day, driving by for months or even years, just waiting for someone to find his handiwork. That's chilling."

Chris didn't have a chance to respond, his cell phone vibrating in his pocket. One look had him sighing out loud.

Stacey.

"Excuse me a minute, Ella. I have to take this."

Chris pulled over into a parking lot. Stacey was a talker and he didn't want to be driving and chatting at the same time.

"Hey, Stacey. I'm at work right now. What's going on?"

"The school nurse called. Annie has a fever. I'm stuck out of town with Ben. You need to get her now."

It was Chris's day to pick her up from school anyway. He would have Annie for three days while Stacey and her new husband were on a business trip. Now it looked like all the fun plans they had would be put on hold until Annie was feeling better.

Casting a sideways glance at Ella in the passenger seat, Chris made a quick decision. He could comb through missing person files and tips from the tip line in the comfort of his own home.

"I'm on my way, Stacey. Don't worry. I'll have her call you when I get her home and settled."

Just like that, his plan for the day changed. He wouldn't

have it any other way. Besides, this was another perk of the job. He didn't have set hours.

He hung up and pulled back into traffic, heading for Annie's elementary school instead of the office.

"We're taking a small detour. Ten minutes. Tops. I promise."

He'd pick up Annie, drop Ella at her vehicle, grab some files, and then head for home. He could do this single working parent thing. He could be a good dad and still find out Jane Doe's real identity. He could handle it all. Luckily, he didn't need much sleep. Or a social life. Or female companionship. Or sex.

Okay, he might miss a few items on that list.

Now…where I can order some chicken soup and have it delivered?

CHAPTER TWELVE

"I THREW UP. Twice."

Annie announced that when Chris buckled her into the backseat of his SUV, tucking her pink book bag at her feet. His daughter's cheeks were flushed and she was slightly more listless than normal but otherwise she appeared to be in good spirits.

Ella looked like she didn't know whether to puke or laugh. He was having the same issue as well. Sometimes Annie was more entertaining than anything he might see on television.

"Did you do that before or after the nurse called your mom?"

Because Stacey hadn't shared that little tidbit of information.

"I don't know. But I threw up my breakfast and lunch. Mom made me toast and scrambled eggs and for lunch I had a peanut butter sandwich. It–"

"That's enough. We get the idea." If he let her she'd go into gruesome detail. She loved gore for some reason. And what was it about farts that made kids giggle? "We have a guest in the car. Annie, this is Ella. Ella, this is my daughter, Annie. Oops, Annalise. She doesn't like to be called Annie anymore."

Ella smiled at Annie and reached over the seat to shake her

hand. He wouldn't have advised that because his little girl was currently infested with germs, and she still had to be reminded to wash her hands on occasion.

"It's nice to meet you, Annalise. I'm Ella."

"What's that short for?"

"Gabriella, but that's quite a mouthful, don't you think? I prefer Ella, but you can call me either one."

"Gabriella is so pretty," Annie said. "It's like a princess name."

Chris had hoped that his daughter was exiting the princess stage. At one point a few years ago she'd worn a plastic tiara pretty much twenty-four-seven, only taking it off to bathe. Even that had been a struggle. She'd argued that a real princess would take a bath with her tiara on. They'd barely won that argument because they didn't have any proof of how royalty actually got clean. Annie had demanded evidence.

"I'm definitely not a princess," Ella laughed. "Not even close."

Chris glanced at Annie in the rearview mirror. If she looked like she was going to boot again, he'd pull the vehicle to the side of the road. "Ella is a television news reporter. She and I are working together on a case."

Annie nodded. "The lady with no name. Can I have a popsicle when we get home?"

Ella's brow raised at Chris. He'd explain later that he didn't share details of cases with his impressionable daughter. She only knew the basics. Pulling the SUV up to the front of the office, he turned to speak to Annie.

"Yes, the lady with no name. And yes, you may have a popsicle when we get home. We have orange and banana. First, I need to grab some files."

He turned to Ella who was gathering up her messenger bag. She'd parked here at the office before their trip this morning. "Looks like I won't be able to go through those tips with you today. I'm sorry about that. If Annie is better tomorrow, maybe we can do it then."

Glancing back at Annie, Ella shrugged. "You're going home to work, right? Why don't I meet you there? I can help you there just as well as in the office."

It wasn't that Chris didn't want Ella in his home. He was fine with it. Pretty much. It was just that he didn't need Annie telling Stacey that there was a woman in his house, no matter how innocent it might be. As it was, he was finding it difficult to be strictly professional with the pretty reporter; he didn't need his ex-wife playing matchmaker, too.

There was also the fact that Annie might be contagious.

"You know you could get sick, right?"

"I never get sick. I was one of those kids who never missed a day of school. In fact, I don't remember the last time I was ill. I really don't."

Chris always had a cold at Christmastime. Every single year. It was annoying as hell.

"On your head be it then. Don't say you weren't warned."

He'd simply remind Annie that Ella was a work colleague,

not a girlfriend. With any luck, she'd forget all about it and not say anything to her mother.

"Why don't you run in and get your work and I'll stay here in the car with Annie?"

That should be fine. What could a precocious nine-year-old say to Ella that might be cringeworthy?

Shit.

He turned his attention to Annie. "Okay, but if you feel sick throw up out of the window."

Her hand might be covering her mouth, but Ella was laughing behind it.

"Sure, laugh now, but when she throws up over the back of the seat it won't be so funny."

He'd been puked on by his daughter more times than he cared to admit. She'd had a fussy tummy as a baby and toddler.

"We'll be fine. Just go," Ella urged. "The quicker you get your files, the quicker we can get Annalise settled and get back to work."

She had a point. He needed to get Annie tucked into bed with her popsicle and a Disney movie.

Then they could start sifting through all of these tips. He could only hope that one of them would pay off.

★   ★   ★

CHRIS MADE ANNIE a little nest on the couch with comfy blankets and pillows so she could watch television while munching on an orange popsicle. In the meantime, Ella had set them up a spot at the kitchen table so they could sift through the calls and emails that had come through the tip line since last night's newscast.

His apartment was on the small side and rather sparsely furnished but quite clean and tidy. The living room had large windows that splashed light on the blond oak furniture and the blue and beige sofa which appeared to be quite new. The only item that looked out of place was a brown leather chair that was soft and worn.

There were no feminine touches like throw pillows or afghans, and only two framed photos on the end table – one of Chris and Annalise, and one of a younger Chris and a devastatingly handsome older man that simply had to be his father. They were practically twins. If this was what Chris was going to look like in twenty years or more, heaven help the ladies of Seattle.

"That's my dad."

Oops. She'd been caught staring.

"I didn't mean to–"

"It's okay. I'm really proud of my dad. He's a small town sheriff back in Montana."

She opened her mouth to tell him she'd known that but then snapped it shut. Should she admit that she'd had him checked out? Would he be angry? There was really only one way to know. Onward and upward.

"I know," she admitted, heat rising in her cheeks. "I...had you and your consulting firm checked out. I needed to be sure that you were legit."

Ella didn't say she was sorry though, because she wasn't. It was her job to be cautious.

"I'm sorry I didn't tell you sooner."

That she could say honestly.

She hadn't upset Chris Marks in the least from the looks of him. If anything she'd amused the hell out of him. His smile had widened and his blue eyes twinkled. She breathed a sigh of relief that he wasn't the uptight type.

"You did? That was smart. Lots of crazy people out there. What did you find out?"

"That you are who you say you are. That you really work for JLJ Consulting and you really are Chris Marks."

"I cannot imagine why anyone would pretend to be me," he laughed. "So you know about Jared, Jason, and Logan too, I would expect?"

"Yes…and Wade Bryson."

Just the mere mention of the serial killer's name wiped the grin off of Chris's face.

"The world is a much better place without him."

"Your dad helped bring him in the first time? And the second time?"

"Logan did it the first time, but all the guys were there this time."

She wasn't exactly sure who *all the guys* were but she had a feeling there was a story there.

"Were you there?"

He shook his head. "I was working as a sheriff in a small

town in Wyoming then filling in for a guy who had been wounded on the job."

"You must have some great stories from that."

"Not really. Are you ready to go through these calls?"

Dismissed. He hadn't been curt or surly about it but he'd been definitive. He wasn't talking about it and he sure as hell wasn't talking about Wade Bryson.

"I'm sorry."

He paused sifting through the stack of papers. "What are you sorry for this time?"

"For mentioning Wade Bryson."

"You don't have to be sorry. We can talk about it if you want but I don't have much to say since I wasn't there. I did hear all about it, of course, so anything I tell you would be secondhand. The press actually didn't do too bad of a job reporting the facts. He was hunting Logan and his family and he did kill a lot of people that didn't need to die. In the end, Bryson didn't want to go back to prison. It was suicide by cop. So the answer to the question you don't want to ask is no, Logan didn't shoot him in cold blood."

Ella had read some of the news stories that had insinuated that Wade Bryson hadn't been armed when Logan Wright shot and killed him. Personally she hadn't put much stock in them.

"I wasn't going to question you about that. I think everyone knows what Bryson was. He wasn't the type to give up." She held out her hand. "Now how about you give me half of that stack and we'll get some work done."

OLIVIA JAYMES

They worked quietly for about an hour and a half, making notes on some of the tips and trying to prioritize the ones that sounded the most promising. Ultimately they would need to check them all out but there were a few that caught their eye right away. While they worked Annalise watched television and ate saltine crackers. She didn't puke.

It was the growling of Ella's stomach that interrupted their productivity. She pressed a hand to her belly, appalled at her digestive tract's annoying behavior.

"Wow, I'm sorry about that."

Laughing, Chris hopped up from his chair and dug into a kitchen drawer, pulling out a couple of takeout menus and placing them on the table. "It's about dinnertime and I'm starved as well. These places are pretty good and Annie can get chicken soup at either. Which one would you prefer?"

"Whichever you and Annie prefer. I'm not a picky eater."

Chris pointed to the brightly colored menu belonging to a mom and pop restaurant she'd never heard of. "This place is amazing. It's all homemade. I highly recommend it."

His smiled dropped and he shoved his hands in his pockets.

"I just assumed you'd stay and eat so we could keep working. You probably need to get home to your boyfriend or husband."

Was Chris fishing for information? Was he attracted to her? She was definitely attracted to him, but hadn't given it much attention because they were working together. Her friends would have urged her to ask him out already. Make a move. As if she knew how to do that.

124

"I don't have a husband or a boyfriend. I am babysitting a cat but he's used to eating dinner late when I get home from work. I've been wanting a dog but I work so much I don't think it would be fair, plus I don't even have my own place right now. So yes, I'll stay for dinner and keep working."

Chris leaned forward and shook his head. "Don't say the d-word too loudly. Annie's been bugging me for a dog. She's also been bugging Stacey as well. One of us is going to cave before too long."

"I had a dog when I was her age. It's a good lesson that your own needs aren't the center of the universe."

Ella had to admit that she was extremely curious about Chris's ex-wife Stacey. What was she like? Was she smart and accomplished? Was she beautiful?

I bet she is. Men as good-looking as Chris don't date ugly women.

Not that Ella thought she was ugly. She wasn't. Television was a visual medium so she wasn't someone that needed to wear a bag over their head. She was attractive and if she really tried with hair, makeup, and clothes, she could look damn good. But she'd never considered herself...beautiful. Her nose was a little too big and her chin too pointy. She was tall and slender though, with long, thick hair. She was also smart and funny. She was a damn catch.

If I do say so myself.

"I work too many hours to get a dog," Chris was saying, pulling her from her thoughts. "I'd love to have one, though.

Maybe…"

His voice trailed off but Ella could finish the sentence in her head. He was thinking that if he had a partner living here it might not be so bad for the canine. She'd thought that a few times herself.

Ella quickly chose a dish from the menu and Chris ordered dinner, which would arrive in a reasonable thirty minutes. At some point, Annalise had fallen asleep in front of the television so Chris turned it down slightly and let her snooze, tucking the blanket around her so she wouldn't get cold. If she was sick, she'd need the rest.

They went back to working the stack of tips but were interrupted again, not by Ella's stomach but by Chris's phone. Grunting, he stood pushing back his chair.

"I apologize but I have to take this."

Ella caught a glance of the screen before he pressed the phone to his ear.

Dad. Tanner Marks, small town sheriff extraordinaire was on the phone.

"Hey, Dad. How's it going?"

Chris hadn't spoken to his father in over a week, which was unusual. They tried to chat every three or four days, each one keeping the other in the loop of what was going on with their life. Chris would talk to his half-sister Amanda from his dad's second marriage – as much as one could talk to a small child –

and his father would talk to Annie, promising her the world when she came to visit. Annie always spent a few weeks with his dad and Maddie every summer.

"Good. It's all good," Dad assured him. The noises in the background indicated that his father was still on duty at the station. "I just got off the phone with Stacey and she said that Annie is sick and with you. Is she okay? Did you want to talk to Maddie?"

His father's wife was a doctor and the sweetest woman alive.

"I've got this covered, Dad, but thanks. I think she just had a little stomach bug. She's sleeping–"

"I want to talk to Grandpa," Annie demanded, jumping up and down next to him and trying to get Chris's cell phone. Obviously, she'd woken up and heard him. "Please. I need to talk to Grandpa."

His dad was chuckling on the other end of the line. "You better hand me over before she excites herself so much she gets sick again."

Shit, Chris didn't want that. He sat his hand on Annie's shoulder to keep her from jumping and calm her down. "I'll let you talk to Grandpa but you need to be a little quieter and calmer. Can you do that?"

Immediately his headstrong daughter was all smiles and obedience. He ought to keep Grandpa on speed dial. "I can be very quiet."

"Now what do we say when we want something?"

"May I please talk to Grandpa?"

His daughter said it so sweetly butter wouldn't have melted in her mouth.

"Yes, you may." He handed the phone to Annie. "Not too long though, because dinner should be here any minute."

Too late. She was already skipping back to the nest on the couch, paying no attention to him. Grandpa was far more important. Chris could only wish that she was that close to his own mother, but that relationship was strained and might always be. Thank goodness for Maddie. She was a terrific stand-in grandmother despite her young age.

Sighing, he sat back down at the table with Ella. "She's got a bad habit of tuning me out when she doesn't want to hear what I have to say. It's not so bad at nine but I'm guessing in a few years this could turn out to be a big problem."

He feared the teenage years, remembering the trouble he'd given his own parents. Paybacks were a bitch.

"She's seems like a normal kid, not that I know that much about children. I'm an only child and my family is very small." Ella smiled and nodded toward the living room. "You're good with her."

He thought about what a mess he'd been when Annie was born. He hadn't been such a great dad then. He had a lot of making up to do.

"I try."

"I think you succeed."

That might be one of the nicest things anyone had ever said to him.

Ella Scott was becoming a dangerous woman and she wasn't even trying. She was smart, funny, ambitious, and most of all, she was kind. She looked damned good, too. It had been a long time since he'd met a woman who had caught his interest.

This one had done it so easily.

CHAPTER THIRTEEN

A S THE EVENING wore on, Ella was feeling more and more guilty about not telling Chris the truth. The whole situation was incredibly personal and frankly, not one she really wanted to discuss with someone she'd met only recently. Heck, she was barely speaking to her own parents at the moment.

But…

He had no idea why this case was so important to her. He'd seemed genuinely puzzled when the delicious dinner was over and he'd put Annie to bed and Ella was still there at his kitchen table digging through all the tips that had come through. He had in fact made a joke about it being his job but that she just must be a glutton for punishment.

It was a way to ask a question without actually saying it out loud.

Why are you still here when you don't have to be?

It didn't help that he'd been so sweet and open with her tonight. He'd welcomed Ella into his home like she was a real friend. She had the distinct feeling that wasn't something he did easily but he'd done it with her. He trusted her and she wasn't sure she really deserved it.

So what do I do?

"You really don't have to stay here and do this. You must be tired by now."

This was about the third time he'd said this in the last hour and a half.

"You have to be tired, too," she replied, dodging the bigger question between them. "If you want to go to bed, I can leave–"

"No," he interjected swiftly. "I want to get this done. I just don't want my workaholic tendencies to make you feel you have to do something you don't really want to do."

"I'm okay," she assured him, rolling her stiff shoulders. "I'm actually kind of impressed. You don't seem tired at all."

He nodded toward the hallway that led to the bedrooms. "It's parent training. You don't get much sleep when you have a kid and you get even less when you're a single parent. Luckily I take after my dad. He never needed much sleep either."

"What about your wife?"

Shit, she didn't have any business asking a question like that, especially as she wasn't telling him the whole truth and nothing but the truth.

"Stacey? She likes a good night's sleep but she was great when Annie was a baby. And for the record, she's my ex-wife. She has a new husband. In fact, she told me that they're going to have a baby."

Studying Chris closely, Ella couldn't see that he was bothered by that information. She'd dated a few divorced men and one of them had definitely still been hung up on his ex.

Wait, I'm not dating Chris. We're...colleagues. That's it.

"That's wonderful for them. Does Annalise know?"

"She does now. She's excited about it, of course." He grinned wickedly. "It's almost as good as a puppy but not quite."

"Nothing is as good as a puppy."

There was silence for a long moment. There were so many questions in Ella's head but she had no business asking any of them.

"Ella, you look like you're about to burst. Just say whatever it is. It will be fine."

"I don't have anything to say."

She didn't sound convincing, though.

"I think that you do. It's okay. I'm not an easily offended man."

Oh, what the hell. It was late, she was tired and not thinking straight. She'd beg for forgiveness tomorrow in the harsh light of day when she made more sense.

"I was just sort of wondering..." Now that she'd brought it up, she didn't know how to explain it. "I mean...Annalise is nine and you're not that old. You must have been married very young."

"I was married young and that was the problem. Plus, in the beginning I was a lousy husband. It took my dad giving me some tough love for me to pull it together. It was just as we grew up, we grew apart. I still think she's a good person and a great mother. We get along pretty well, too. We didn't have one of those nasty bitter divorces, thank goodness. We try and keep it together for Annie."

Ella's cheeks burned with embarrassment. "I'm so sorry. This is really none of my business. I don't know what's got into me tonight asking you all of these personal questions. It must be all of the caffeine I've drank today."

They had put away quite a bit of coffee, although come to think of it, it had been Ella who had drank most of it.

"I'm not bothered by questions like these," Chris said with a shrug. "It's not a huge secret, to be honest. I'm divorced and I spend most of my time working or with Annie. That's about it. I do like to watch football sometimes though, if I have the weekend off. I'm actually boring when you get to know me."

Somehow Ella doubted that. Chris appeared to be intelligent and well-spoken, and a decent investigator. Definitely not a misogynist. Most men wouldn't have let her join the case. How did she know that? She worked with a bunch of guys that would have actively sabotaged all of her efforts. She'd learned quickly never to talk about her work or to trust that they just wanted to help her. And Galen had given juicy assignments to males much greener and less experienced than herself.

"I guess I'm pretty boring, too. I work and hang out with friends or family. One of my girlfriends said I needed a hobby."

"You don't have any hobbies? Not one?"

"Do you have any?"

A quick glance around his small living space didn't reveal a thing.

"I like to fish. I like working with my hands, too. I used to refinish furniture when I had a big garage."

Ella didn't hear much past the fact that he liked to work with his hands. Which, of course, had her looking down at those hands. Large and strong with calloused fingers. Her mind instantly went to thoughts of an intimate nature and she had to take a gulp of her now cold coffee to cover her flaming cheeks.

Don't think about the nice man doing naughty things. Bad Ella.

"What about a girlfriend?"

Jeez, what the hell was that? It was as if she was possessed and had no control over her own mouth. What she needed was to smack her forehead against the kitchen table. Repeatedly. Until she made better choices.

Thank goodness the question didn't seem to faze him in the least. Laughing, Chris shook his head.

"When would I have time? Between work and Annie that takes up most of it. Plus, most women don't like being dropped at the last minute so I can go chase a bad guy. My mom hated being the wife of a lawman and she never made any secret of it. The crazy hours and the crappy pay don't make for domestic bliss."

"You must be doing okay. A two bedroom apartment in the Seattle area isn't cheap," she observed. "Not that I'm asking anything about your financial situation because I'm not. My parents always said not to talk about politics, money, or sex."

Now she'd mentioned sex so it was back on her mind. Again. She was staring at his hands. Again. Shit. Clearly, she was delirious from too much caffeine and not enough sleep. She was acting like a woman that hadn't been around a good-looking guy ever in her life.

"That's one of the reasons that I'd like to hold onto my new job. But seriously, I'd work for a lot less just to get to be close to Annie. I miss her when she's not here." He stood and walked to the sink, rinsing out his coffee cup. "I think I'll go check on her. I'll be back in a minute."

Watching Chris disappear down the dark hallway, Ella took a deep breath and then let her head drop down into her hands. He'd been so friendly and open. No guile whatsoever. What she could see was what he was. He wasn't on some macho kick, he wasn't trying to prove her incapable. He only wanted to do a good job on this case and be a good dad.

Chris Marks was a good man. She could see it.

And she was lying to him. That guilt she'd shoved away all day and evening was right back, squeezing at her chest. She didn't feel good about it. In fact, she felt absolutely awful.

The truth will set you free.

It was a saying her dad liked to use at times like this. She'd never questioned him, always assuming he was right. She might feel better if she told the truth.

But it's personal.

Chris had answered some personal questions tonight without batting an eyelash.

It's painful.

A divorce probably didn't tickle but he hadn't shirked from

her nosey questions.

Does he even need to know?

At first, she'd thought the answer was a resounding no. Her possible connection to Jane wouldn't make a bit of difference. But that wasn't true. If her DNA showed that she was a family member, that narrowed down who Jane could be.

And yes, that might actually help them figure out who she was.

The more Ella denied the need to tell Chris the more she managed to convince herself that it had to be done.

She was still arguing with herself when Chris walked back into the kitchen.

"She's asleep," he said, walking back to the refrigerator and pulling out two bottles of water. He handed Ella one and opened the other. "With any luck she'll sleep through the night and feel better in the morning. She told me that some of her friends at school have had this. It didn't last long."

"That's great," Ella said, her mind still whirring with possibilities. Talk or don't talk? She hated when she wasn't decisive. Time to do something difficult. Step out on a ledge and take a chance. "Chris, we need to talk."

His brows pinched together and he sat down at the table. "Okay, is everything alright?"

Taking a deep breath, she plunged in, not allowing her own emotions to turn her back.

"Not really. There's something I need to tell you. It's important." He still looked confused. "It's about the case."

"Okay…"

Here we go. The truth will set me free. Maybe. Probably. Could be. Damn.

"And my connection to it."

★ ★ ★

ELLA HAD EXPECTED Chris to be angry that she'd kept her possible connection to Jane Doe a secret.

No, that wasn't the truth. She'd expected him to be livid. Really pissed the hell off. After all, she might be a walking, talking clue as to Jane's identity and she was withholding it.

He'd surprised her by being…calm. Maybe he didn't hear her correctly, or he wasn't comprehending what she was saying.

"Do you understand what I'm saying?" she finally asked when he'd been silent for what felt like hours but was probably only a ten or fifteen seconds. Her whole body was tensed as if ready for the verbal blow she was expecting.

"I do. You think Jane Doe could be a relative, perhaps even your own mother. Your parents admitted that they didn't tell you the truth about your adoption." He reached across the table and patted her hand. "I'm so sorry about that, Ella. I can't imagine that was an easy conversation for you and your mom and dad."

Wait…Chris was sympathetic?

"You're not mad?"

Okay, blurting out questions wasn't the best idea but Ella was outspoken and honest to a fault. She didn't practice little

138

games and she was getting the idea that this man didn't, either.

"Why would I be mad?" Chris stood and paced the small area between the table and the kitchen counter. "This was incredibly personal, so of course you wouldn't go around telling someone who is practically a stranger to you."

Except that right at this moment, Chris Marks didn't feel like a stranger. He felt like a friend. A good one.

"I could be the key to solving the case."

He stopped in front of her, their knees brushing. "True, but you're more than just a clue. You're a human being."

Frowning, she scrubbed at her cheek where a few tears had fallen as she'd made her confession.

"Do you take Xanax or something? You're so calm and cool. I thought you'd be pissed off."

His brow quirked up. "Really? Through some painfully won wisdom I've learned that I can't control and fix everything. I have to learn to adapt every now and then. I thought you'd be mad at me for stirring up trouble in your life. Looks like we're both surprised."

"My life is fine," Ella insisted, her throat beginning to grow tight. "Just great. A-okay."

I'm a lying sack of crap.

Chris didn't believe her because she didn't even believe herself. She'd been desperately trying to give herself a pep talk since that conversation with her parents but the fact was her normally well-ordered life was in shambles, her parents were upset, and she wasn't all that happy, either.

More tears began to well up in her eyes and her stomach tumbled in her abdomen. There was bile in the back of her throat and she smacked her hand over her mouth to keep from heaving up her dinner. Then Chris would be the only person that hadn't puked that day.

"It's all out of control," she blurted out, the tears falling at a faster rate. "Everything is just out of control."

Chris did what pretty much every man did when faced with tears. He panicked. At least that's what it looked like to Ella, his eyes growing wide and his neck turning red.

"Hey, it's okay," he said, awkwardly patting her on the back from where he stood. "It's going to be alright. Your parents love you and everything is going to be fine."

His attempt at comfort only served to make her feel even more awful because now she was getting sympathy for being a wimp.

"It's not going to be fine," she replied through sobs, hiccupping when she tried to calm down. "It's all as bad as it can be. I was so smug, you know? I thought I had it all under control but I was just fooling myself."

She didn't know what she'd said that made the difference but suddenly Chris's expression softened and he pulled his chair next to hers. He sat closely, his side pressed into hers and his arm wrapped around her as she cried into his cotton t-shirt.

"I know all about fooling myself," he crooned, running his hand down her back in a soothing motion. He probably did the same thing to Annie. "I know all about thinking that I have everything in the world under control but the truth is I don't know shit and it's all falling apart. But it's not that bad, honey. I promise you. You're going to get through this and be even stronger when you're done."

"You don't know that," Ella said, taking a shuddering breath and scrubbing at her wet cheeks. "You can't possibly know that it's all going to be okay."

"Let's just say that I think that it will."

She lifted her head, looking into his sympathetic blue eyes. "I was so smug. I thought I knew it all. I've met other people who have been adopted and many of them talked about wondering who they were or what their biological parents were like but not me. I thought I knew it all. I thought I was above it, which when I look back at it is a really snotty little attitude to have. I guess the karma bus backed up into my driveway and dumped a pile of shit in my yard."

"You'd been misled. That's not your fault. And I think the karma bus is busy with people who really deserve it. Like those people that don't merge until the last minute even though they saw the sign at the same time you did but they thought they could just cut in and get ahead of everyone else."

She sniffled and he pulled out a large white handkerchief from his jeans pocket. "I hate those people. I never let them in."

He dabbed at her face before handing her the handkerchief. "Neither do I. Now do you want me to get you a glass of water?"

"How about a whiskey? I could use a drink."

"Sorry, no can do. I don't keep alcohol in the house. I can

get you a soda, though."

She nodded, her face brushing the soft material of his shirt. Taking a lungful of oxygen into her lungs, she also inhaled his distinctive scent. She couldn't quite put her finger on it. There was citrus, and maybe some spice, but that wasn't all. It was warm and comforting, like wrapping a soft blanket around her shoulders on a chilly day and she didn't want to let it go, needing its feeling of refuge from a world that had gone quite cold and cruel.

Chris Marks was the epitome of solid ground. He exuded protection and safety, letting her lean on his broad shoulders if only for a few minutes. When he rose to get that drink she grabbed onto him, not ready to let him go.

"Don't–Don't go yet." She shoved the handkerchief onto her eyes, not wanting him to see her face. "I just…"

Ella wasn't ready to admit out loud that she needed Chris to hold and comfort her like she was a child. But she did. She could at least admit it to herself.

"Okay, honey," he said, his tone soft and soothing. "I'm not going anywhere until you want me to. We can just sit here as long as you need to. Do you want to cry some more?"

"No," she said, almost laughing at his question. "I do not want to cry anymore. I didn't want to cry to begin with."

With her head buried in the crook of his neck, she couldn't see him nod but she could feel his chin on the top of her head. She took another whiff of his scent and felt her muscles relax slightly. It had been far too long since the last time she'd been held as she'd cried. How long? She couldn't even remember. She'd been a child, that was for sure.

"I'm okay," she said, pulling away and sitting up straight. She instantly missed the warmth of his skin and the closeness. She had to fight the urge to go right back where she'd been, tucked safely into his strong arms. "I'm so sorry about this. I'm so embarrassed."

Or at least she should be.

"You've got nothing to be embarrassed about. You have good reason to be upset, honey," he said, pushing back a strand of hair that clung to her damp cheek and tucking it behind her ear, his skin rough and warm. "Life is uncertain for you right now. That would throw anyone off their game."

It might but that wasn't why she was crying. She was upset because...

"If I'm not who I think I am, then who am I really?"

It was the most ill-constructed question ever asked, but Chris seemed to know exactly what she meant.

"You're the same person you were before you met me. None of this changes that."

She wanted to believe him but at the moment his encouraging words rung hollow.

Who was Ella Scott? And more importantly, what should she do now?

CHAPTER FOURTEEN

THE SUN WAS barely up when Chris opened his front door the next morning. Reed and Kaylee stood on the other side wearing matching expressions of concern. They were also bearing coffee and breakfast as if Chris wasn't domestic at all. At one point that would have been true.

The smells from the bags were waking him up, however. Bacon. He was sure there was bacon. Or sausage. Either way, his stomach growled in anticipation.

"Come on in. Annie's just beginning to wake up."

Last night when Chris had called Reed to tell him the latest, Kaylee had offered to watch Annie so that he could work today. She'd insisted actually, and he'd accepted with gratitude. His daughter would be in excellent hands.

He stepped back so they could walk past him. His place wasn't large so the kitchen was only a few feet away. Reed set the bags on the table along with the three paper cups of steaming hot coffee – which smelled like heaven – while Kaylee shrugged off her raincoat.

"I'll go check on Annie. See if she needs any help getting

dressed or doing her hair."

"She's going to want Aunt Kaylee to French braid her hair again," Chris warned with a smile. "She's been trying to learn to do it herself. Lord knows I can't do it."

"If you can tie a tie, you can French braid her hair. You just don't want to." She took one of the paper cups and disappeared down the hallway.

Kaylee might be right.

Reed held up his phone. "Jason just sent me a text on the way here. It's all set up for nine-thirty this morning."

It was a DNA test. For Ella. After the bomb she'd dropped on him last night Chris hadn't managed much sleep. He'd been a little too busy calling his bosses to update them on the new information. He'd also spent a great deal of the night thinking about what this all meant for Ella. And Jane. They might be family. Jane might even be Ella's own mother. It was almost too far-fetched to be believed but it was true.

And all because he'd seen her on television and she'd looked like the drawing. What were the chances? A million to one, easy. And yet, here they were.

"How on earth did Jason get this set up so quickly? In the middle of the damn night?"

Reed simply chuckled and reached for the two paper cups, handing one to Chris. "As a former government agent he has connections. I guess those connections don't sleep or maybe they're in a different time zone. Either way, it's all systems go. They're going to put a rush on the results. Normally it takes weeks but somehow he's convinced them to make this a priority. He's called in some favors."

"Are they sending it to the FBI lab?"

"No, a private one. Easier to control the timing." Reed slapped a hand on Chris's shoulder. "You did good, rookie. Your long shot lead has paid off. You might actually figure out who Jane Doe is."

Yes...and no.

"Have I?" Chris questioned, his mind still in a tussle with his conscience. "I may have ruined Ella's life with all of this. That doesn't feel good."

"You didn't ruin that young woman's life. She knew she was adopted, right?"

Chris nodded. She had but...

"And her parents lied about the circumstances of the adoption?"

"Yes, they told her she was the daughter of her father's dead sister. She died of cancer and they'd always said that they'd adopted her because of that."

"Now she knows that's not true," Reed replied. "Truth will always win out, Chris. Remember that. No matter how hard you try to bury something, the truth will rise up. You can deal with it or you can let it clobber you. It's your choice. And now it's your girlfriend's choice."

"She's not my girlfriend."

The reply was automatic but to Chris's surprise it didn't make him feel any better to say it.

"She's your friend then. This isn't your fault. You're helping her find the truth. If she wants to know who she is, a DNA test is a good place to start."

Just who was Gabriella Scott? Chris didn't think it started or ended with her DNA. Who she was as a person was more than that. It was about Ella's innate curiosity or her gentle kindness with a sick child. It was her hell for leather attitude that made her show up at an old detective's house to dig into a story and then hang on when anyone else would have been discouraged. It was the way she hadn't given in when they'd given her shit assignments because she was a girl. And it was how she'd pretended last night that she wasn't tired when she'd practically been falling asleep at his kitchen table.

"I just don't want her to be hurt from all of this."

Eyes narrowed, Reed's lips quirked up. "Are you sure she isn't your girlfriend? Maybe she should be."

"It's not like that."

Reed just shrugged before dipped his hand into one of the delicious smelling bags. "If you say so. Now how about we have some breakfast? You have a busy day today. You're getting closer to finding the truth about Jane Doe."

Yes, but at what cost? Was the price too high? Only time would tell.

THE TRIP HAD been eerily quiet. Too quiet. It made Ella even more tense than she'd been when she'd climbed into the vehicle.

Chris was trying to be respectful but at this point in their rather strange relationship they probably didn't need the niceties.

Or maybe he was so put off by her crying jag last night he wanted to drop her by the side of the road and never see her again.

"You can ask about it," she finally said, studying his profile as he drove. Chris was a good driver, which wasn't a surprise as she'd found he was good at just about everything. Being an investigator, being a dad, and yes…being a friend.

He could have blown his top last night when she'd found the courage to tell him the truth but instead, he'd been nice. And sweet. And understanding. Shit, he'd been sympathetic, too. When she'd cried, he'd dried her tears with a real handkerchief from his pocket. Who on earth carried a real hankie anymore? When she'd chided him about it later, he'd said it was a habit he'd picked up from his father.

"If you don't want to talk–"

"It's fine," she interrupted. "So I'll just tell you. They took a cheek swab at the clinic and that was it. They said I'd get the results back soon. It was a swanky private clinic, too. Your boss must have quite a bit of pull."

"Jason called in some favors. It's not going to take weeks to get back your results. He's put a rush on it."

"It's been more than thirty years so I'm not sure that it was an emergency but I am glad that he did. I'm anxious to find out."

That was an understatement. She'd pressed Chris to call his

boss last night when she'd finally made the decision to try a DNA test.

"Did you talk to your parents?"

"I stopped by their house this morning to tell them," Ella said, remembering her mother's tears and her father's stoic visage. They'd ended up hugging and crying together. Ultimately their family ties were strong even though they'd all been thrown for a loop. It wasn't going to be easy but somehow they'd work it out. "They said they would support me in whatever I wanted to do. Of course, they kept apologizing which was awkward. I told them they don't need to keep doing that."

"I haven't met them but it's clear that they love you, Ella."

"I don't doubt their love," she replied softly, her hands wrung together. "And I love them, too. More than they can imagine. They've given me a wonderful life and I'll always be grateful for that but I have to find out the truth."

There was a small silence before Chris spoke again.

"I feel like I should be apologizing, too. I've…put your life into turmoil. I never meant to do that. I hope you know that. I was just trying to put a name to Jane Doe. That's all."

Last night as she'd tossed and turned in bed, she'd thought a great deal about how Chris had brought chaos to her once fairly peaceful existence. But wasn't there a saying?

Ignorance is bliss.

Her strong curiosity wouldn't let her just shrug her shoulders and move on with her life. She couldn't do that. Even if Jane Doe wasn't any blood relation, Ella already felt a responsibility to help Chris find the truth.

"You were just doing your job. If you hadn't contacted me, you would have been ignoring a clue. If there's one thing I've learned about you these last few days is that you leave no stone unturned."

Which was why they were in the car driving together in the first place. They were headed to interview their first tip.

Sheri Martindale. A seamstress that had called the tip line saying that the picture looked just like her best friend from thirty years ago.

"I just want you to know that I'm here for you."

After last night she didn't have any doubt that Chris would be there no matter what. He was an old-fashioned type of guy. Ella had assumed his kind had all disappeared like the woolly mammoth but here he was sitting next to her, worrying about her and wanting to protect her. For the first time in a damn long time, she'd felt cared for and cherished by a man. Her last few relationships hadn't really included comfort or sensitivity.

"You get the good guy badge today."

Chris just laughed as he pulled into a parking space. "I'm no Boy Scout. I just recognize a person in pain. I've had my share as well."

She wanted to ask but they had arrived at their destination and there was work to do.

"I'd kind of like to forget all about this for an hour or two. I just want to concentrate on the job at hand."

He pushed open his car door. "Then let's go ask some questions."

The condo community was large and there were several streets of identical buildings. Chris had driven almost all the way to the back – building J108. This place hadn't been here thirty years ago. The trees were too small and the exteriors far too new. Ella rang the bell and waited, taking in the flowered wreath on the door and the rabbit statue near the bushes. When it opened a smiling middle-aged woman stood on the other side.

"Sheri Martindale?" Ella asked, extending her hand. "I'm Ella Scott and this is Chris Marks."

"I'm Sheri. Come in, come in," the woman replied, stepping back so they could enter. "Can I get you some coffee or tea?"

With a murmur of thanks, they both shook their heads and followed her into the living room, settling onto the flowered sofa. The room was bright and airy with lots of light coming in the big picture window that looked out onto the small front yard. Sheri sat down on a chair opposite them, her hands folded into her lap.

In a way, she reminded Ella of her own mother. Around the same age and height. Both women had a few shots of silver in their hair and some lines around their eyes. Ella would place Sheri around fifty-five or six.

"Thank you for coming to see me," Sheri began, her hands wrung together until the knuckles were white. "I'm sure you must have received lots of calls."

Chris immediately took control of the interview, pulling the drawing from his messenger bag and placing it on the coffee table. "I'd like you to take a much closer look at the picture, Ms. Martindale. Do you still think it looks like your friend?"

"Call me Sheri." She picked it up and stared at it for a long time, one finger tracing the outline of Jane's face. "Yes, that's Kelly. It looks just like her. She was my best friend."

Sheri's expression had gone from fairly happy to unutterably sad just that quickly.

"Kelly...?" Chris prompted, scribbling in a notebook. Ella preferred technology.

"Perkins," Sheri said. "Her full name was Kelly Elizabeth Perkins."

Ella placed her cell phone on the table between them. "Do you mind if I record this? It makes it easier later."

"No, go right ahead. It's fine."

Now that Ella had Sheri's attention she had all of it. The older woman's gaze was riveted to Ella's face.

Ella waited for Sheri to remark on the resemblance but she didn't, simply shaking her head and turning back to Chris. "Do you think your Jane Doe is Kelly?"

"I don't really know yet. We'll need to do much more investigation before I can say for sure. Can you tell me a little bit about your friend, Sheri?"

Licking her lips nervously, the woman nodded. "Kelly and I met at a job I had right out of high school. We were both waitresses at one of those chain restaurants out by the highway. She was just a year older than me and I guess we sort of bonded. We worked the same shifts and Kelly had a car so she often gave me rides to and from work. Eventually I saved up enough money to buy my own but we still spent a lot of time with each other. We went shopping together and we spent most of our off time together."

Sheri's hand flew to her mouth and she jumped up from the couch. "I have photos. I pulled them out yesterday. They're on the kitchen counter. Let me get them."

She sped out of the living room and almost as quickly was back, holding several photos in her hand. "I thought I had more but these were all I could find."

With a shaking hand, Ella accepted them from Sheri. This was a big deal. It was one thing to look at an artist's rendering but these were real photos of a person that might or might not be related. They also might be photos of a person who had been murdered.

Bless Chris, he sat patiently while Ella looked at them. He had to want to see them as much as she did but he didn't so much as peer over her shoulder.

She'd say thank you later.

One was the two women sitting on the hood of a car, each holding a can of soda. It was sunny and they were dressed for a warm summer day. The second was the two women all dressed up for an evening out. Big hair, big shoulder pads, and lots of eye makeup up and blush.

Yes, Ella had a strong resemblance to Kelly Perkins. The photos weren't great and the colors had faded over the years but she could see it. It was there and unmistakable.

But it was the last picture that shook up Ella the most. Her breath caught in her throat when she the photo of Kelly standing sideways…showing off her pregnant belly.

"Kelly had a baby?" Ella asked, her voice shaky. Her throat was tight and her stomach clenched in her gut.

"She did," Sheri replied. The older woman was studying Ella again, this time quite openly. "A daughter named Krystle Elise. You know…like the character on Dynasty. She would be thirty-two now, I think."

Krystle. That might be my real name.

"So let's get back to your story, Sheri." Chris was putting the conversation back on track. Good thing too, because Ella wasn't capable of doing it at the moment. "You met Kelly Perkins right out of high school at a job. What happened after that?"

Sheri briefly glanced at Ella again but then turned back to Chris. "We became best friends over the next few years. We were practically sisters."

"So you knew if she was dating anyone? If she had any enemies? Things like that?"

Shifting on the chair, Sheri appeared uncomfortable. "I loved Kelly, and I don't want to speak ill of the dead. She had her issues but she had a big heart."

Ella's attention was instantly snagged by the word *issues*. "What kind of issues?"

Clearly Sheri didn't want to tell them, wringing her hands together again. Chris tried to give her a reassuring smile. "You can't hurt your friend now, Sheri. But you can help her by being completely honest with us. If our Jane Doe does turn out to be Kelly Perkins then we're going to need to know a bunch of personal information to be able to finally find out who did this and bring them to justice."

The older woman seemed to collect herself, her lips firming into a line. "Kelly had some...problems. She liked to drink and party. She liked to have fun."

Fun. That one word could mean a whole lot of different things. From Sheri's reluctance to *speak ill of the dead,* it looked like Kelly might not be the most fine and upstanding citizen Seattle had ever known.

Just what had Kelly Perkins been into?

CHAPTER FIFTEEN

C HRIS HAD LEANED forward, his elbows resting on his knees. Ella had placed the photos on the table, now more interested in hearing about Kelly than seeing still pictures of the past.

"What kind of partying did she do?"

"The usual kind," Sheri replied quickly, her tone insistent. "Parties, bars, dancing. She loved to go out and have a good time."

Slipping his hand between him and Ella, Chris placed it over Ella's, lacing their fingers together. He was about to start asking some tough questions.

"Were there men there?"

"There were always men there. Buying drinks and asking her to dance."

"Was one of those men the father of Krystle?"

Ella hand gripped his tightly, her nails digging into the skin.

"Oh no," Sheri exclaimed. "That was Tim Wagner, Kelly's sometimes boyfriend. They met in high school and they sort of dated in between her other boyfriends. He was a good dad.

Krystle spent most of her time with him and his mother."

"Because Kelly liked to party and drink?" Chris asked, glancing at Ella at his side. Her face was paler than normal but outwardly she appeared calm.

More awkward shifting on the cushion from Sheri. She didn't want to answer this one either.

"Kelly loved Krystle. She really did...but she...I guess you could say she didn't take to motherhood all that well. She wasn't ready to settle down. She used to talk about Krystle all the time, though. She just wasn't very good taking care of someone."

"But Tim was? Did he resent having to take care of Krystle?"

"No, he adored Krystle and he was a great dad. His mother adored her, too. She watched Krystle during the day while Tim was at work. He was a mechanic. He took over his dad's shop." Sheri sighed. "Kelly never appreciated him. He was too nice. She liked the bad boys."

Bad boys? Was that a euphemism for criminal element?

"Do you know any of those bad boys' names? Especially any that Kelly might have been dating when she disappeared?"

"I don't remember. Kelly didn't talk about them much when she was with me. The last year before she disappeared I didn't see her much, though."

Chris's gaze was drawn back to the photos. The smiling woman with long dark hair stared back but couldn't speak, couldn't tell her own story. She could only be described through another's eyes. The killer had taken away her voice. He wanted to give it back.

"Can you tell me about the day that she disappeared?"

Sheri's gaze dropped to the floor, her fingers absently rubbing her cheek. "By then I was working the cosmetic counter at a department store. Better pay and much better clientele. I really liked it. I got off work about six and Kelly was waiting for me outside the store. It was a surprise because as I said I didn't see her much then. We didn't have plans but she convinced me to go grab some dinner with her. I called my boyfriend and let him know that I was going to be later than I thought. I told him the store had asked me to work late."

Her cheeks had gone pink. "He wasn't the biggest fan of Kelly. He said she was a troublemaker and that I should stay away from her."

"So you didn't want him to know that you were spending the evening with her?"

"Yes, he would have been mad." Sheri's gaze moved from the floor over to the mantle where several framed photos resided. "I told him later and he was mad but he got over it. In all the years we've been married, I've never lied to him again. I made a promise that day."

Chris's gaze followed hers to a portrait of a much younger Sheri in a white dress and veil with a handsome young man.

"That's your husband?"

Smiling, Sheri nodded. "Ned. He's at work right now. He's a stockbroker. That's our wedding day. Those other pictures are our kids and that last one is my two grandchildren. I think they look like my husband."

"You have a lovely family." Chris scribbled a few more notes. "Can we go back to that night? What did Kelly talk about that night?"

"She hated her job. She was still waitressing," Sheri explained. "Not at the same place, though. She said the tips were better at this sports bar downtown. I don't even remember the name. Gilley's? Gilligan's? It was something like that. She was complaining about her job. She said her boss was handsy and that he grossed her out. She said the customers were nice, though."

"Her boss? What was his name?"

Chewing on her lip, Sheri shrugged. "I really don't remember. I think it started with a 'B'…maybe? She hadn't talked about him all that much. She hardly ever talked about work actually."

That was code for Kelly got fired a lot. Chris would lay money on that if he was the betting kind, which he wasn't.

"So you had dinner and she complained about her boss. Where did you eat?"

"Gianni's on Fifth. They had the best lasagna."

"Then what happened after you ate?"

"I needed to get over to Ned's place and Kelly said she had a late date."

"Did she say with whom?"

Sheri shook her head again. "No, she didn't mention it and I didn't think to ask. She had so many boyfriends. They came and went so I never got to know them or anything."

"So you walked out of the restaurant with her?"

"Yes, we got in the car and she drove me back to the store so I could pick up my car."

"Then what?"

Sheri frowned. "I got in my car and drove away."

"Did Kelly drive away?"

"I'm sure she did. She had a date."

"But did you see her drive away?" Chris wanted it specifically laid out. No vagaries. "Which way was she going?"

Sheri blinked in confusion a few times. "Well...I...no. No, I didn't see her drive away. I pulled out ahead of her. When I looked back she was still sitting in the empty parking lot. I assumed she was putting on lipstick or touching up her hair before she left."

An empty parking lot after dark. Not the safest place in the world.

"And that was the last time you saw or talked to her, correct?"

Sheri's eyes filled with tears. "Yes, I kept calling her but she never answered. She didn't have an answering machine so it just rang and rang. Eventually, Tim called me looking for her. He couldn't get ahold of her, either. That's when we both were really worried. He went to her apartment but she wasn't there. Her car was gone, too. So he went to the police."

"Did he file a missing person's report?"

"I think so. But nothing ever came of it. Eventually I lost touch with Tim. It was harder to keep in contact back then. No email or texting. No internet."

Sheri swiped at a stray tear making its way down her cheek. Her hands trembled visibly and she looked quite distraught. Genuinely so. Chris could be a cynical bastard at times. The closest people to the victim were often the ones he ended up arresting.

Mental note. I need to talk to Tim Wagner.

"Sheri, what was Kelly wearing that night that you saw her last?"

The older woman paused before answering, her brows drawn together. "Stone washed jeans. A striped blouse."

"What about jewelry?"

"The usual. She had a plain gold chain that she wore around her neck and birthstone studs in her ears, and of course the long chain earring from the second hole."

"Second hole?"

Chris didn't know what that was.

Ella pointed to her ear. "Some women have a second hole put in their ears. See? I have one. I rarely use it, though."

Sheri was nodding. "Yes, that's it. Kelly had this one long earring that she liked to wear all the time. She's wearing it in these photos."

Taking a close look at the pictures, Chris could see for himself that Kelly was wearing what appeared to be a long chain with gold balls that reached almost to her shoulder.

It must be an 80s thing.

Thinking back to the inventory of Jane's belongings he

didn't remember seeing any sort of earring documented. She had been wearing jeans and a striped blouse, though. He was actually sort of excited about this interview. Kelly and Jane could very well be the same person, but it was way too early to celebrate. They had many more people to talk to.

"Is there anything else you can tell us about Kelly? Anything that we should know?"

Sheri dashed away another tear. "Yes, there is. Kelly was a fighter. She would have fought to live, and she would have fought hard. If she's your Jane Doe, then whomever did this probably got the ass kicking of his life because she there is no way she would have gone quietly."

That was assuming that Jane had seen her killer coming and wasn't taken by surprise. Or that Kelly was Jane.

He had a hell of a lot more work to do before he could say they were the same. There were more secrets to uncover but they had a place to start.

Tim Wagner. The most dangerous person in a female's life was the man she loved.

Had Kelly's sometime boyfriend finally become tired of her wicked ways?

CHRIS WAS TAPPING out a text to his office while Ella sat in the passenger seat of his car, her mind replaying their conversation with Sheri Martindale over and over again as she stared at the photos in her hand.

"Don't, Ella."

Looking up, she could see the concern in his expression but right now she didn't want it. She needed to feel all of these emotions even if they weren't good for her in the long run. The strangest emotion was that she didn't feel any connection to Kelly Perkins. None at all.

"Don't do this to yourself." He placed his hand over hers, his flesh warm where hers was cold, before gently tugging the photos from her nerveless fingers and tucking them into a side pocket on his messenger bag. "We don't know that Kelly was Jane. This is only the first person we've talked to. I have to tell you that we're going to talk to a hell of a lot more people and if you get like this after every one then I'm not sure you should be accompanying me when I do this. You're going to destroy yourself if you wonder every single time if this was a relative. It's not healthy."

"I know," Ella admitted. "But those photos look just like me, don't they? Now I see what you saw."

"You didn't before?"

She tried to shrug as if she didn't care. "I just thought I resembled a drawing. It was the pictures that made it all so real. Kelly Perkins could be a blood relative. She could even be my mother."

"Or she could be someone that looks like you. Everyone has a twin, that's what they say."

"Since when do you want us not to find out who Jane is? You sound doubtful."

"We have to be sure. We have photos but we don't have much else."

She could practically see the wheels turning in his head. It was funny how they'd known each other such a short time but they could read each other like a book.

"Just because Kelly wasn't a good person doesn't mean that I can't be related to her."

The age-old question reared its ugly head. Nature or nurture? Was it blood or environment that shaped who a person was? If Ella and Kelly were family, how much personality did they share?

"It doesn't mean that you are, either." Chris sighed and rubbed the back of his neck. "The whole issue here is that Kelly and Jane aren't here to tell us about themselves. All we're going to get when we do these interviews is someone's *opinion* about them. And everyone's got an opinion. They also often have an agenda to make themselves look better in comparison. So what you're hearing may not even be true."

"You think Sheri is lying?"

"Maybe. Maybe not. But the brain does funny things as time passes, Ella. She's had thirty years to think about Kelly and that last night. Thirty years to forget details, embellish others, maybe even add some to make a better story. All we know is what she told us. Until we have corroboration that's all it is...a story."

A story. That might not even be true.

"I should know that," Ella sighed, letting her head fall back against the seat. "I'm a goddamn reporter, after all. Eyewitness testimony is the worst."

"It is. I'm not saying Sheri is lying, and I'm not saying she has a personal agenda. We just need to take her story with a grain of salt."

Ella pointed to the phone he held in the other hand. "Did you send your office a message about Tim Wagner?"

"I did. I also sent a message about that earring. I didn't see anything in the police inventory report about it."

"That's why you doubt Jane is Kelly."

Chris gave her a lopsided smile. "That's just one of the reasons I have questions. And I have questions because I'm a cop."

"Not really."

"Close enough." Chris started the engine and backed out of the parking lot. "Are you ready for our next stop? I can drop you at the office if you don't want to do this."

"No way. I'm going."

The need was even stronger, more forceful now. She had to know the truth. No matter what it was.

CHAPTER SIXTEEN

T HE NEXT STOP was Henry Johnson, a little gray-haired man in an assisted living facility. Henry was a smiling, cheerful man who invited them into his apartment and offered them lemonade and shortbread cookies. When they said no thank you, he dove into the plate himself, munching on one as he answered Chris's questions.

"What was your daughter's name, Henry?"

"Sarah. Sarah Johnson. She was eighteen when she disappeared. She went to visit a friend one day and never came back."

Ella was beginning to realize just how many missing persons there were just in this area alone. Chris had a printout from the computer pages long of women that had gone missing within a five-hundred-mile radius in the two years before Jane's body was found.

"No communication? No letters or calls?"

Henry shook his head, his happy smile vanished. "Just gone. We looked for a long time. We talked to all of Sarah's friends and we put up posters in the neighborhood but we never heard anything. It was like she'd disappeared off the face of the earth.

For years after that I looked for her in a crowd, wonder what she might be doing. But eventually you lose hope. I always felt something bad must have happened because my Sarah would have never left like that. No word and all."

"Do you have any pictures of your daughter?"

Henry pointed to the bookcase against the wall. "Over in those photo albums. Do you mind? I don't get around like I used to. Damn arthritis."

"I'll get them." Ella jumped up, glad to be able to move around and be useful. Sitting and thinking wasn't the best way to spend her day and all it did was give her a nasty headache. "Both of these?"

"One of them is the kids when they were little…Try that blue one. I think that's it."

The album was large, heavy, and a little dusty. She sat back down and opened it up on her lap, faded pictures tucked into the brittle plastic pockets.

A younger-looking Henry. A pretty dark-haired woman that was probably Sarah's mother.

A teenaged boy that resembled his father, and a teenaged girl who resembled the drawing.

Sort of.

But not like Kelly had. This was a more superficial resemblance. Both had long dark hair and a pointed chin but the eyes and nose weren't quite right.

Chris leaned over to see as well. "Is this Sarah?"

"That's my Sarah and her brother David. Good kids. A little

wild but nothing too crazy."

There were pages of photos of them as a family. Christmas. Easter. Birthdays.

"Where's David now?" Ella asked, paging through the album and pausing when saw a picture of brother and sister together posing next to the tree in Christmas pajamas.

"He's a corporate attorney in New York City. Successful, too. I'm sure Sarah would have been as well. They were smart kids. Good grades. I was proud of them."

Chris was scribbling in that notebook again, his gaze on his writing and not on the photos. He was the smart one. She, on the other hand, was fascinated by the pictures of this everyday seemingly normal family.

Were they her biological family? As before with Kelly, Ella didn't feel any sense of connection. No tug of familiarity. If she'd thought that somehow she'd just *know*...she was completely wrong. There was nothing, just a blank feeling that all of these people were strangers. Which they were in reality, but somehow she'd fooled herself into believing it might be different.

"Can you tell me what Sarah was wearing the last time you saw her?"

Henry shook his head sadly. "It was too long ago. I don't remember."

"You said you talked to her friends. Did they have any idea where she might be? Any names?"

Henry shook his head again. "I just don't remember their names. I'm not as young as I used to be."

"Did you call the police? File a missing persons?"

"I did, but I never heard anything. Like I said, we eventually just gave up." Henry's brows raised. "Do you think it's my Sarah? She needs to be put to rest finally. We never had a service or anything for her."

"I don't know," Chris replied, tucking his notebook back into his bag. "If I had someone stop by tomorrow would you be willing to give a DNA sample, Henry? They'd just swab your cheek and that would be it. It's the easiest way to tell if you're family to the deceased."

"Absolutely. I'm here every day pretty much. Don't get out like I used to." He gave Ella a smile and a wink. "It's nice to see a pretty face around here."

Chris asked a few more questions and then they bid Henry goodbye, climbing into his car and heading back to the office. They had some research to do. Chris wanted to speak to David Johnson, and he wanted details about Tim Wagner.

They had far more questions than answers.

WHEN CHRIS DROPPED her off at the station later that day, Ella wearily plodded back to her cubicle, wanting to get some of her thoughts down regarding the case.

Not about her and the case. Just the case.

It wasn't going to be easy but she had to be professional about this. Somehow she needed to find a way to divorce herself from the process of finding out Jane's identity and simply be a reporter, telling the audience the facts. No judgment, no gut feelings. Just facts.

And the facts were in short supply at the moment. After a day of interviewing people, they didn't know much more than they did this morning when she'd been filled with coffee and optimism. They had a few leads to follow up – which was a positive turn – but it was all still up in the air.

What did I expect? To solve a thirty-year-old case in one day? Not likely.

It would have been nice, though. It was her impatient nature. She wanted the truth and she wanted it now. Life didn't work that way and Jane's identity wasn't going to be any different.

Flipping open her laptop, she began typing out notes from the day. Facts only. No impressions or feelings. She summed it all up with their next steps.

"I thought you'd gone home already."

Galen was leaning over the short wall of her cubicle, a steaming cup of coffee in his hand and the usual scowl on his face. Seriously, the man never slept. He was here no matter how early she came in and here late into the evening.

"I just got here, actually. Thought I'd take a few minutes and write down some notes from today."

"Productive?"

That was Galen's standard question to all his reporters. What he really meant was did she waste her – and technically his – time today.

"It was, although it's early in the investigation. We talked to some of the people from the tip line."

"Anyone we could put on air?"

Heavens to Betsy no.

"It's too soon to say who might be good for the story," she replied instead of the flat negative she wanted. This was her boss, after all. "We have a hell of a lot more tips to follow up on."

Galen took a sip of his coffee and then rapped the cubicle wall with his knuckles. "I'd like you to do an update tomorrow. Ninety seconds. We'll flash the picture and tip line again plus some commentary from you."

"Right. Got it."

This was her job and she'd begged Galen to let her cover this story. She needed to do her damn job.

"Maybe get that guy to answer a few questions on camera. Put a face to the investigation."

Wait...

"Chris? You want to put him on the air?"

He'd hate that. He didn't like attention. She'd learned that quickly.

"Sure, why not? Is he ugly or something? Kind of stupid? Little slow?"

Not in the least. Chris was too handsome, if anything, and very smart.

"No, he's just more of an under the radar kind of guy. I don't know if they want the attention."

"Whatever you decide but I want to put a personal spin on

this story. The loss, the unknown for all of these years. How the public can help…that sort of thing. They eat that shit up. I want a regular update on this murder case. People love killers and forensics." He leaned farther over the cubicle wall. "This could be very good for your career, Ella. Play this right and it could take you far."

Her throat tightened with an unnamed emotion. She wasn't sure if it was good or bad but she was becoming too used to being in turmoil. She didn't even question it now, simply enduring it until the next wave came over her.

"I suppose it could," she managed without choking. "This case…means a lot."

His eyes narrowed at her reply. "Just take some advice, okay? From a guy that's been doing this for a damn long time. Don't let it get personal. Don't let it get into your head. That victim has been dead for a long time and nothing you do is going to bring her back to life. Report the news and move on to the next story. Don't make someone else's problems your problems."

With that Galen turned and strode away, his footsteps fading on the tile floor. He would be in his office working until the wee hours.

As for his advice, Ella would love to have taken it but it was simply too late. These might be her problems whether she wanted them or not. She'd chosen to go after the truth and there was no turning back now.

CHAPTER SEVENTEEN

T HE NEXT MORNING, Chris took a gulp of his way too hot coffee – his second of the day – and felt it burn all the way to his stomach. He needed to let the damn thing cool off a bit but he desperately needed the caffeine. He'd slept like shit last night, his brain far too busy to let him rest. Realizing he wasn't going to get any more sleep he'd come into the office as soon as he'd dropped Annie at school.

Taking a bite of his cruller, he picked up his phone and punched some numbers. He needed to talk to the former detective Wallace Wade and it was finally a decent hour to call. Chris's mom had drilled it into her son's head that it would be rude to call before eight in the morning.

It was seven-fifty-nine. Close enough. The guy ran a bed and breakfast. Chris was betting he didn't get to sleep in very often.

"I hope it's not to early to call. I had a question I was hoping you could answer."

"Hell, no," Wally's voice boomed on the other end of the line. "I was up with the chickens. What can I help you with?"

"I know I'm testing your memory here but I was wondering

if you remembered Jane Doe's belongings including one earring. It would have been a long gold chain. I didn't see it in the inventory of personal possessions but I know that sometimes small items like that can be overlooked or lumped together under the generic term jewelry."

It was a long shot, but Sheri had been adamant that Kelly had been wearing it that night. If it wasn't in her belongings, it was an indication that Jane and Kelly might not be the same person.

"I can't say that I remember that, no," Wally replied. "But that was a long time ago and my memory isn't what it used to be. Funny, I can remember riding bikes with my brothers around the neighborhood but I can't remember what I had for breakfast yesterday. I think it was pancakes but I'd have to ask the wife to be sure."

"That's okay, Wally. I was just checking. If you remember it later will you give me a call?"

"I sure will. Now don't be a stranger. You and your friends stop by anytime. I have other stories I can tell, and if you come later in the day we can all have a beer."

They could have a beer. Chris would have a water or soda.

"I bet you do. We'll do that soon. Thanks again, Wally."

They ended the call and Chris made a checkmark on his to-do list. It was far too long to finish in one day, hell, even two or three days, but it felt good to actually mark an item as done.

The office was starting to come to life, although non-attendance didn't mean they weren't working. Knox had an early meeting with a witness today and Jared often worked from home when he was doing deep research.

Logan had been in his office on the phone but he stuck his head out now, motioning to Chris.

"Do you have a minute?" Logan asked. "I have some info from Jared."

"Sure." Standing, Chris headed for his boss's office, closing the door behind him. "What do you got?"

"Quite a bit. Might as well sit down. You may or may not like some of it. First of all, we checked into Henry Johnson and his daughter Sarah. Jared talked to David, Henry's son. He said that his dad is...how do I say this? Delusional. Apparently Henry Johnson was a real son of a bitch for a parent and Sarah took off the minute she graduated from high school. David wasn't far behind but he keeps in touch with the old man. Sarah doesn't and she has good reason. She took the brunt of her dad's temper and she's not the type to forgive and forget. He said that he heard from Sarah a few years ago. She reached out to him and was alive and well and living in Chicago with her husband and two children. He doesn't know if she's still there but she was fine. I asked Jared that when he has a chance to track her down and get her address and phone number for the son so they can reconnect."

"I guess that's one off of the list," Chris said with a sigh. "And it's good news that Sarah is alive. I can cancel Henry's DNA test. What should I tell him?"

"You don't have to tell him anything. His son is going to call

him today. He apologized this his father wasted our time."
Logan rubbed his chin. "Getting old is hell. Johnson's mind has
created an entire scenario to deal with his daughter's absence."

"Except the truth."

Logan nodded solemnly. "Agreed. It's probably difficult for
the man to admit that he drove his own child away."

"He seemed like a nice guy, too. Friendly, jovial. I never
would have guessed."

"Those are the ones you have to watch out for."

Logan would know.

"I also have news about Tim Wagner," Logan continued.
"He's passed on. Years ago. Leukemia. The daughter would have
been less than two years old. His mother had a heart attack
about a month later, but an adoption was already in the works.
He must have known that his mom couldn't take care of the
little girl."

"And Kelly was already dead," Chris croaked. "Ella could be
that little girl."

"It's possible."

Logan then picked up a piece of paper on his desk, holding it
out. "The interns worked late last night and found the missing
persons report for Kelly Perkins. Interesting thing about it is that
it wasn't her friend that filed it. It was her husband. Steve
Adams."

Husband?

"I'm floored," Chris admitted. "This is the first we've heard
of a husband. Sheri never mentioned him."

"Maybe Sheri wasn't that good of a friend after all," Logan observed. "Remember all we have is her perception of that time. Like Henry Johnson, she may have changed it up a little. Either way, we have a name and address on the guy. I'm guessing you'll want to talk to him."

Right away, if not sooner.

"Thanks, I will. I have a lot of questions for him."

Logan's hand was on another folder but he didn't move it from its spot on the desk. "I have something else for you. I wanted to give it to you when your friend Ella wasn't here."

That didn't sound good. What could possibly be that bad?

"Okay, but now I'm a little nervous about it."

The corner of Logan's mouth turned up. "I simply wanted you to take a look at it and decide if you wanted to show it to her. This is your case and she's helping you so I'll trust your judgment."

That was good...being trusted and all. But it still didn't tell him what Logan had in the folder.

"Thank you."

This time Logan did hand him the folder. It wasn't thick, but it was full of official-looking forms. Before Chris could identify the contents, Logan spoke again.

"It's Kelly Perkins' police file. She had a record."

Shit.

"Please let me she had a lead foot or that she parked in front of fire hydrants."

"Sadly, no. Try possession and prostitution."

Chris's head jerked up. "A prostitute? She was a hooker?"

"And a user. That poor girl lived a hard life and frankly, I'm not surprised she ended up young and dead. The odds weren't in her favor."

"Fuck," Chris muttered under his breath. "No wonder you didn't want Ella to see this."

Logan nodded. "If this is her mother...well...it's not a pretty parental picture. It does, however, shine new light on what might have motivated someone to kill her. She ran with a sketchy crowd from the looks of things. I've included the names of people she was arrested with."

A crowd Chris was going to investigate.

"I know what you're thinking and I'm afraid the news is bad there, too," Logan warned. "You want to talk to her friends but both Jared and I scoured every database we could find and we could only turn up one person that was still alive, and she's currently serving a stretch for manslaughter. I guess you can talk to her. She might have something to say."

"Live fast, die young."

Chris hadn't realized he'd said it out loud until Logan shook his head. "The last part of that is *leave a pretty corpse*. We know that didn't happen. From what our research turned up, Kelly Perkins lived on the edges of society. But I do have what might be good news."

"I could use some," Chris replied, a cynical tone in his voice. "What is it?"

Logan was smiling now. "It's Robert Trask. I pulled his

background and guess what I found? Way back in the eighties he was busted for soliciting a prostitute. I don't know if it was Kelly, but I think that's a funny coincidence. And you know what your dad says about coincidences."

The same thing all the guys did. That coincidences weren't as common as people thought they were.

"Looks like I have two places to visit today."

Ella would want to go along with him. How did he tell her about Kelly? Should he even tell her? Then again, there might not be any connection at all between them.

What should I do?

CHRIS DROPPED THE file on his desk and headed straight for the coffee pot in the corner of the office. He didn't make it. Knox stepped into his path wearing one honked-off expression.

"We need to talk."

Sidestepping the other man, Chris reached for the carafe. He wasn't in the mood for Knox's shit today, not after the conversation he'd just had. "Why?"

"We're supposed to be working together, but I haven't heard shit from you in two days."

"You didn't ask so I haven't made it a point to tell you. We're both busy on our cases. You haven't given me an update on your case, either."

The less they saw of each other the better as far as Chris was concerned.

"Arrogant asshole."

The words were muttered under Knox's breath but Chris could clearly hear them. He was sure that he was meant to. Slamming the empty cup down on the counter, he whirled around and was nose to nose with Knox. His frustration with this investigation had started him down this road but Knox was a jerk.

"Do you have a problem?"

"Yes, I do. With you. You're–"

"Knox. Chris. Get in here."

Logan's voice cut through the haze of their discord and made Chris realize that they were standing in the middle of the office.

Fuck.

With heads hanging, Chris and Knox entered Logan's office and didn't bother to sit down. They both knew why they were there and it wasn't for a friendly chat. They were going to get a new asshole chewed.

And that was if they were lucky.

"What the fuck are you two doing out there?" Logan demanded, his blue eyes icy. "I know you two aren't fond of each other but you need to understand that I don't care about that. I care that you two can work as a team."

"He–"

"You–"

Chris and Knox both started speaking at the same time but Logan waved them off. "Don't bother. You think I don't know why you two are at each other's throats? Do you honestly believe that I didn't check out both of you completely before bringing you in? Shit, I know what you ate for dinner last night and what brand of socks you wear. So this is what's going to happen. I'm going to leave the office and you are going to stay here and talk this out until you come to some sort of understanding where you can work with one another. I fucking mean it, too. You stay here until you settle your shit. I don't want it oozing out onto this team. Am I understood?"

Knox stepped forward. "If I could just say—"

"No, you may not." Logan leaned down, his knuckles resting on his desk. "You know what you can do, though? You can decide whether you really want this job. Both of you. If you don't want it and you don't want to settle this bullshit argument between the two of you then you're welcome to pack your shit and go. Your choice."

Chris and Knox stared stonily at one another, neither saying a word. Logan finally sat down and pointed to the chairs on the other side of his desk.

"Sit the fuck down."

They both sat and waited to be fired.

Logan sat back and steepled his fingers. "Now let's talk about the elephant in the room. Who wants to start?"

"I think—"

"He can't—"

"I'll start," Logan replied loudly over their voices. "Thanks to the current sheriff, who was a deputy at the time, I know a bit about this situation. You were working a string of robberies and

Knox didn't listen to Chris when it came to who may have perpetrated the crime. Making a long tedious fucking story short, Chris was right about the suspect who was eventually arrested. Have I left anything out? Do enlighten me."

"The robber was a friend of Knox's. That's why he got away with it so long."

"That is not–"

"Quiet," Logan bellowed. "No arguing. Knox, was the reason you didn't bring in the robber was because he was a friend?"

"No," Knox snarled. "And I did bring him in. He had an alibi."

"A lousy one," Chris shot back. "It sounded lame and it was."

"It was still a corroborated alibi. Once it started to fall apart, I brought him in again. Friend or no friend. I arrested him and he went to jail. End of story."

Logan's brow rose as he turned to Chris. "Is that the end of the story? It sounds like it all worked out in the end. So why are you still harboring a grudge against Knox?"

Rubbing the back of his neck, Chris counted to five before he answered. He couldn't get to ten. He was too pissed off.

"He put his friend before his deputy. If this had been a murder investigation, he might have gotten someone killed. How can I trust him to have my back?"

Knox hopped to his feet, scraping his fingers through his hair. "I've got your back. I've always had your back."

"You took Alvin's word over mine."

"I've known him since we were in kindergarten."

"I was your deputy and you didn't trust me."

Knox started to answer and then shook his head, pacing back and forth in the small space before finally facing Chris.

"You were my best deputy."

"Didn't seem like it."

"You were," Knox insisted. "Maybe I should have listened to you sooner. If you're upset about that, I'm sorry. I can't go back and change any of it."

The words came tumbling out before Chris could stop them.

"You didn't listen to me because I'm Tanner Marks' son. You constantly threw that up in my face. You wouldn't let it go."

Silence. No one said a word. It stretched out until the tension was almost too much.

"Is that true, Knox?" Logan asked at last, tapping a pencil on the oak desk. "Did you not want Chris to be right because he's Tanner's son?"

Knox's head fell back and he muttered something under his breath that no one could hear.

"I was just busting his balls about his dad. I didn't want Chris to be right because then Alvin would be a criminal. I didn't want him to be fucking guilty, Logan. Shit, he had a wife and two kids."

Chris's teeth snapped together. "I'm so fucking sick of you talking about my dad."

Rolling his eyes, Knox groaned. "At least you had a dad. I would have given anything growing up to have had a dad like yours."

More silence. This time, though, it was Chris that felt like shit.

"I didn't know that."

Knox shrugged, his gaze on his boots. "Because it wasn't all that important."

Logan stood and came around his desk. "I think it's time for me to exit the room. Take as long as you need."

He left the room, closing the door behind him. Chris and Knox simply stood there for a long time, not looking at each other or speaking. It was Knox that finally broke the silence.

"You left after that case. Just quit and walked away."

"I didn't feel respected."

"I respected you so much I recommended you for the sheriff's job in Oak Springs."

Chris's head jerked around, his eyes wide with surprise. "Oak Springs? I never knew that."

"You didn't get the job but you should have. It was local politics that kept you out. They ended up hiring a cousin of the mayor. With that kind of bullshit, you probably had a lucky escape when you think about it." Knox gave a heavy sigh and slumped against the desk. "I've got your back, Chris. Always. Even if you are a pain in the ever-loving ass."

"Back at you, asshole," Chris sniped, but the air didn't feel so tension-filled any longer. "What in the fuck do we do now?"

Knox wagged his finger at Chris. "We walk out of here acting like we still hate each other. I don't know about you, but if

Logan thinks he was right – again – he'll be fucking insufferable. Deal?"

"Deal. But actually, I still kind of hate you."

"I hate you too, and it works for us. Let's get some breakfast. I'm starved."

"I'm driving."

Knox pulled his keys from his jeans pocket. "Fuck you. I'm driving. We'll take my truck."

"Fine. You can pick up the check, too."

"Cheap bastard."

It was a start. It wasn't going to go away in an instant but for the first time in a long time Chris was confident that Knox was on his side.

Friends? That was taking things a little too far.

WHEN CONFLICTED THERE was only one person that Chris wanted to talk it out with. His dad.

They'd spent a good portion of Chris's young adult years at loggerheads but things were different now. The respect was mutual and when they did disagree they talked it out like adults.

It was kind of funny that now Chris was an adult with a job, a kid, and more responsibilities than he cared to name how his father started looking and sounding like a genius.

The office wasn't the most private of venues so Chris stepped outside, his jacket zipped against the cool breeze. A light rain was falling but then this was Seattle. His dad picked up on the second ring.

"Morning, son. Is everything okay with Annie?"

"She's fine," Chris assured his father. "That stomach bug was only a twenty-four hour virus. She went to school today and Stacey is going to pick her up in the afternoon. Actually, I was calling for a bit of advice. I don't suppose you've got any wisdom for me?"

His dad chuckled on the other end of the line. "The older I get the less sure I am that I'm right about…well, just about anything. But I'll give it a shot. What's going on? Is it that case you're working on?"

Chris had given his father the lowdown a few days ago without going into great detail.

"Jared and Logan dug up some stuff about the possible victim."

"I take it that the *stuff* you're referring to isn't positive?"

"She wasn't citizen of the year, and that's the issue. This woman might be my Jane Doe but she also might be Ella's family. Perhaps even her own biological mother."

"And you're wondering how to tell her?"

"I'm wondering *if* I should tell her," Chris corrected. "Does she really need to know? The DNA test might come back as not a match. Then it doesn't really matter."

But in a way it did. Both he and Ella were becoming personally attached to Jane. They wanted to see her identified and her killer found. She deserved to lie in peace.

"You want to protect your friend? Make sure she doesn't

have to deal with any hurt?"

The minute his father asked the question, Chris knew what he had to do.

"She's already been through so much."

It sounded as lame as it truly was.

"It's commendable that you don't want to hurt her, Chris. Is she the delicate type?"

"No." The idea was laughable, actually. "She's pretty tough but she's vulnerable, too. I just…don't want to cause any more hurt than I already have."

And that was the crux of it. Chris had inflicted a wound and he didn't want to do it again.

"I think you know what you need to do, son, but I'll give you my opinion if it's important to you. I would always err on the side of honesty. Eventually the truth will come out and she may not thank you for trying to protect her. I know Maddie would have my ass in a sling."

Maddie was about half the size of Chris's dad but she didn't take any shit. She'd worked in an emergency room in Chicago and she was tougher than she appeared.

"I have to tell her the truth."

"It's probably a good idea. You want to save her from hurting, and that's admirable, but you can't shield people from the truth. Now bullets…that's something you can shield people from, but let's hope this case doesn't come to that."

"It's a thirty-year-old cold case, Dad. I doubt I'm going to have to worry about that. Thanks for the advice. Even if I didn't want to hear it."

His dad laughed. "You didn't really need my advice. You simply needed to trust what you already knew. In fact, you haven't needed my advice in a long time."

His throat growing tight, Chris had trouble replying. "I still need you, Dad."

"It's always good to be needed. Now tell me when we're going to see you and Annie again."

"We'll come visit. Just as soon as I close this case."

CHAPTER EIGHTEEN

C HRIS HAD BEEN uncharacteristically quiet during their drive to see Robert Trask. Normally, he liked to talk about the weather, the traffic, how hungry he was, and what he'd read in the paper that morning. Today? Not so much.

When he'd picked Ella up he'd smiled and greeted her normally but then he'd completely shut up. This behavior had set off alarm bells in her head and fifteen minutes into the drive it hadn't improved.

"You're awfully quiet this morning. Are you feeling okay?"

Jerking his gaze from the road, Chris nodded.

And still didn't say anything.

"You're starting to freak me out here, Marks. What's going on? I usually can't shut you up but now your lips are buttoned tight. Something isn't right."

To her surprise Chris didn't answer, instead pulling into the parking lot of a big box store. He parked at the back away from the other cars before turning off the engine.

"I have to tell you something."

Clearly, but he wasn't getting on with it. The tension had

built between them and all she wanted to do was bust through it.

"Are you pregnant? Is it mine?"

Pinching his brows together, Chris looked confused. "Huh? What?"

Maybe a joke at this particular moment wasn't the best idea, but that's what she did when it was tense.

"It was a joke," she explained, twisting in the seat so she was facing him. "I was trying to make you laugh. I guess it wasn't all that damn funny. I have a peculiar sense of humor. Ignore me."

A smile bloomed on his handsome face, growing wider until he threw back his head and laughed.

"I think your sense of humor is just fine. And no, I'm not pregnant." His smile faded. "But I do need to talk to you."

She didn't like the look on his face at all. This was bad news. She'd make another joke about only having a few months to live but she didn't want to get him off track again. Her heart beat loudly in her ears but she managed to look calm.

"So far you've done a lousy job of it. Spit it out, cowboy. Whatever it is, I can take it. Did you get reassigned to another case or something?"

If so, she'd investigate on her own.

Reaching behind the driver's seat, he pulled out a folder and handed it to her. "Logan called me into his office this morning. Jared dug up some information about Kelly."

"And it's not good news."

She didn't say it like a question because it wasn't one. She could easily see that whatever was in that folder sucked.

"Tim Wagner is dead. He died from leukemia not long after Kelly. He was in the process of putting Krystle up for adoption."

If she was Kelly's child, this might mean that she didn't have any remaining biological relatives. That was bad news but it didn't warrant the expression he was currently sporting.

"There's more though, isn't there? There's something else you need to tell me."

"Kelly had a police record."

Ella replayed the words in her head over and over again to try and make heads or tails of them. She'd heard him clearly but she kept wanting his statement to mean something else. Because if he was bringing it up, Kelly hadn't been arrested for protesting global warming. Or whatever people were protesting in the late eighties. Nuclear power, perhaps?

"So just say it." Her fingers tightened on the file. "What's in here?"

"Drugs," he answered, his voice soft. "Prostitution."

I should have known.

"That's why we're going to see Robert Trask? He was arrested for soliciting a prostitute so we're going to see if he knew Kelly?"

"Yes, that's why. We're also making a second stop. The man who filed Kelly's missing persons report said he was her husband."

A husband, too. What else did Kelly Perkins have in store?

"This is certainly the day for surprises."

"I hesitated to tell you but I figured you'd want me to be

honest."

"I do want you to be honest. Lying to me..." She shook her head. "Not after how my parents lied to me. I just can't deal with that anymore. I'd rather have the honesty even if it's not good news. I'm not some dainty little flower that has to be protected."

"That's what I told my dad."

Chris had talked to Tanner Marks about her?

"What did he say?"

"That Maddie would have his hide if he lied to her even if he was trying to protect her. He was right."

"Is your dad right a lot?"

"All the damn time. It's annoying as hell."

"My parents are right a lot, too."

Her parents had done a bad thing, but that didn't make them bad people. They'd made a mistake and they were paying for it. Her trust in them had eroded somewhat and it would take time to build that back up. In the meantime, she was still their daughter and she loved them.

"You don't have to come with me today," Chris offered. "It would be okay if you wanted me to drop you back at the station."

"I can take whatever they're going to say. I mean...the DNA hasn't come back yet. I don't want to get all angsty for nothing. We're making a bunch of assumptions here."

Although the more that Ella looked at those photos of Kelly the more she was convinced that they were indeed family of some sort. It was simply too eerie. Like looking into a mirror.

"I just don't want to see you hurt or upset."

There was an earnestness in his eyes that said the same. He was worried about her. Hell, she was worried about herself. But in the end, she'd be fine. Because anything else wasn't an option. She was no victim and she wasn't about to start now.

"Thank you. Now let's get going. I can't wait to see what Robert Trask has to say for himself."

Ella didn't like liars. She hadn't thought much of the man when she'd met him the first time and he hadn't improved upon learning more.

Had he killed Kelly Perkins and then pretended to find the body? What would his motivation be? Had he grown tired of waiting for someone else to find her?

THEIR SECOND WELCOME at Robert Trask's home was slightly chillier than the previous. His smile wasn't as easy and his body language wasn't as open. Still, he welcomed Ella and Chris into his office again but this time he didn't take a seat on the other side, instead remaining standing near the window.

What Chris had to ask him wasn't going to make the situation any better.

"We appreciate you taking the time to speak with us again," Chris said. Ella sat at his side but they'd discussed how to deal with the delicate topic. Man to man seemed like the best idea. "We do have one or two more questions for you."

"Fine, but I do have a busy day," Bobby replied pointedly. "I have other appointments."

"This won't take long." Chris shifted in his chair, glancing briefly at Ella. Might as well just go for it and deal with the shrapnel as it came. "It's come to our attention that you have an arrest record. We really need to talk to you about that."

Bobby's face instantly turned crimson, and his shoulders straightened and tensed. "I don't see that it's any business of yours. It doesn't have anything to do with finding that poor girl back then. God rest her soul."

"That's exactly what I want to do. Let this woman rest in peace, but to do that I need facts. You were arrested for soliciting a prostitute, and we have reason to believe that our Jane Doe might have also been a prostitute."

Bobby's head jerked up, his eyes wide. "You know who she is? After all of these years?"

Mental note to self. Robert Trask doesn't seem happy about that development in the case.

"It's not confirmed," Chris said. "But it's one of our possibilities. Now can we get back–"

"Let me stop this line of questioning right now," Bobby said, his hand making a cutting motion in the air. "You think that maybe I knew that girl? That I was one of her clients? No way in hell. Not even a possibility."

"How can you be so sure?" Ella asked, finally looking up from where she was taking notes. "Maybe you should look at the picture–"

"I don't need to." Bobby laughed but he didn't look happy. "Now listen to me because I'm only going to say this once. I know that I wasn't that girl's client because she wasn't my type. Do you know what I mean?"

It took a second for Chris but it dawned on him as Bobby continued to stare at the two of them, his brows raised.

"She wasn't your type," Chris repeated. "In other words, you were seeking out a...different team?"

With that Ella understood, her frown replaced by a nod.

"I was in an experimental phase in my life. Need I explain more?" Bobby, finally relaxing, leaned a hip against the dark oak desk. "The police officer took pity on me and made the report sound like something it wasn't. Back then... Let's just say it was a different time. People weren't as open-minded as they are now. You can ask the cop that arrested me. It's the truth."

Chris would ask the cop but he really didn't need to. He could tell that Bobby Trask wasn't lying. There was no deception.

"I will check, if you don't mind. I'm sorry that we had to ask you about this, but as I'm sure you can imagine we have to dot every–"

"I understand," Bobby broke in, his expression sober. "I get it. Do you really think you know who she is?"

Yes. And no. Chris was an optimistic son of a gun. It was his nature to believe.

"We've made some progress thanks to the public tips we've received. When we do confirm her identity, we'll let you know."

And when we put her killer behind bars, you can watch it on the news.

Next stop…Kelly's husband.

CHAPTER NINETEEN

S TEVE ADAMS WAS a man who had lived a hard life if his appearance was anything to go by. Tall and rail-thin, his face was gaunt, lined, and pale. His steel-gray hair was clipped close and the front receding. Chris would put his age at close to seventy but the short biography that Logan had given him said that he was closer to fifty-five.

Frankly, he looked as though a puff of wind might blow him over completely. The way his clothes hung loosely on his frame made Chris wonder if the weight loss was recent, indicating an illness.

Chris had called earlier in the day, not wanting to show up unannounced. Steve was welcoming as he showed them into his shabby apartment, the furniture as worn and faded as the man himself.

They sat down in the tiny living room and Steve picked up an old shoebox from the end table and handed it to Chris. "Photos. I thought you might want to see them. Some of me and Kelly and some of just her."

As much as he wanted to look at them, the woman sitting

beside him probably wanted it even more so he passed the box into Ella's eager hands. But as he was doing that, it appeared that Steve's attention had been captured by the female in the room. He was staring, his mouth hanging open in shock.

"Krystle...?" he breathed, his hand covering his heart as if it was giving him pains. "I never thought...you look just like her. It's like having Kelly alive again."

Steve's voice was choked and Chris could see the tears glistening in the older man's eyes. Ella too looked like she might cry, her lips trembling with emotion. Chris placed his hand on hers, squeezing her fingers in support.

"My name is Ella," she said simply, her voice barely audible. "Ella Scott."

Steve frowned but didn't seem convinced, his gaze still taking in her familiar features. "I'm sorry. You just look so much like her..."

Time to redirect. Ella wasn't comfortable under the scrutiny.

"Did Krystle spend a lot of time with you and Kelly?" Chris asked, rubbing his thumb against her wildly beating pulse. She was far more affected at this moment than she was letting on.

The older man shook his head, his eyes sad. "Just a few times. Krystle didn't spend much time with Kelly. She couldn't really take care of a little baby."

Ella had abandoned the photos, instead staring at this man that had known Kelly.

"Why don't we start from the beginning," Chris suggested, giving Ella's hand another gentle squeeze. Her skin was cold but she held onto him tightly. "How did you and Kelly meet?"

Steve dragged his gaze from Ella reluctantly. "Through a few mutual friends at a party. We hit it off right away and started spending as much time together as we could."

Since Ella was far too distracted to take notes, Chris pulled his notebook and pen from his messenger bag and scribbled a few notes. "Was Sheri Martindale one of those friends?"

Making a face, Steve shook his head. "I only met her once. She didn't like me or any of us, really. She thought we were a bad influence on Kelly."

"Were you?"

"Maybe, but she was a bad influence on us, too. Kelly didn't want Sheri to know all of the things she did. She played a part with Sheri. She could be herself when she was with me."

"Is that why she married you? And when and where did that take place?"

Logan and Jared had done a quick search and hadn't found any record of the marriage in King County.

His pale skin turned pink. "About that...well...when I put in the missing persons report I said that I was her husband so they would give me information but we never actually got married. We talked about it but we never did it. Didn't seem important at the time."

That cleared up several of Chris's questions so he skipped ahead.

"How long were you together?"

"About a year. I met Kelly soon after she had Krystle." It

only took a mention of the name and Steve's attention turned back to Ella. "You look so much like her."

"Everyone has a twin they say," Chris said loudly to pull the man's gaze back to himself. Ella was squirming again, clearly uncomfortable. He was second guessing his decision this morning to bring her but she'd done so well before. Somehow this was different. Maybe because of what they'd learned about Kelly today? "We know that Kelly had a police record."

That did it. Steve turned back to Chris, his cheeks even pinker than before.

"Yeah...right...about that...we both had run-ins with the cops but I've been clean for years."

Seeing the glazed look in Steve's eyes, Chris didn't think that was exactly true.

"Such as?" Ella prompted when Steve didn't elaborate. "Drugs? Solicitation?"

He was already shaking his head before she finished the question. "Now I never wanted her to do that. She only did it a couple of times when she was between regular jobs. I told her not to and that we could get money some other way but she said it was the easiest. Stealing was wrong."

They'd had a strange set of morals but it looked like it had worked for them.

"If she sold herself, what did you do?"

Ella's tone was chilly, her lips a tight line.

"You know...stuff. I did what I needed to do...I bartended in the same dive where Kelly waitressed. I ran errands and stuff for the owners."

Chris caught one word in particular. "Errands? What kind of errands?"

"The kind where you don't ask too many questions. Take the package, don't look in it, deliver it, and keep your mouth shut. They paid good, too. They were good guys."

I highly doubt it.

"And you did this so you had money for drugs?"

Ella's question was enunciated carefully. She was trying hard to hide her disdain but Chris could see it in the set of her shoulders. She'd taken a dislike to the man across from them.

"Not the hard stuff," Steve replied, his hand reflexively reaching out to rub his opposite arm. "That's not who we were."

Chris didn't know how Steve categorized illegal pharmaceuticals. What was hard? It didn't matter, to be honest.

"And Kelly's friend Sheri didn't know about all of this?"

"I don't know what she exactly knew. I think she suspected but she liked to fool herself into thinking that Kelly was a popular girl who just partied too much."

Chris would have to loop back with Sheri.

"Can you tell me about the last time you saw Kelly?"

"Yeah...sure..." Steve nodded, his gaze traveling back to Ella. "She showed up at the bar late one night. She was supposed to be there for her shift at six but she didn't make it until nine. I covered for her and we weren't too busy so it wasn't a big deal. I asked her where she'd been and she said dinner with a friend. We worked until closing. She was tired so I told her to go on home and I'd close up the place. She wasn't there when I got there. I never saw her again."

At this point, Chris was going to assume that the dinner had been with Sheri.

"Was she driving that night?"

"Yes, but they never found the car. The cops made me report it stolen but it didn't turn up."

Chris made a note to check that.

"So she disappeared between the bar and your place?"

"Yes."

"Were you worried?"

"Not at first."

"Not at first," Ella repeated. "Where did you think she was?"

"You know…" Steve shrugged. "I just thought she got a call from someone and went out to party. She'd be home eventually."

Ella clearly hadn't met a whole lot of lowlifes in her journalism career but Chris had come up close and personal with them during his law enforcement years. In comparison, Steve wasn't that bad. His situation was more sad than anything.

"How long had she been gone before you reported her?"

"Three days. I remembered from a television show that you had to wait that long."

State laws varied but at least he'd remembered something.

"And you never heard anything else from her? No letters or postcards? Nothing?"

"Nothing. She just…like…vanished. I kept thinking she'd

be back. Kelly...she was the restless type. I just always thought she'd be back but she never did. After awhile I lost hope. It never occurred to me that she was hurt or dead. Never."

Steve looked heartbroken, not attempting to hide his emotion from Chris and Ella.

"Do you remember what she was wearing, Steve? I know it was a long time ago but it would be helpful if you can."

Running his fingers through his short-cropped hair, Steve nodded. "I do remember because Kelly was worried about spilling beer on her shirt. It was her favorite outfit. She tied an apron on that night and she usually didn't do that. I think I have a picture... Do you mind? Can I see the box?"

Ella handed over the shoebox and Steve sifted through the photos, finally pulling out one. "Here it is. This was the first night she wore it. We were going to a party. She didn't have a lot of clothes but she loved this outfit."

Chris accepted the picture, studying the smiling woman sitting next to a much younger Steve Adams. It was faded but it clearly showed the striped blouse and stonewashed jeans that Chris had seen in the crime photos, right down to the brand tags on the back pocket of the pants.

He was pretty damn sure that his Jane Doe was Kelly Perkins. A ripple of excitement ran through him because this meant that they actually had a shot at finding the killer. Jane might get to finally rest in peace.

Ella tapped the photo. "She's wearing the earring."

Chris held up the picture for Steve. "That night she disappeared…was she wearing the long earring?"

"Yeah, she wore it pretty much every day. All the time. She only took it out to sleep. She said she didn't want it to get caught on the pillowcase."

And yet it hadn't been found. Had they simply overlooked it at the dump site? Chris didn't want to place too much emphasis on this small detail but it nagged at him. He didn't like inconsistencies. It kept him from being one hundred percent sure about her identity.

"Steve, can I borrow these photos? I'll make copies and bring the originals back to you. I promise I won't damage them."

At first, Chris wasn't sure he was going to give permission and then he nodded. "Yeah, sure. It's just all I have left of her, you know?"

"I understand and I'll be very careful. I'll bring back the originals in a couple of days, okay?" He slipped the photo back into the box and carefully closed the lid. "Steve, can you tell me the names of the guys that owned that bar you worked in? Maybe some of the regular customers?"

It was a long shot, especially if Steve's memories were twisted from whatever substances he might have been imbibing at the time, but to Chris's surprise he reeled off three names in an instant. Chris quickly wrote them down, putting stars next to their names. He wanted to be sure that Logan and Jared checked them out. They didn't sound like law-abiding, legit businessmen.

"I don't remember the customers much," Steve admitted. "But I remember my boss. He wasn't the type you would forget."

They might even be the type to commit a murder.

In the meantime, he'd put a name – a real name – to Jane's face. They were one step closer to the truth.

CHAPTER TWENTY

"NICE PLACE."

Ella laughed at Chris's dry tone. He was currently staring up at her building and taking in the fancy neighborhood.

"I'm housesitting," she explained, climbing out of his vehicle. "It doesn't belong to me. The last place I lived in I shared with two other roommates, remember?"

"So you stay here all by yourself?"

"Just me and the cat. He doesn't hog the bathroom so we're okay."

He followed her into the building and up the elevator to the top floor. There were two loft apartments on this level. One to the left and one to the right.

Ella turned right when they exited the elevator and dug into her purse for her keys while juggling her small leather backpack. Before she could put the key into the lock Chris had insinuated himself between her and the door, pushing her behind him.

"Stay here," he said softly. "Don't move."

It took a moment to register that he'd pulled a gun out from under his jacket. She hadn't even known he was carrying a weapon, although she should have assumed it. He was like a grown Boy Scout, always prepared for any situation.

And what was the situation now?

She couldn't see around his wide shoulders but he slowly opened the door that was supposed to be locked and that's when she was hit in the head with a clue by four. The gun hadn't done it but the unlocked door had. Her heart went straight to sixty miles an hour.

"I didn't leave the door unlocked this morning."

"I didn't think you had. Now stay here and call 911."

"I–"

Placing his finger over her lips, he shook his head then slipped in the front door, leaving her out in the hallway. Sweating. It was pooling on the back of her neck and under her arms as her overactive imagination played out several scenarios each one worse than the last, and every one of them ending with one or both of them lying in a pool of blood.

She had to remind herself to breathe. Inhale. Exhale. Focus. Don't wander. Stay in the moment in case Chris needs help.

Although she didn't have a fucking clue what she'd do if he did. She wasn't armed and she was no black belt. She did have some pepper spray in her backpack.

That. Get that out and be ready.

Where the hell was he? She hadn't heard anything and she didn't know if that was good or bad. Had a bad guy knocked him out silently? She couldn't hear a struggle. Ella had her ear pressed against the wall when Chris reappeared.

"It's clear but a mess. It looks like you had company. You'll need to check if anything is missing. Did you call the cops?"

Oops. No. She'd been trying to breathe.

"I was about to do that."

To his credit he didn't roll his eyes. He holstered his weapon under his jacket and pulled out his phone.

"I can do that. You go on in and check for missing items."

"I'm not really good in a crisis," she admitted, crossing over the threshold with him on her heels. "I sort of just freeze up. You're probably not like that."

"They frown on that in the police academy."

He had the phone pressed to his ear but he kept glancing her way as she walked around the living room, taking in the destruction.

It was the only word she could think of that truly fit. Couch and chair cushions slit open, pillows torn apart, drawers hanging open, drapes pulled down. Nothing had been left untouched. It was the same in the kitchen and all the other rooms. They'd been so thorough that if she'd been hiding a winning lottery ticket they would have easily found it.

"I was supposed to make sure nothing happened to the place. I was supposed to be watching the apartment. Holy crap, I have to find Merc."

An inane statement at such a moment but it still hadn't quite sunk in that she'd been robbed. Someone had broken into the apartment while she'd been out. She felt...violated. It was disturbing to even think about. Had they been watching her for awhile, getting to know her daily routine? Had they been waiting for her to leave this morning? It creeped her the hell out.

"Merc, Merc," Ella called, practically sprinting from room to room. Tears had begun to fall as she pictured the worst but then she heard a loud meow coming from somewhere in the bedroom. "Oh my God, Merc. Where are you?"

Another loud meow. This time from the bed. Kneeling on the floor, she peered under the bed and found herself looking into two golden eyes. Thank goodness, Merc had had the good sense to hide under the bed.

"Come here, kitty. Everything is going to be okay."

To her surprise, Merc launched himself into her arms, clinging to her like a lifeline. He must have been terrified.

"No one can expect you to watch their home twenty-four-seven. It's unrealistic." Chris said, tucking his phone away. "No one can do that. Is anything missing?"

Good question. One she'd been asking herself as she'd toured each room, more slowly now that she'd found the cat. The answer was far more murky.

"Well…no. Not that I can find yet. The television is still here. All the small kitchen appliances are in place, and I can't see anything missing but they must have taken something. I had my laptop with me."

"What about jewelry? Did you have anything of value?"

Ella shook her head, her gaze still scanning around the room. "No, I only have a few things and I'm wearing them. A necklace and a pinky ring. That's it."

"Clothes? Shoes?"

"I didn't notice anything." She pointed to the gigantic television on the wall. "They left the most valuable thing in the whole place. That has to be expensive."

Chris had that look on his face. The one where he was thinking about something and the wheels were turning in his head. She'd spent enough time with him to know that he'd tell her about it soon but to give him a little space in the meantime.

She watched him as he walked around the living room and kitchen, picking up an item here and there that had been tossed on the floor. Eventually he came back to stand in front of her, a frown on his face.

"It doesn't make any sense."

"I agree. Maybe they got the wrong–"

"They didn't get it wrong," Chris said with a shake of his head. "They did this to scare you. And maybe me, too. They wanted to rattle you and get you off balance."

"They've succeeded," Ella replied tartly. Her breathing and heart rate was still elevated. The entire situation had her looking over her shoulder. "I'm totally creeped out. What were they looking for?"

Chris walked over to the front door where he dropped his worn brown messenger bag just inside.

"They might have been looking for this."

"Your notes?" She didn't quite comprehend what he was trying to say. "Can you just say whatever it is you're thinking and stop making me guess?"

So much for patience. After seeing her home ransacked, it was in short supply.

"What I'm saying is that my theory is that whoever did this did it to scare you away from the Jane Doe case. Or they may have been looking for your case notes. Or mine. I doubt they were all that fussy."

It sounded far-fetched. Kind of. She'd never investigated any story important enough that people might want to warn her off. Dog shows and beauty pageants had their own drama but usually not the deadly sort.

"That's an out there conclusion you've jumped to. Maybe the burglar was inexperienced? Or confused? Maybe they were drugged out of their minds?"

It was a strange day in her life when it was preferable that crazed druggies had broken into her home, but Chris was shaking his head before she even finished her sentence.

"This wasn't random or not thought out, honey. I wish it was but whoever did this methodically ransacked your apartment. They went room by room and threw shit on the floor and sliced through pillows and cushions. They created maximum damage without really doing anything else. No threatening notes on the walls, nothing actually stolen. Think about it, Ella. Think about how long it would have taken someone to do all of this damage, hell, even two people. They had a plan, they came in and executed it. The same actions were taken in every room. That's not random or confused."

He made a good argument, one that Ella couldn't poke any

holes in. Now she was even more freaked out. This wasn't good by any stretch of the imagination.

"Why? Why me? Why not you?" She slapped her forehead and groaned. "That didn't come out right. I don't mean that I wanted this to happen to you. I'm just wondering as to why they came here."

"No offense taken. And to be honest, we don't know that they haven't been to my place, too," he pointed out. "We'll know when we get there. That's our next stop after we deal with the police."

"*Our?*"

"Do you think I'm leaving you here alone after this? No way. You're staying with me until we get to the bottom of this."

Ella wasn't a woman who took orders easily. Her first instinct was to argue about his high-handed protectiveness but then a little voice in the back of her head reminded her that she was creeped out and didn't really want to be alone. Would it be so awful to stay with him for a night or two? It would take time to put this place back together and the mattresses and couch were slashed. Unless she wanted to bunk on the floor, she couldn't sleep here.

But she didn't want to give in too easily... She didn't want Chris to think he could order her around and she'd just fall in line.

She looked around the shambles that surrounded her. "I don't know about that. I mean...maybe I should stay here."

"You cannot stay here," Chris replied firmly. He wasn't

being pushy but there was no give in his tone. The laidback guy she'd come to know was nowhere to be found. She'd run into an immovable brick wall instead. "It's too dangerous. If someone is trying to scare you off of this story then this might only be the opening salvo. The next could be much worse."

Some reporter she was. That hadn't occurred to her. Shit and fuck.

Give in gracefully. You don't really want to be alone here.

"Well...I guess I could stay with you. I could call my parents but I don't want to alarm them."

The mere thought of telling her mom and dad what had happened sounded like a terrible idea. They'd freak and then she'd freak more and...

She'd warned Chris she wasn't good in a crisis.

"Pack a quick bag." Chris peered out the window as the sound of sirens grew closer. "Once we deal with them we'll go check my place. If they've hit there, then we'll have to find a safe house."

A safe house? What kind of alternate reality had she entered? Did someone really want her to drop this story? And if so, why? It was a cold case from thirty years ago. It didn't make any sense.

Had they struck a nerve with one of the people they'd spoken to? Had they already talked to the killer and didn't realize it?

Her ringtone broke into her dark thoughts and she accepted the call without even looking to see who it was. The voice that asked for Gabriella Scott was unfamiliar but as she continued to listen to what they were saying she realized that her long day wasn't over. Not even close. When they were done, she hung up but didn't put her phone away.

Still holding it, she stared at her screensaver, a picture of Ella and her parents in front of the Christmas tree. Taken a few months ago, they were smiling and happy, not knowing any of this shit was coming at them. Life was great and always would be. Right? Not so much.

The sirens were close now but she barely registered any of the sounds around her. Her mind was still processing... It was only when Chris gently took the phone from her hand that she realized she was visibly shaking.

"Honey, what's wrong?" His arms closed around her, pulling her against his warm and strong body, but her fingers, toes, and lips still felt numb, as if she'd been out in the cold too long. The numb feeling was beginning to spread through her limbs making them feel heavy and slow. "Talk to me."

"That was the DNA lab."

She was proud that she'd been able to form words considering she couldn't feel her lips.

"What did they say, honey?"

Chris's voice was soft and gentle and for a moment she allowed herself to lean into his strength. Just for a moment. She'd be strong in a minute or two. She didn't have any choice.

"The test results came back. Jane was my biological mother."

CHAPTER TWENTY-ONE

DEALING WITH THE cops had been a pain in the ass but Chris had done his best to be patient. It wasn't their fault that Ella's world was imploding while they were trying to get a statement. They said they'd pull any surveillance video from the camera at the entrance and exit but that's about all they could do. For an expensive neighborhood, the building security left something to be desired. His own building had even less but then he had a gun on the premises. And he knew how to use it.

After the police left Chris had helped Ella pack a bag, bundling her and the cat into his vehicle as quickly as possible without actually pushing her toward the door. Having her place ransacked would have been bad enough but now she had to deal with the emotional aftermath of the DNA results. Somehow in his mind, he'd simply assumed that Ella had to be some sort of family to Kelly. The resemblance was just too strong to be a coincidence.

Besides, Chris – and his dad – didn't believe in coincidences.

She didn't say much on the drive to his place, busy watching out of the window as the scenery passed by. Every now and then the cat would meow from his little carrier but other than that no one spoke. Chris didn't interrupt her thoughts, keeping himself quiet as well and letting her deal with it however she needed to. He didn't have any answers for her situation so the least he could do was shut the hell up and give her some peace.

When they arrived at his apartment, he again made her wait outside while he checked it out but it appeared completely untouched. Inviting her in, he took her bags without comment, setting them beside the couch in the living room. She'd be staying in Annie's room tonight and he was relieved that they'd made it a more "grownup" space. Done in soft pastels, the bed was a full-size with a butterfly-themed comforter. At least Ella would be comfortable and not sleeping on a tiny mattress.

She opened the cat carrier and the small tabby sprang out and immediately found a comfy spot on the couch where he could see outside.

"I'm going to order us some dinner," he said, digging into the kitchen drawer and pulling out a stack of menus. "Did you want to take a look or should I just order a bunch of food and we'll share?"

"That sounds fine," she replied without saying which part sounded that way, the former or the latter. He didn't ask again. "I'm going to use the bathroom if you don't mind."

"Of course not. Take your time."

Ella disappeared down the hall, leaving him literally holding three menus. He picked his favorite and dialed them up, ordering enough food for a small army. They could stow the leftovers in the fridge. He did this quite often so he wouldn't have to cook for a few days. He liked to cook when Annie was there but it wasn't all that fun just for himself.

Even when she came back into the kitchen he kept his distance, giving her physical space as well as emotional. He wasn't going to add to any pressure she might be feeling.

Sitting down at the table, Ella scrolled through her phone but apparently wasn't all that interested in what she saw. Listlessly, she placed it on the table and turned her attention to Chris who was loading his breakfast dishes into the dishwasher. He'd been in too much of a hurry this morning to take care of them.

"Do you have any whiskey?"

He quickly finished wiping up the counter before answering. "Sorry, I don't keep alcohol in the house."

"Right. You said that before. Sorry."

She reached for her phone again but then stopped, heaving a heavy sigh. This was probably Chris's moment to say…something but for the life of him he didn't know what. There wasn't anything he could say that would make Ella feel better. She had to work through this the hard way.

"I didn't expect those results."

Chris froze at her words, a million questions on the tip of his tongue but he wouldn't allow even one of them to be spoken. This was her show and he was only the audience. He'd let her take the lead.

"I mean…of course, I knew it was possible, especially after I saw those photos of Kelly. We look like twins and what are the odds of that? But I just…I don't know. I guess there was a part of me that kept holding out hope that the original story that my parents had told me was true. That I was Dad's sister's baby and they adopted me after she died. I know that sounds stupid because they told me themselves that it was all just a story, a lie to make me feel better, but I wanted it to be true, Chris. I really wanted it to be real. It was all so loving and romantic and it made me feel special. But the truth doesn't make me feel like that. It makes me feel…"

That was the most words Ella had spoken since she received the news. It was good that she was working through it, but it had to be far from pleasant.

"It makes me feel unloved…and…ordinary. There's isn't anything special about me, and isn't it pathetic that I counted on that my whole fucking life?"

He couldn't keep quiet, not when she was talking about herself like that.

"You are special. What makes you think that you're not?"

Ella rolled her eyes and huffed out a breath. "You sound like my parents or one of my teachers. *Each one of you are special in your own way. Love yourself.* You think I'm special? Is that because I'm the daughter of a drug-addicted hooker?"

This was going downhill on a sled.

"You don't know what Kelly was. Not really. All we have are people's opinions."

"That police report isn't an opinion. She was a prostitute to support her drug habit. Not exactly Mother of the Year."

"And she knew it," Chris replied, coming to sit down next to her at the table. He reached for her hands, entwining their fingers together. "She knew she wasn't a great mom so you lived with your dad. She must have loved you very much. She was sick, Ella. Addiction is a disease."

Snorting, Ella wrinkled her nose. "Does that make it better?"

No, but it was an explanation. The world certainly needed more of those.

"She made some bad choices and she paid for them. Perhaps even with her life. That doesn't make her evil. It sounds like she didn't have anyone in her corner helping her to clean up her life."

"I know I should feel sorry for her…"

Ella's voice trailed off so Chris finished her sentence.

"But you don't."

"I suppose you think that makes me a real bitch."

"I think that makes you human. I'm also guessing that you can be a bitch every now and then, just like I can be an asshole. We all have that side of ourselves, but I don't expect you to hear news like this and less than an hour later be all fine about it. You're hurting and mourning but you think you're wrong to do it. You think you're not supposed to. Trust me when I say that you can't go around something like this, you have to plow forward and go right through it."

"No matter how painful?"

Her tone was full of sarcasm but that was the hurt talking.

"Life is painful," Chris replied simply. "Not all the time, but it can be. No one gets to avoid it or pretend that it didn't happen. You have to deal with it."

"I'm trying but you're not making it easy. I can only deal with it a little at a time."

There wasn't any way he could make it better for her. He didn't have that kind of power.

"You can deal with it however you want to. I'm not trying to tell you what to do."

"Yes, you are." He opened his mouth to deny it but she waved away his excuses. "You're being a typical male and trying to solve my problem. Has it occurred to you that I don't want to solve it? Maybe I just want to wallow in it for awhile. Did that occur to you?"

It did not. He wasn't sure that her characterization of the situation as a *problem* was even a good one.

"Maybe I'm just being a guy but when someone tells me they have a problem, I assume they want to solve it. If you don't, that's fine, though. It's just—"

He broke off, not knowing how to put his thoughts into words.

"It's just what?" she prompted. "Go ahead and finish it."

It was a lousy idea. He should probably order her a chocolate cake and tell her she was pretty but what the hell? Life could be painful at times and he might be finding that out in the next few minutes when she smacked him upside the head for what he was about to say.

"Technically…you're the same person you were before the phone call, and before this case. You're Gabriella Scott, reporter and house sitter. Your biological parent doesn't change that."

She gave him a look that would have felled a lesser man. "You're dumb as a stump, aren't you? I can't believe you actually said those words. That they came out of your mouth but I heard them loud and clear. You think that I should be fine because *nothing has changed.* Well, fuck you, because everything has changed and if you can't see that then you're a fucking idiot."

So I was right. I should have stayed quiet.

"You're absolutely one hundred percent correct. I don't know shit about your situation. I've never been in it before and even if I did, I probably still wouldn't have the right thing to say to make you feel better. What I'm trying to say – and badly – is that deep down who you are is unchanged. Yes, your life has changed and that may change some parts of you but who you are – who you really and truly are – as a person is solid as a rock."

Ella seemed to think about what he'd said and he thought he might be getting somewhere until she tugged her hands away and sprung to her feet, walking over to the small window overlooking the street. Even from a few feet away, he could see the tears glistening in her eyes. They were far overdue.

"Then tell me, since you know everything, *who am I?* Because I thought I knew who I was and I don't anymore. So please tell me and be specific. None of that flowery language where we're all special and wonderful and the world is rainbows and kittens."

She wanted to do this? Get into the nitty gritty? Okay, he could do that.

"How about I tell you a story first? About me and my dad."

Chris wasn't the type to talk about his personal shit but he could give up a little privacy to help someone he cared about.

And he cared a hell of a lot for this woman who was clearly in a great deal of emotional pain. She'd slipped under his defenses with a minimum of fuss. But here they were. He would do whatever he could to help her through this.

Even talk about himself.

CHAPTER TWENTY-TWO

"I 'M A RECOVERING alcoholic. I've been sober for seven years, three months, and fifteen days. This is my second attempt, by the way. I was doing pretty well on my first attempt and but I fell off the wagon, set fire to it, and then drank a bunch of whiskey while I watched it burn. The next day I felt like hell so I tried again. I take it one day at a time but so far so good."

Ella couldn't believe her ears. It had sounded like Chris had said he was an alcoholic, which couldn't be. He was the personification of chill, laidback, and practical. He was the proverbial Rock of Gibraltar in a storm.

"I don't think I understand," she said, shaking her head in denial. "That…can't be."

"Why not?" he challenged. "Because I don't act like I'm addicted to alcohol? Because I'm not hanging from the chandelier with my pants down around my ankles? Not everyone acts the same, Ella, and I'm embarrassed to admit it but I just might have swung from a light installation at one point. Doubt I'd remember it, though. There's a whole bunch I don't remember, in fact."

Searching his face, she tried to evaluate the veracity of his words but he appeared to be totally sincere.

Chris was an alcoholic. Okay…she hadn't seen that one coming.

Maybe she should have, though. He'd told her twice that he didn't keep booze in the house. She simply hadn't put it all together.

"So you're an alcoholic. Are you trying to say that you're like my biological mother or something?"

Smiling, Chris shook his head. "No, I'm saying that I'm like you, Ella."

Her brows flew up and her mouth fell open. "I'm not an alcoholic. I barely drink at all."

"I'm not talking about that. I'm talking about not knowing who we are. That's what we have in common." He settled back against the couch cushion and patted the one next to him. "Come sit with me and I'll tell my story. I warn you it's kind of boring but it has a decent ending."

Mercutio the cat must have also wanted to hear the story because he jumped from the arm of the couch right into Ella's lap. She stroked his soft fur and murmured in his ear, listening to him purr.

"Growing up, I struggled with living in my dad's shadow," Chris began. "He was something of a legend in the little town I grew up in. He was the football hero in high school, married the head cheerleader – that would be my mom, and even went into the military. When he came back he became the sheriff. Not just any old run of the mill lawman, either. Everyone said he was the best sheriff ever. He was amazing and there was supposedly nothing he couldn't do. It seemed like he knew everyone and everyone knew him. And they all adored and respected him."

"Sort of the opposite of Kelly," Ella observed. "I'm not sure how this story pertains to me."

"Give me a minute and I'll get to that."

"Sorry."

"To me it was strange that because everyone in town knew him they thought they knew me. They thought I should be just like him. A veritable chip off the old block. Hell, one better. They thought I should be his clone. Look like him, talk like him, think like him. I didn't have an identity of my own and especially in those troubled teen years that became a huge problem. I wanted to separate myself from my dad. I wanted to show everyone that I wasn't him. But I went about it all wrong."

Chris had alluded to some wild behavior before but this sounded more serious than a few teenage pranks.

"I became rebellious at the best of times, and a complete asshole at the worst. After I got married and we had Annie, it didn't get any better. I was a lousy father and husband, I couldn't hold down a job, and I spent most nights and weekends hanging out with my buddies drinking and getting into fights. I resented him for being perfect and then I resented him when he wasn't. All in an effort to create an identity separate from my father."

Ella couldn't imagine that this man sitting next to her was

the man he was describing.

"Did it work?"

Chuckling, Chris shrugged. "For some it did and for others it didn't. I learned that people see what they want to see. One of the things I had to learn the hard way was that I couldn't control how others perceive me. I could only control myself. That's tough enough."

It was still different, though.

"It's not quite the same. My biological mother was a mess and your father was a hero. Two different sets of circumstances."

"My dad had his own demons. He was an alcoholic, too."

She hadn't expected that. Chris was full of surprises today.

"Your dad was an alcoholic. How...I mean...did the town know? Did you know?"

"Dad was what you might call a functional alcoholic. He only drank when he wasn't working and he managed to keep the two separate. He was gone a lot though, so I had my suspicions when I was young. As much as I wanted to be separated from my dad, when it came time to deal with my own demons I walked right into his footsteps. It was him that got me into a rehab down in Arizona, helped me clean up and become a decent husband and father. He never gave up on me even when I'd given up on myself." Chris leaned forward, his expression intent. "I'm only telling you this because you need to understand that who you are is not defined by those around you. It's also not defined by some DNA strands. I have a lot in common with my father but I am not him. His issues are not my issues and vice versa."

"I want to believe that. But how will other people—"

"Fuck 'em," Chris replied firmly, not letting her finish. "Just fuck 'em. There will always be people who want to judge you. They'll do it no matter what and they'll make sure that you come up wanting in some way. Don't let them shake what you know in your heart is true."

"What if I'm like her?" Ella's voice trembled as she voiced her fear. "What if I screw up my life like she did?"

It was the old nature versus nurture argument, and she didn't have an answer. She only knew that she'd thought she was one person a few days ago and now she was someone entirely different.

"What if you don't?" Chris asked. "We'll never really know the whole truth of Kelly's story, Ella, because she's not here to tell it. Even then, just like the story I told you, it might be full of biases and rationalization. I'm sure my dad would tell you a different story about my youth. We have bits and pieces of who she was but we don't know her dreams or her fears. We don't know the things she tried and failed at. We don't know her successes. I don't think it's fair to judge her all these years later."

Ella's fingers trailed through Merc's silky fur. "Not everyone is going to think like you do."

"So fuck 'em," he repeated with a grin. "Don't let a few people's opinions run your life. I did and I can tell you that it didn't turn out well. It was only when I stopped caring what others thought and started caring about what I wanted that my life truly turned around. I had to do it for me. Not for my dad, or Stacey, or even Annie. For me."

"I don't want other people to run my life," Ella admitted, a lump building in her throat. "But I can't help wondering who I am right about now. I thought I had all of the answers."

"That has to have knocked you off of your feet. You thought you were the same flesh and blood family as your parents and now you found out that isn't true. But Ella, that wasn't that long ago. You've been so busy with this investigation you've barely given yourself time to digest it all and figure out how you feel about it."

How do I feel about it?

"I'm angry at my parents."

She didn't like saying it but it was true.

"That seems natural. They lied to you for a long time even if they thought it was for your own good."

"I still love them," she said swiftly, her fingers curling around Merc's sparkly blue collar. "They're still my parents. I'm just mad."

"And you've told them that?"

"Yes, they seem to understand."

"That sounds healthy then. You've expressed your feelings and they've heard you. Time will sort it all out, I would imagine."

"I don't trust them as much any more."

That was the hardest to admit. They'd shattered her trust and she was scrambling to get it back. Chris, on the other hand, was nodding as if it was totally natural.

"The day we find out our parents aren't perfect is a tough one. I remember seeing Dad drunk and it messed with my head for a long time. I'd thought he was perfect and invincible, just like the town. But seeing him as a flawed human being has made us closer. I just had to get over my anger at him. I was so mad because if he wasn't even close to perfect then what chance did I have?"

"Exactly!" Ella nodded in agreement, going up on her knees on the cushion, her excitement making her antsy. She couldn't sit still and Merc jumped down to the floor, clearly disgusted with her behavior. Chris had verbalized the thoughts she hadn't been able to describe or understand. "Our parents are supposed to teach and guide us, but if they're messed up then aren't we by default? And how much of Kelly's mess did I inherit? Because I seem to have plenty of my own without adding hers."

Chris picked up the feline and placed him on the edge of the couch. "Let me just say that in the years that I've been in law enforcement I've seen a hell of a lot of screwed up parents and the kids don't always turn out the same way. They have a tougher time in life, that's for sure, but it's not preordained that they're going to be like their parents. It seems to me that your mom and dad gave you a pretty solid start in life, better than most kids. I think you'll be fine." Chris paused for a moment. "In fact, I know you'll be fine. You've got a hell of a lot more level head than I ever did. I was one angry jerk and I blamed everyone for my problems except me. No one thought I was going to straighten up and look at me now. I'm the most boring man on the planet."

Ella might have agreed with that statement when she'd first met him but she wouldn't say it now. Chris was fascinating with all sorts of layers that she was only beginning to pull back.

"When did you get so wise, Chris Marks? I feel like I've just had a session with a therapist. Or Yoda."

Apparently he found that incredibly hilarious because he threw back his head and laughed, the sound traveling all around the room. It was rich and throaty and it made him even more attractive than he already was.

Maybe it was because what he was saying was…kind of helping. A little bit. She still felt like hell but at least now she was reminded that lots of people felt that way and they got through it. It wasn't like she didn't know that, but she'd forgotten it for a little while, instead wallowing in her misery.

I'm not alone.

"I'm not wise in the least, and I hate to give advice but frankly it looked like you needed some even if it wasn't all that good."

"Actually it helped," she admitted. "You've helped me realize though that I can't avoid this, and I'm a world class avoider. I can avoid and ignore just about anything until it's a moot point."

"But you can't do that with this. It's not going to become moot."

She shook her head. "No, that won't work here. There's only one way forward and it's full steam ahead. No taking a shortcut or a bypass. It sounds…painful."

Grimacing, Chris rubbed his stubbly chin. "I hate to say it but it might get worse before it gets better, but just deciding that you're going to get out the other side is a huge step forward."

Having taken that huge step, Ella was now exhausted. She had a hell of a lot of emotional work ahead of her but was it so bad that she just wanted to rest? She'd work on her mental health tomorrow. Tonight she didn't want to think about it.

CHAPTER TWENTY-THREE

ELLA TWISTED UNDER the covers and punched her pillow a few times more than necessary to fluff it up. She couldn't sleep. She could blame it on an unfamiliar bed or her empty stomach but those weren't the reasons she wasn't drifting off to dreamland.

It was the deep sense of violation that she couldn't shake after having her apartment ransacked.

Why? Why had they done it? Was Chris correct in thinking that they wanted to discourage her from pursuing this investigation? It was a plausible argument and she didn't have anything to counter it.

People...*strangers with ill intent*...had pawed through her belongings with their grubby mitts. They'd touched her clothes and her bed. They'd put their hands on every throw pillow and cushion in her home. She might not have picked out and bought that couch herself but she'd sat there every night and ate dinner while watching television. She'd stumbled into the bathroom in the mornings and made herself coffee in the kitchen. It was her *home* and *sanctuary* and it had been invaded. If she couldn't feel safe there…

There was no real reason not to feel secure. Logically Ella knew that. Chris had a gun, after all, and he was an experienced lawman. He wasn't about to let anyone break in and hurt them. But she couldn't shake that uneasy feeling. The one that kept her awake and staring at the windows wondering if anyone could climb in. She'd actually crawled out of bed to see if they were locked more than once.

This is crazy and a total waste of time.

Throwing back the covers, Ella swung her legs out of bed and placed her bare feet on the pastel butterfly rug next to the bed. She couldn't just lie there and wait for sleep that would never come while slowly going out of her mind. She needed to move around, maybe get a drink of water or check her email. Whatever, it didn't matter. But lying in bed counting sheep was useless.

Shoving her feet into a pair of warm socks, she padded into the kitchen in her flannel pajama pants and t-shirt. These were her favorite comfortable pants to lounge around the house, plus there was a unicorn on one of the legs. It was pastel and silly with long eyelashes and a sparkly horn but it always made her smile. Even now when life was looking a little too grim.

She poured herself a glass of water from the pitcher in the refrigerator, lighting up the tiny space. Closing the door, she turned to head into the living room to check her email but stopped short, a strangled scream erupting from her lips. She almost dropped the glass as her heart stopped dead and her blood ran cold.

Clutching her chest, Ella gasped and coughed, shaking in her wool socks. It took a moment before she could speak to the man that was standing in the middle of the kitchen, a flashlight illuminating his face.

Chris.

"Jesus motherfucking Christ, don't ever do that again. I almost fucking died right here in the damn kitchen from fright. What the fuck are you doing creeping around the fucking house? Shouldn't you be in bed dreaming of catching bad guys or something?"

He snapped off the flashlight and flipped the switch on the kitchen wall. The room was now almost bright as day. Things didn't look so scary or sinister in fluorescent lighting.

"Got quite the potty mouth when you're scared. I kind of like it." Chris set the flashlight on the counter. "And I wasn't creeping around. I was checking for noises."

It was then that she realized that he was also carrying a gun in his other hand which was also placed next to the flashlight. This was the second time he'd been packing heat and surprised her.

Wait…he'd had a gun.

"You could have killed me," she croaked, pressing a palm to her chest once again. Her heart had not only resumed beating at some point but now it was galloping as if being chased by demons. "Shit, I could be lying in a pool of blood right now. Are you crazy? You can't go walking around like that."

Her voice had gone up a few octaves and she sounded hysterical. But shit…she might have been shot.

"I couldn't have killed you because I never had the gun pointed at you," Chris explained in a far more reasonable tone than her own. "The first rule of gun safety. Don't point at anything you don't intend shooting. I had a gun, Ella. I didn't intend to shoot it."

"Unless you had to," she completed the sentence for him. She was still shaking in her socks. "What if you'd mistaken me for a burglar?"

"The second rule of gun safety is don't shoot at dark figures that you can't identify. Once again, you were never in any danger. I wasn't even close to discharging my weapon."

Her heart was still beating like a brass band in a parade.

"What if you'd touched the trigger by accident?"

Shaking his head, Chris placed his hands on her shoulders, their weight pleasant and reassuring.

"We're not going to do this, Ella. I'm not going to stand here in this freezing cold kitchen in my bare feet and answer your what-if questions all night. You're going to have to take my word for it that you were never in any danger. Now let's get to the important part of this conversation. Are you okay? Are you sick?"

No and no. No, she wasn't okay and no, she wasn't sick.

"I'm not sick."

It was the easiest answer.

"I couldn't sleep."

That was true as well.

His expression softened and he stepped closer, the heat radiating from his body making the room far warmer than the actual temperature. But as always, he kept his distance at the same time. Even if it was only a few inches. He was always the professional. Right now she wanted more. She wanted him to hold her and tell her everything was going to be fine. She didn't care if he was lying to her; she needed to hear it. She'd believe him if only for tonight. Tomorrow, of course, was another story.

"I should have expected that. To be honest, I had trouble falling asleep, too."

With his brown hair sticking up every which way, he looked like a sleepy little boy.

"I'm not sure I believe you. You look like you were sleeping just fine."

"When I finally fell asleep." He reached for the refrigerator door. "Are you hungry? I can heat something up. Or thirsty?"

She held up her glass of water. "Got something already, although I have no clue why it's not broken all over the floor."

Chuckling, he pulled open the refrigerator again. "How about I make you some of my dad's famous hot chocolate? Guaranteed to make you feel better and help you sleep."

"Guaranteed by whom?"

Rummaging in a cabinet, Chris pulled out a saucepan to go with his gallon of milk. "My dad, of course. If you don't like it, I'll give you his phone number."

While it might be interesting to talk to Chris's dad, it probably wasn't a great idea to do it in the middle of the night.

"Can I help?"

"Naw, I got this. It's easy." He pulled out a kitchen chair. "This won't take long. While I warm the milk up you can talk to me."

"About what?"

"About anything. When Annie has a bad dream, I make her hot chocolate and we talk. Eventually, her nightmare seems further away and she's able to sleep."

Fantastic, Chris was equating her with his young daughter. It was probably the unicorn pajamas.

It had snuck up on her…how much she wanted his approval. But mostly how much she wanted…him.

"Why don't you go curl up on the couch and I'll bring your cocoa to you."

Too tired to argue – and not sure why she would to begin with – Ella plopped down on the couch. She was simply out of sorts when she didn't sleep and it made her irritable. There was no reason to start a fight with Chris but she kind of wanted to. At least it would keep her mind occupied.

Idiot. That's why he wants to talk to you. To get your mind off of the break-in.

There was a fluffy blanket folded over the arm of the sofa and she tugged it over herself, tucking it in around her feet. She didn't really want to watch television but the sound in the background might help. She clicked it on and turned it to cable news out of habit, keeping the volume low. One of her co-workers from the station was animatedly talking about the weather. It was going to be chilly tomorrow.

Where in the hell was Chris? He was supposed to be making hot chocolate but–

"I rummaged in the cupboard and found the Milano cookies that I keep hidden from Annie. I thought you might be hungry."

Sighing, she smiled and murmured her thanks. She was jumpy and impatient. She'd almost given him a rash of shit for taking a few extra moments in the kitchen. He'd only been a few feet away but she was ready to admit that she didn't want to be alone.

"You keep them hidden?"

He placed the saucer of cookies and the two steaming mugs on the coffee table in front of them before sitting on the couch. Not too close. Once again, he was completely professional. Except this wasn't really a professional moment in their lives. They were both wearing pajamas. Hers had a fantasy character on them and his were dark blue with gray stripes paired with an old gray t-shirt.

"In a box of shredded wheat cereal. She wouldn't go near that."

Ella reached for her cocoa. "So what do you want to talk about?"

"I'm not picky. What do you want to talk about?"

You. I want to know more about you.

"Tell me something most people don't know about you."

I sound like some kind of groupie. Crap.

He tapped his chin, a smile playing around his lips. "Hmmm…that's a good question. Let's see…I'd eat nothing but junk food if I thought I could get away with it. Like those cookies."

Picking up a cookie, he held it up before taking a huge bite out of it.

"You can get away with it." It was amusing to watch the way he clearly relished the sweet treat. "You're an adult. You can eat chocolate cake and ice cream for breakfast if you want to. There's no one policing this, Chris."

Her gaze wandered down to his lean middle, his flat abs outlined under the worn cotton. He might love sugar but it didn't appear to be a problem. She should be so lucky.

"I'm policing it. I don't want the issues from eating a crappy diet. So I'm careful. Luckily, I like to be active. But it's fine to have a treat now and then. What about you?"

"I like chocolate but I'm more of a salty snack sort of person. Popcorn, chips, those sorts of things."

"So now it's my turn."

For what? Oh right.

"Ask me anything. At this point, you know more about my life than just about anyone in the world."

Her words came out bitter instead of the "whatever" attitude she'd been going for, but frankly, she was a lousy actress.

"I think something more is bothering you than the break-in. Do you want to talk about it?"

She didn't even have to think for a split second about the

answer.

"No."

"No?"

"No," she repeated, her tone firm. "And stop being so calm and reasonable. It's pissing me off."

His brows rose in question but he didn't verbalize it. She couldn't blame him. He was probably thinking that he needed to sit there very still until she was done having a tantrum or whatever it was that she was doing.

It was just all too much.

Kelly, her parents, the investigation, the break-in, and...Chris. She couldn't handle all of that and how she was beginning to feel for him, too. There wasn't enough brain bandwidth to deal with it all. She was losing her mind and he was sitting there as if everything was fine and dandy. He'd said he could be an asshole. How did that switch get flipped?

She couldn't sit still anymore. She needed to move around or walk or something. It was like she could jump out of her own skin. Her adrenaline raced and the blood roared in her ears. She couldn't lie here any longer and keep her sanity.

Springing up from the couch, she intended to stand and pace the living room but it didn't work out that way. As graceful as a newborn foal, her legs and feet tangled up in the blanket she'd tucked around her earlier. Arms flailing, she pitched toward the floor which was flying up to meet her but at the last minute she was granted a reprieve.

Two strong arms caught her, wrapping around her waist and

lifting her at the last minute. Instead of a goose egg on the forehead and a few bruises she was being cuddled against Chris's strong torso, feeling safe and warm. There was only one thing to say to him.

"Goddamit, Chris Marks. I fucking hate you sometimes."

CHAPTER TWENTY-FOUR

JESUS FROG IN the afternoon, Ella was in a mood. She had every right to be, of course, but that didn't mean that it wasn't a challenge dealing with her. Chris had been on his best behavior this evening and it wasn't easy. He'd tossed and turned before being able to sleep, the mere thought of her in the bedroom next door driving him crazy. This attraction was becoming a problem.

He wasn't always the most patient of men. Most of the time he could be laidback and relaxed but he could get his buttons pushed just like everyone else. Stacey had known exactly how to do it and she'd done it on purpose many times just to get a reaction from him. That's how he knew that Ella was doing the same thing. She was upset and apparently she didn't want to be upset all by herself. If she kept pushing him, she might get her wish.

"You're welcome."

He lifted her up so he could get the blanket untangled from her legs, and then set her firmly on her feet.

"Did you hear me?"

Her tone was aggressive and clearly this normally mild woman was fixing for a fight. Alrighty then. Who was he to deny her?

"I did. Did you want to tell me why you fucking hate me or is this a guessing game? Because I just love that at two in the morning."

He put a sufficient amount of sarcasm in his reply so she would know that she was walking a fine line. Not that she was in the mood to care but it was only fair to warn her.

Her shoulders stiffened and she lifted her chin, poking him in the chest with her finger. Even her cheeks had turned red. She was pissed.

"No guessing required," she replied, her tone matching his. "I'll tell you why I hate you."

"Then tell me."

"I will." Her voice was louder and her finger was still pressing against his heart. "I'm mad at you because you're so calm, cool, and collected when my life is falling apart. How can you be so fucking perfect all the time?"

She gave him another hard poke in the sternum.

"You make me want to trip you when you walk into a room just to see you struggle a little bit. You make me want to scream just to get you to yell back at me. My life is in shambles and I feel like the biggest failure in the world and you're like Ghandi. So patient and kind and sweet and it makes me sick because I don't feel kind and sweet at all. I feel…shit…I don't know how I feel. I just know that I feel something and I don't think that you do. How could you when I'm so fucked up?"

The immediate silence between them was louder than any argument. Chris replayed her words in his head over and over until he could recite them from memory. Ella, for her part, looked like she wanted to run but instead had frozen in place. Her eyes were wide and panicked and if her brain was telling her to flee her feet weren't cooperating.

If she ran, he'd run after her.

Because he was feeling something, too. It wasn't the right time in his life, it sure as hell wasn't convenient, but dammit...Ella had wormed her way into his heart. And he wasn't nearly as pulled together as she thought he was.

"First of all," he began, ticking off his first reply on his fingers. "I am not even close to Ghandi. I can have a temper at certain times and I have to remind myself not to lose my patience. I'm getting better as I get older but I still have a ways to go. In fact, I almost punched Knox in the face the other day when he was giving me shit about my dad. That wasn't mature or calm or even wise. I just might have ruined my chances of getting this job."

Ella's eyes were still wide but now she was smiling. "You almost punched him?"

"Yep, he took it pretty well, though. Logan ripped us a new one though, for fighting. He basically locked us in a room until we worked it out."

"Are you okay now?"

"We're getting there." He held up two fingers. "Now...second of all, I apparently still have issues about my dad.

I'm proud to be his son but I don't want to live in his shadow. Which is why I was mad at Knox. Remember, I did say that I'm working on that."

This time she didn't interrupt so he plowed forward. Being a coward wasn't an option at the moment. He'd better cowboy up because this was it.

"And third." He held up three fingers, his pulse speeding up with excitement and fear. He didn't want to screw this up. "Just so we're clear, I feel something, too. I doubt I'm a decent prospect as a boyfriend because I'm divorced with a kid and I'm a recovering alcoholic, and let's face it, we're ass deep in this case but I think that I might be falling for you. My timing has never sucked so much."

"I thought you were perfect," she said in a small voice. "That's awfully intimidating."

"I'm not even close. I was trying to impress you. For the record, I think you're pretty intimidating. Smart, pretty, funny. I was just trying to keep up."

Her smile widened and his heart squeezed so tightly in his chest it was painful. "I was impressed, but I like you more this way. Are you really messed up?"

"Hopelessly," he assured her. The finger poking him in the chest was replaced with her hand pressed flat against him. He could feel the warmth of her flesh even with his t-shirt in between them. "I'm just making life up as I go. I don't have a clue."

"You really had me convinced."

"Like I said, I was just trying to impress you."

She took a step closer and he could smell the coconut scent of her shampoo. "I was trying to impress you too, but I was doing a lousy job of it. I wanted you to think I was a better reporter than I really am."

"You're a damn good reporter."

She shook her head. "No, I'm an okay reporter. I'm not sure I'll ever be great."

"I'd definitely want to hear terrible news from you."

"That's the sweetest thing any man has ever said to me."

Neither one of them said anything, both still unsure as to what all of this meant. It was Ella who finally broke the silence.

"So what do we do now? Do we kiss? Do I wear your letter-man jacket around campus? Do you think they'll talk about us at school tomorrow?"

This woman was amazing. Feisty, funny, and she didn't let him get away with much. She'd sure as hell never be boring.

"I left my letterman jacket back in Montana but I wouldn't mind a kiss."

★   ★   ★

ELLA HAD THOUGHT quite a bit about what it would be like to kiss Chris Marks. She'd imagined it several ways – soft and slow, fast and hard, tentative and searching, wet and wild. She'd been way off base.

It was easy to tell that Chris had done this a time or two because he didn't hesitate once she gave him the go signal.

Cupping her face, he leaned down to capture her lips, his breath warm against her cheek. This was a man confident in his kissing skills and for good reason. He knew what he was doing. She'd bet cash money that he'd had plenty of practice. A man as good-looking as he was probably had to fight them off when he was younger. Or now even. She'd seen waitresses giving him the eye but he didn't seem to notice.

His tongue gently swiped at her bottom lip and she opened up, letting his tongue explore and tickle the roof of her mouth. His arms had pulled her closer and she could feel the heat of his body and the thump of his heart, in perfect rhythm with her own racing pulse. He took his time, in no hurry to move on as if cherishing her lips was the most natural thing in the world, something he did every day. Her universe narrowed to only the two of them, everyone else fast asleep, and she clung to his wide shoulders so she wouldn't fall into an embarrassing heap at his feet.

When their first kiss was finally over, her head was spinning and her knees jelly. Damn, he packed a punch. From the expression of pure male satisfaction he was wearing, he was feeling pretty damn happy, too.

"That was…" She didn't quite know what to say but it felt like she should say something. This shift in their relationship was big. Huge. Momentous.

"Yeah," he agreed, although she hadn't really said anything. "That was…"

Neither of them moved, content to simply stare into one

another's eyes. After a few minutes though, Ella was ready for more. She wanted Chris to kiss her again. She wanted to kiss him back. She wanted…

"We could go back to bed," she suggested. There was no way Chris would suggest it himself. That whole cowboy gentleman crap had been pounded into him from birth. She loved his chivalry but it was a gigantic orange cone at this moment, a barrier keeping them apart.

His brows pinched together and his hand reached out and smoothed a stray strand of hair back from her cheek. The mere brush of his fingers sent tingles down to her sock-clad toes.

"Do you think you can sleep now?"

"No."

"No? Then why–"

He broke off, a smile beginning to bloom on his face. He was starting to get it. She'd put his slowness down to being exhausted. Looked like they weren't going to get much rest tonight, either. They'd need massive amounts of coffee in the morning.

"I need someone imperfect to tuck me in. Know anyone who can do that?"

He bent his head so they were nose to nose. "Baby, I'm the man for the job."

She was counting on that.

CHAPTER TWENTY-FIVE

U SUALLY THE FIRST time with a man was incredibly awkward and uncomfortable. Ella didn't have dozens and dozens of first times under her belt but she'd had her fair share.

Sometimes to help herself relax she'd have a few glasses of wine and it would loosen her up a little bit so she wouldn't be so shy, but that wasn't an option. She simply wasn't the type to confidently toss her clothes aside and stand in the middle of Chris's bedroom bare-ass naked, just as bold as brass. She hadn't been brought up in a house that encouraged casual nudity, or any other type of nudity, to be perfectly honest. There was a time and a place for all of that.

So it was a shock how easily her clothes seem to melt off of her body under Chris's skillful but gentle hands. Between his passionate kisses and teasing touch she barely noticed as her unicorn pajamas ended up in a pool at her feet along with her t-shirt, thick wool socks, and cotton panties.

Her normally freezing cold toes were toasty warm as the entire temperature of the room seemed to have become decidedly tropical. She was thrilled to shed the extra layers and luxuriated in her nude flesh against his cool sheets.

Ella reclined against the pillows and watched fascinated as Chris shed his own clothes. First the t-shirt was pulled over his head, revealing a muscled torso and ridged abs. She had to curb the instinct to reach out and trace his stomach with first her fingertips and then her tongue. For now, anyway, but she definitely wanted to do that at some point. In the faint light of the bedside lamp, his skin was golden and infinitely touchable, covered in a soft dusting of silky dark hair that disappeared under the waistband of his boxers.

He was the one currently undressing yet his attention never wavered from Ella, his gaze sweeping her from head to toe and then back up again. In the dim light, she couldn't see his blue eyes but she could feel the warmth as if he'd physically touched her.

"You're so beautiful, honey," he said, his voice deep and hoarse. The outline of his cock was pressed against the cotton of his boxers, letting her know in no uncertain terms that his words were not empty. "I can't wait to make love to you."

He wouldn't have to wait if he'd simply hurry up, and she almost told him that but then her mouth went dry when he stripped down completely. Holy smokes.

Dropping down onto the mattress, he crawled up her body, his skin brushing against her own and sending tingles to all the right places. It had been way too long since she'd felt the weight of a man on top of her.

Not able to resist any longer, she ran her fingers down his

spine, delighting in the gasp that escaped his lips at her mere touch. She lost her train of thought, however, when that clever mouth of his found a spot at the base of her neck that had her writhing underneath him in pleasure.

"I'll catalog that under successes. What about here?"

His lips leisurely traveled to the sensitive skin behind her ear, nipping and sucking until she was arched flush against him.

"Easy," she choked, her fingers digging into his biceps. "You don't play fair."

"Neither do you, honey."

His lips wandered down Ella's neck to the curve of her breast before his tongue made a lazy path to the already pebbled nipple. He laved at the sensitive bud, his fingers plucking at the other until she was a panting mess, her hands anchored onto the back of his head to keep him right where he was. Preferably forever.

A bar of arousal began to build in her abdomen with each stroke of his fingers and tongue. Her eyelids fluttered closed and she allowed herself to simply revel in the attention for a few moments. She could feel the blood flying through her veins and the flames lick at her over heated flesh. If a human being could die from pleasure she was taking her last breaths.

But Chris was far from done with her.

Hallelujah.

Pressing open-mouthed kisses down her quivering belly, he pushed her thighs apart with his shoulders. His breath was warm on her most intimate flesh and for a split second she was self-conscious, but it simply couldn't last when Chris was doing devilishly naughty things with his tongue and sending her spiraling higher into the stars.

At first, he teased, not letting her tumble over the cliff but her moans and pleas for mercy must have done the job because suddenly he was *there*, exactly where she needed him to be. His mouth closed over her clit sending her directly into orbit, her thighs clamping onto his head and her toes curling with pleasure. It was a star-spangled, multi-colored light show behind her eyelids as her orgasm washed over her and she was breathless and smiling when it was over, her limbs heavy as her heart slowed rate slowed and her breathing resumed.

Oxygen is good.

Sex is better. We need to do this a lot.

"That was…"

"Yeah, it was…"

They were having that conversation again where they didn't finish their sentences yet knew exactly what the other person was trying to say.

"Are you okay, honey?"

A full sentence. Clearly he could recover faster than she could. Oh wait. She was the only one that had climaxed. She'd need to rectify that immediately, if not sooner. She was no slacker between the sheets and she wanted to make Chris feel this blissful.

She sort of had a plan, too.

Pressing her palms against his chest, she pushed him onto his back and threw her leg over him so she was straddling his lean hips. His brows shot up in surprise but then he smiled, reaching up to wrap a strand of her hair around his finger.

"You have a very determined look on your face, honey."

"I am determined."

Bending down, she brushed her lips across his flat abdomen, watching the muscles jump under her touch. A surge of confidence ran through her, knowing that she could affect him so strongly. She pressed kisses down his treasure trail, her long hair tickling his stomach until she reached her final goal.

He was long and thick, the skin like velvet but hard as iron underneath. She wrapped her hand around him and began moving her hand in a rhythm that was as old as time. His eyes drifted shut and a soft groan escaped his lips. Leaning down, she gave him a long lick from root to tip.

His reaction was instantaneous.

His fingers curled into her hair and his entire body bowed off the bed, his heels digging into the mattress. "Honey, that felt amazing and I'd love for you to do even more, but if you keep that up this evening is going to end far sooner than either one of us would like."

Giggling at the compliment, she ran her tongue up and down a few more times and reveled in feeling this confident and strong man tremble. "I'm okay with starting again."

"I'm not."

Just like that she was flat on her back. He'd flipped her over so quickly she hadn't even realized it until it was done. His hands flat on the bed, he hovered over her, their bodies brushing against one another as he leaned down to capture her lips with his own. Arousal fizzed in her veins like the finest champagne, the bubbles popping one by one like fireworks on the Fourth of July.

Ella was so caught up in the kiss she didn't hear him reach into the bedside table until he'd pulled away to tear open the foil packet with his teeth. With shaking and eager hands, she helped him roll on the thin layer of latex and was probably more of a hindrance than anything, but they managed without making it awkward. She was using protection as well and was glad that she didn't have to make a fuss about him wearing a condom.

Positioning himself between her thighs, he nudged at her entrance while his lips and tongue played a game of tag with her own. He pressed forward slowly, giving her ample opportunity to change her mind or simply to get used to his size. He stretched her deliciously, not painfully and she savored the sensation of being so completely filled when he was in to the hilt.

Heaven.

His breath was warm against her cheek when he spoke. "Fast and hard or soft and slow? Ladies choice."

"Can I have both? Soft at the start and then hard and fast at the end."

"We can do that, honey. Why don't you wrap those gorgeous legs around my waist?"

That sounded like an amazing idea so she did as he began to move, pulling out slowly just as she'd requested before thrusting back in a little faster and harder. With each stroke her arousal built as he unerringly found that spot inside of her that made her crazy. Clever man that he was, he was quick to recognize his luck and aimed relentlessly for it over and over again until she was sailing among the clouds, her body not even touching the bed underneath her.

She ran her hands down his damp back and anchored her fingers at his hips, her nails digging into the flesh. She needed...more.

"Faster," she urged, lifting her hips to meet each thrust. If she angled her hips just so... Yes, that was better. He was stimulating her inside and out now and she was going to explode soon. Very soon. "Harder now."

With a grunt, Chris did as she bade, slamming into her again and again, his face a mask of concentration and his jaw tight with the effort. Their bodies were bathed in sweat and their fleshed slapped together loudly in the silence, punctuated by their breathy moans and barely intelligible words. He could have been speaking a foreign language and Ella wouldn't have known. Or cared. She only wanted one thing and that was for him to fuck them both into nirvana.

"Now, Chris, now."

Trembling on the brink, she reached down to touch her clit but Chris's hand was already there, his skilled fingers circling the sensitive mound. It didn't take much to push her over the edge. Waves of pleasure wracked her body and her back arched off the bed, her head thrown back in pure ecstasy. The world tilted and whirled around her, making her dizzy like a roller coaster, so she hung on to him for dear life until the wild ride was over.

At some point Chris reached his peak as well, his mouth plundering hers as his muscular frame shook with the force of his climax. At the end he froze above her, his entire body taut and his eyes closed as if trying to make the moment last a little longer. He exhaled noisily and then collapsed on top of her, quickly rolling on to his back and tucking her into his side.

Ella couldn't have moved if the apartment was on fire. So completely exhausted and sated, all she wanted to do was lie here with Chris floating on a cloud of pleasure for as long as she possibly could. Tonight? Tomorrow? A week from now? She didn't know how long it could last but right now the entire world was trapped outside of this bedroom and it was only the two of them. No worries, no problems. Just physical pleasure and happiness.

And for now, she would enjoy it. There was plenty of time for the real world to catch up with them. There was no way to avoid it. But she could pretend for a few hours that it didn't exist.

★   ★   ★

AWARENESS CAME SLOWLY the next morning. Chris wasn't quite awake but he wasn't asleep either, just sort of drifting in between. He knew that he wasn't alone. Ella's pert little derriere was pressed up against his morning wood and her long hair was lying on his face, tickling his nose. He blew on it but it didn't shift, still tickling so he had to actually move, which made him wake up even more.

The weak morning sun could be seen through the slats of the blinds, casting shadows on the bedcovers. Seven? Maybe seven-thirty? He didn't normally get up this late but they'd barely slept last night so it wasn't a surprise. He ought to get up and get going. There were a million things to do and it was going to be a busy day. But…

Surely they could take a few minutes for just themselves.

Ella's head was pillowed on his bicep and at some point his arm had fallen asleep, all pins and needles. Luckily his right arm was good to go and he reached around and insinuated a finger between her legs, finding her already wet and ready.

Drawing circles around her clit, he watched as she slowly woke, her eyelids fluttering and a low moan dragged from her lips. With a wicked grin, he slid two fingers inside of her tight channel while his thumb strummed her swollen bud.

That did it. Now she was moving around restlessly, but not wanting to admit she was awake.

"I guess you're not a morning person, huh?"

Wrinkling her nose, she delicately grunted in response but he wasn't sure whether she was agreeing or telling him to fuck off.

"I can stop if you want me to."

Her eyes popped open and her lips tightened into a line. "If you stop, I'll kick you out of bed, Chris Marks."

Laughing, he did stop so he could reach into the nightstand and retrieve a condom. "Give me a minute and I'll do better than that."

"Sixty seconds. Tops."

"You're bossy in the morning. Interesting."

It was probably more like ninety seconds by the time he ripped open the foil square and rolled it on. At least this time Ella didn't try and help him out. Last night there had been far too many fingers and it had taken twice as long.

If last night was fast and furious, this morning was as leisurely as a stroll by the lake in July.

It wasn't that he was any less aroused or that he wanted her any less. Hell, if anything now that they'd made love he wanted her even more. But he also wanted to savor this time with her because he knew that they'd be apart most of the day.

In his position as the big spoon, he could easily reach all the important spots so he curled close around her and plucked at one hard nipple while slowly circling her clit with the hand, all the while pumping in and out as if they had all day to laze in bed. Or maybe not.

A wave of heat ran through him and the pressure began to build in his lower back, telling him in no uncertain terms that he sure as fuck didn't have all damn day and he was going to detonate any minute now.

"Honey, are you...?"

"Yes," she breathed, reaching back to pull his head down so their lips could fuse together. Quickening his pace, his tongue explored her mouth and his fingers rubbed at her clit. He could feel her climax building as her body stiffened and her fingernails dug into his scalp. She tore her lips from his and panted his name as her orgasm hit.

"Chris."

It was a beautiful song to his ears and he fell over the cliff right after, her voice the catalyst. Her channel clamped down on him, dragging a groan from his throat. His orgasm ran through him like a waterfall, gentle at first and then crashing waves at the end. When it was over he sucked oxygen into his starved lungs and pressed kisses to the warm skin of Ella's shoulders. She felt soft, warm, and she fit against him perfectly.

He was falling hard and what surprised him the most was that he wasn't even scared by it.

CHAPTER TWENTY-SIX

ELLA HAD TO go into the office to work on her update for the evening news so that meant that Chris was paired with Knox again. The two men were getting along better but they still liked to snipe at each other and probably always would. As usual, Knox had insisted that he drive. Chris had decided it was easier not to argue. Today at least. Tomorrow might be different.

Alan Maxwell, Kelly's former boss, owned several restaurants and nightclubs, but in the last ten years or so had made most of his income from real estate. They were meeting him at his home, a swanky condo in the downtown area.

"Parking in this part of the city sucks," Knox groused as they pressed Maxwell's doorbell. He'd been bitching about it for the last ten minutes. "In Montana we didn't have any parking problems."

"If I give you ten bucks will you let it go?" Chris asked. "Even the doorman was giving us strange looks, you were so loud about it."

"It's highway robbery," Knox protested. "And I don't want your money."

"I offered to drive, but you insisted."

Knox didn't reply as the door swung open revealing an older man with graying hair, dressed in jeans and a navy crew neck sweater. He was a few inches shorter than Chris but carrying more weight. He greeted them warmly and invited them in.

"Please come in and sit down. I have to say that I was very intrigued by your call, Mr. Marks. I haven't heard Kelly's name in at least thirty years."

The decor in the condo was ultra modern and blindingly white. Chris would never in a million years live in a place like this. In fact, he'd bet money that Maxwell didn't have pets or small children come through here. But he'd been invited to sit down so he would, praying that there was nothing on the back of his jeans or on the bottom of his boots.

"Please call me Chris," he invited, perching on the edge of a snow-white sofa cushion. Knox seemed just as uncomfortable, not relaxing back but sitting straight up. "This is my associate Knox Owens."

"Nice to meet you." Maxwell shook Knox's hand. "Now what can I do to help you?"

"We're investigating the murder of a Jane Doe from about thirty years ago," Chris explained. "We've come to the conclusion that Kelly Perkins is that Jane Doe. Now that we've identified her, we're working on finding who might have killed her."

Maxwell's eyes widened and his mouth fell open. "Kelly? Little Kelly is…dead? Oh my God, that's terrible."

Hopping up from the chair he'd been seated on, Maxwell didn't seem to know what to do with himself. His shock seemed genuine, at least to Chris. So far.

"Perhaps we should start at the beginning," Chris suggested. "How did you meet Kelly? How long did she work for you? That sort of thing."

Patience was a virtue, Chris had learned when questioning people. Give them lots of rope and if they were guilty of something they just might hang themselves. It was tough to stay quiet but it was better to listen.

Gripping the back of a chair, Maxwell shook his head. "I honestly don't remember how I met Kelly. She probably came in looking for a job and one of my managers hired her. She was a nice girl and a decent waitress. She was late sometimes and called in sick a little too much, but she was nice to the customers. They liked her."

"How well did you know her?"

"Acquaintances," Maxwell shrugged. "I wouldn't call us friends, more *friendly*. Like I said she was a nice girl."

"You seemed pretty shaken up when I told you she was dead."

"Well…yeah. I don't like to hear about anybody being murdered." The man scraped his fingers through his thinning hair. "What…I mean…how…did it happen?"

"You may have seen it in the papers," Knox replied, breaking his silence. "Remains found by the road outside of Seattle, hands cut off so no identification could be made."

Maxwell paled, his grip on the chair tightening until his knuckles were white. "Oh God…that's awful. Just…shit. I don't know what to say. Are you going to arrest her boyfriend? What was his name…Steve? That's it. Steve. I don't remember his last name."

Now this was interesting. Chris was definitely going to follow up with more questions.

"Why would you think we were going to arrest Steve Adams?"

"Adams. That's it." Maxwell came around the chair and sank down into the cushion. "I just assumed…"

"Yes?" Chris prompted. "Why did you assume that?"

Sweat had popped out on Maxwell's forehead. "They used to argue. A lot. Sometimes Kelly would come in with a black eye or bruises on her arms. I asked her about it one time and she shut me down, said it was no big deal. It was clear she didn't want to talk about it."

"So you let it go?"

Maxwell straightened. "Hey, I talked to that little peckerhead about it. I told him that men don't knock their women around but he swore up and down it wasn't him."

"But you suspected that it was."

"She wouldn't talk to me about it but she talked to one of the other waitresses, Connie Chastain. She told me that it was Steve hitting Kelly. It got better for a little while after I talked to him but then it got bad again."

"Did you talk to him about it again?"

Maxwell wearily shook his head. "Frankly, I didn't want to get involved in the drama. With Kelly there always seemed to be drama in her life. And then it wasn't long after that she just stopped coming to work. Eventually I had to replace her."

"So let me get this straight…a waitress that worked for you was being abused by her boyfriend and then one day she disappears. I don't suppose you thought to alert the authorities or anything?"

Shifting on the cushion, Maxwell appeared uncomfortable. He should, dammit.

"Steve said that Kelly had taken off." Maxwell's gaze bounced back and forth between Knox and Chris. "I thought it was a good sign that she'd left the loser. I thought maybe she'd get her life together, if only for her daughter."

They were going to have to speak to Steve again. He'd left out a whole hell of a lot of information.

"You knew about her daughter?" Knox asked.

"Yes, but I never saw the girl. Just a few photos that Kelly brought in to show Connie. The baby lived with her dad, thank goodness. Kelly was a sweet girl but she wasn't mother material, if you know what I mean."

"You mean that she was an addict," Chris replied, a hard edge to his voice. "You had to be aware of it."

His shoulders slumping, Maxwell nodded. "Okay, fine. She was an addict, but I don't think she did anything harder than pot and alcohol. Not that I knew of, anyway. She'd disappear for a couple of days along with her stoner boyfriend and then come back like nothing even happened. I thought about firing her a couple of times but like I said, the customers really liked her. That's why I didn't think much of it when she stopped coming in altogether. I even waited over a week to replace her in case she came back."

Chris had no idea substances Kelly might have dabbled in but her pictures didn't show the tell-tale face or body of someone on hard drugs. Or at least no hard drugs for a long period of time. If she'd "graduated" to something stronger she hadn't been doing it for long.

Now that Chris had to go back and speak with Steve Adams he wasn't in the best of moods. Ella always talked about how patient he was but she just hadn't spent enough time with him.

Chris stood and walked over to where Maxwell was standing, invading his personal space. He wanted to make sure this guy knew just how fucking serious this was.

"Now if I go talk to this Connie is she going to tell me the same things you have? Because I don't want to come back here."

Swallowing hard, Maxwell nodded. "She'll tell you about Steve's temper. Honest."

That was great but that wasn't what Chris was alluding to.

"Fine. Will she also back up your statement that you and Kelly were only acquaintances? That you didn't know her very well? Or is she going to tell me something different?"

A trickle of sweat rolled down his forehead. "Hey, I may have made a pass or two, pinched or made a grab, but who hasn't? Right? I mean, these girls were flaunting it in short-shorts and tight t-shirts. But we never – I mean – she and I never – you know. It was just a little slap and tickle. She had a boyfriend even if he was a total loser."

Knox stood as well, his expression sour. "So it's okay to grab a boob or pinch their ass if they have a boyfriend but sex is off the table. Unless she wants it, right? Nice philosophy of life you have there."

Maxwell tried again to defend himself. "Those girls knew how to get big tips. They weren't virgins."

And that makes it okay?

Arguing the point with a guy like Alan Maxwell was a waste of breath. They weren't going to change his mind, although he did at least have the grace to look a little embarrassed.

"One more question. The last time you saw Kelly did she act differently at all? Mention any new friends or maybe even a new club where she liked to party?"

Maxwell shook his head again. "Not that I remember. She worked and then went home. She and Connie talked about some movie they wanted to see that weekend but I don't remember what it was."

Pulling a business card from his pocket, Chris held it out. "Call me if you remember anything else. Even the smallest detail might make a difference to our investigation."

Trailing behind Chris and Knox, the man tucked the card into his pocket before opening the door. "Do you really think that you can find the guy that did this? All these years later? He could be dead or in jail for all you know."

Chris crossed the threshold but then turned back to answer. "That's true but he could also be walking around free as a bird thinking that he got away with it. He thinks that after all this time that he's safe, and that no one cared enough about an anonymous Jane Doe to try and find out how her life ended. I'd like to show him he's completely wrong. There's no statute of limitations on murder for a reason."

Leaving Alan Maxwell standing in his doorway gaping like a fish, Chris and Knox headed to their vehicle. They needed to talk to Kelly's friend and then it would be back to Steve Adams. If Connie corroborated Maxwell's story, Adams had a hell of a lot of explaining to do.

CHAPTER TWENTY-SEVEN

IF CONNIE CHASTAIN-MARCH had slung beers in her youth in a dive bar, she'd left it far behind. Chris and Knox caught up with her at her suburban home, a comfortable ranch style in a middle-class neighborhood. Their research told them that she'd eventually earned a real estate license along with her husband Ted March. They had three grown children, two grandchildren, and three Corgis who happily greeted them at the front door. Chris was more a dog person than cat person and was happy to pet the wiggling canines.

"Alan called me."

That was the first thing Connie said but she didn't seem upset about it. She was smiling, welcoming them into her home as if they hadn't called her only a few hours ago asking to discuss a friend from over thirty years ago.

The walls were covered in photos of her family along with a large wedding photo in a gold frame of a much younger Connie in white lace and satin, holding a huge bouquet of pink roses. Today she was wearing casual slacks and a striped cotton sweater, her now gray-tinged hair cut short.

Knox leaned close to Chris so she wouldn't overhear. "I wish he hadn't done that. We don't know what he said to her."

"Hopefully we'll be able to tell if she's lying or covering for him."

Chris and Knox took a seat at the March kitchen table along with Connie.

"I appreciate you meeting with us on such short notice, Mrs. March," Chris said, pulling out his notes from his messenger bag. "You said that Alan Maxwell called you. Are you two still in touch after all of these years?"

Chris tried to make his question sound completely innocuous, as if the query was idle curiosity.

"Please call me Connie. We see each other from time to time, although less as the years have gone on. We're both in the real estate business. In fact, it was Alan that urged me to take the licensing exam. He had contacts that would hire me if I passed."

A perfectly plausible explanation but their friendship made anything she said less credible. Did they have the kind of relationship where one would lie for the other?

Connie twisted a ragged tissue between her fingers. "Alan told me about Kelly. I just...I just can't believe it. All these years she's been dead and we didn't know. Do you know who did it?"

Knox gave Chris a sideways glance that said it all. Alan had done more than just call Connie to warn her they were going to talk to her. It sounded like they'd had quite the conversation.

"Not yet but we're looking into it," Chris replied. "Alan said you and Kelly worked together and were friends. Is that correct?"

Connie nodded, her eyes tearing up. "It is. I really liked Kelly. She had some issues but she was a sweet girl. She had a smile that could light up an entire room. People loved her."

If Kelly was like that, she'd passed those traits onto Ella. She was the same, although she might not appreciate Chris comparing her to her troubled mother.

"Did Kelly confide in you about any personal problems she may have had?"

"You're talking about Steve," she replied knowingly. "They had a volatile relationship but they couldn't seem to stay away from one another. One of them would break it off and then a week later they'd be back together again. There were other men in between but she always went back to him."

Chris wanted to talk about Steve but he also wanted more information about one item that didn't seem to be clear.

"Our understanding is that she also had a substance abuse problem. Is that true?"

Her cheeks turning a bright pink, Connie squirmed in her chair. "We were young and we liked to party. I guess Kelly had trouble controlling it. I know that Steve did because when he got drunk or high he became a different person. A not so nice person."

"High?" Knox asked. "Can you be more specific?"

"Cocaine."

Connie's answer was short and clipped. "I see," Knox said. "And did Kelly also do coke?"

At first Chris didn't think Connie was going to answer but

then she exhaled slowly, dabbing at her eyes with the tissue. "We all did at the bar, although some more than others. I'm not proud of it so don't think that I am. I have kids and when they asked me about drugs I told them to stay away. They can never know what I did back then. I could never tell them…"

Her voice trailed away as a silvery tear ran down the older woman's face. Since Chris had a heap of stuff in his past that he wasn't proud of he could understand her reticence to come clean with her children. But someday in the future when Annie asked him if he'd ever gotten drunk or done something stupid, he was planning to tell her the truth. Age appropriate truth, of course.

"Tell me more about Steve and Kelly's relationship," Chris invited. Her statement negated Maxwell's belief that Kelly didn't get into anything harder than pot and booze. "You said it was volatile and they broke up more than once."

"Several times," Connie said with a nod. "Really, I lost count. They were always arguing and making up. That's why I didn't think anything of Kelly disappearing. I thought she was finally getting away from him. She was afraid of Steve. Now I see that she was right to be."

Choking on a sob, Connie grabbed another tissue from a box on the counter. "I'm sorry. This is just so distressing. All these years…"

"You thought she left town?"

"Yes, a fresh start, so to speak."

"What about her daughter?"

Taking a shaky breath, Connie's shoulders sagged. "Bless

that little girl. Kelly knew she wasn't a good mother. She was wrong about almost everything else in her life but she got that one right. She knew the father would take care of the baby and raise her right."

"Tim died a few months after Kelly," Chris said. "His mother passed on soon after. The toddler was put up for adoption."

Connie's hand flew up to her mouth, her eyes round with distress. "Oh no. No, no, no. If I'd known, I would have–"

She broke off and sighed heavily. "Who am I kidding? I wasn't capable of raising a child back then, either. But I would have tried. Krystle was the sweetest thing. So pretty and always smiling. She had Kelly's smile."

I think she still does. It's beautiful.

"You said that Kelly was afraid of Steve. When we talked to him he was really broken up about her disappearance and death."

Her lips tightened into a thin line. "Playacting. He could pretend to be the most loving boyfriend in the world and then black Kelly's eye the same night. If he's upset then it's out of guilt. You don't have to look far for who killed Kelly. It was Steve. I'd bet my life on it."

That was a firm declaration, and it was clear that Connie believed it.

"Did he ever threaten to kill her? Did you ever hear him say it?"

"No," she admitted. "But I did hear him say that if she left him she'd regret it. That's sort of the same, isn't it?"

Close enough. Time to talk to Steve Adams again.

★　★　★

SITTING AT HER desk, Ella watched one of the television monitors on the wall as it aired the story update she'd filmed that morning. She and a cameraman had driven to the body dump site and filmed during a lucky break in the weather. Even after all this time as a television reporter, Ella didn't enjoy watching herself. She could only see the flaws, not the positives and she cringed again today. She wasn't fond of the sound of her recorded voice, although at least she wasn't expected to be happy and perky for this story. For once, she could be sober and serious.

I should have stuck with newspaper work.

In the segment, Ella stood in front of the body dump site, dressed in a navy blue suit with her hair and face made up. Holding a microphone, she'd recited the scripted update she'd written early this morning over her first cup of coffee, highlighting the progress that had been made because of the forensic rendering and a renewed investigation.

"This is Ella Scott for Channel Thirty-Six News."

"Not bad."

Galen had snuck up on her and was now leaning on her cubicle wall and carrying a steaming coffee cup. His gaze turned to the television for a moment and then back to her.

He wasn't smiling but he wasn't scowling either. That was progress.

"Thank you," Ella replied. "It's good to have made progress

in the investigation."

It was now public knowledge that Jane Doe had been identified as Kelly Perkins, but Ella hadn't told anyone her connection. Least of all Galen. As he reminded all of his employees, he was their boss, not their best friend.

Even if he had welcomed the personal revelation, he would have insisted she become part of the story and that was something she didn't want to happen. She'd made a sort of peace that she was part of the *investigation*, but telling others – strangers – wasn't going to happen. Not yet. Maybe never.

"You've shown a real grit that I didn't know you had, Ella. A persistence that's impressed me. This story has really opened my eyes about what kind of reporter you could be."

About time. When Ella had been laid off from her newspaper job and taken this one, she would never have thought that she'd still be proving herself.

"Thank you," she said again. "I appreciate the compliment. This was a fascinating story."

She had a gift for understatement. Galen, however, wasn't paying much attention to what she was saying. He appeared to have an agenda of his own.

"Do you have any others?"

Was he asking what she thought he was asking?

"More?" Ella stammered. This was huge. Huge. "Are you offering to let me do more stories like this?"

"If you want to. You seem to have a nose for what interests our audience."

Holy hell.

"I'll do that. Right away. Thank you, Galen."

There were a few people at the station who weren't going to be happy, but she'd deal with them later. This was her chance and she was going to make the most of it.

He checked his watch. "Great, why don't you meet me in my office in about an hour? We can talk about your new assignments. I want you to start on a new story immediately."

"That's—" Wait, right now?

"Is it a problem?" Galen's brows were pinched into a frown. "I'm not sure I'm following. You found Jane Doe's identity. Good work. You're done. Now you can move on to something new."

"We—I mean, Chris hasn't found the murderer yet."

"So? You can cover it when he does. If he does. Are you even close?" He cocked his head, his gaze intent. "Is an arrest imminent?"

"Well...no," she admitted, although it pained her to do so. "I don't think so but I've never worked on a murder investigation before so I could be wrong. But now that we actually know who she is we have a much better chance of finding out who did this."

Galen took a sip of his coffee. "That's true. Listen, Ella, I feel like I've given you a great deal of freedom on this case, more than I've given to others. I've basically let you become part of the investigation team but they can't have you forever. You have a job to do here. When they find the killer, I promise you can report on it but I think that needs to be the extent of your involvement. Reporting, not investigating. It sounds like they're not even close, to be honest."

Once Galen made up his mind it was damn near impossible to get him to change it, but every now and then he would if the reporter made a good argument. She wasn't going to give up easily, but it required her to tell him about her apartment. It was an item she'd kept to herself but it wouldn't reveal anything too personal if she told him.

"I didn't tell you this before but my apartment was broken into and ransacked. They didn't take anything but they destroyed whatever they could. Chris thinks it was to scare me into dropping the investigation."

Galen's brows rose in surprise. "That's news, Ella. You shouldn't have kept this to yourself. Your safety – and the safety of all of my reporters – is important to me."

Sighing, Ella tried to reason with him. "I don't want to become part of the story and I sure as hell don't want whoever did it to think that I'm spooked or scared. I don't want them to think they've had any effect on my life at all."

"That's very brave of you."

"It's not all that brave. Besides, if you think about it what they did was rather cowardly. They came and messed up my apartment when I wasn't there. They didn't want to face me so why should I be scared?"

Rubbing his chin, Galen nodded in agreement. "You make a good point there, although now I'm going to worry about you.

Frankly, it's another reason to step back from the case. It's not your job to find the killer, Ella. That belongs to the cops. You have a job *here*."

His emphasis was clear. She needed to be available to take daily assignments, not running around interviewing people about a thirty-year old murder.

"Does this investigator really need you, Ella?" Galen asked. "I'm not trying to be unkind here but he's a professional, right?"

Did Chris truly need her? No, he'd do fine by himself.

"He could handle it without a problem. I was working with him to get it all first-hand."

"If you were writing a book about the case then I'd applaud the dedication but at most you're going to do a sixty-second segment. Tops. Probably less. Unless the killer is the mayor or the governor. Then we'll cover the perp walk all the way through the trial and the verdict. That would be a hell of a bestseller." Straightening, he took another sip from his coffee cup. "Meet me in my office in about an hour. We'll talk about some new assignments."

In other words, the discussion was over. Full stop. She was lucky, really. Galen generally didn't *discuss* anything. He gave an order and expected it to be followed. He'd been humoring her and he was now done. She had to fall in line or he'd find someone that would. There were always plenty ready to take her job if she didn't want it.

And she did want this opportunity. Right? She'd been so sure before but now...

She wasn't as happy and thrilled as should have been. There was no rush of joy or adrenaline. She should have felt more, but instead she'd barely felt anything at all. Something inside of her had shifted and now she was questioning everything.

Who am I? And what do I want to be when I grow up?

CHAPTER TWENTY-EIGHT

ELLA'S PHONE BUZZED a few hours later to let her know that Chris had arrived to pick her up. She'd been heads down for the last hour looking through old newspaper articles.

Stretching her arms over her head, she yawned widely. Despite being exhausted, she was excited to see Chris again. After last night, she was ready to admit that she wanted this relationship to work out.

Because she was falling in love with him.

Stuffing her laptop into her oversized bag, she zipped it closed and walked through the corridors to the front of the building. From the lobby, she could see Chris standing outside, his back to her. A tingle ran up her spine and her steps quickened in response. She couldn't wait to spend time with him again. She'd never quite had this same connection with anyone else.

She pushed the door opened and he quickly turned around, his face lighting up with a smile that was just for her. Damn, he was good-looking.

"Hey, how did it go today?"

Before she could answer he wrapped her in a big, warm hug that had her instantly relaxing against him and the stresses of the day melting away. She wanted to turn her face up for a kiss but they were standing in front of her work building. Probably not the best idea.

"It was good. Galen's going to let me do some of my own stories."

Even saying it out loud didn't make it completely real. She kept waiting for her boss to laugh and tell her it was all a joke and that she had a charity car wash to cover tomorrow.

"That's great." Chris's face split into a grin, but then it fell when she wasn't smiling, too. "Or not? Aren't you happy?"

"I can barely explain it. I thought I would be deliriously happy and I am."

His brows shot up. "Really? Because you don't look deliriously happy."

"I am…and I'm not, all at the same time. I guess I'm confused. I thought it was what I wanted."

"And now you're not sure?"

"I'm not sure," she admitted, pulling her coat closer around her. The sun had gone down long ago and it was cold outside. "Maybe I'm still in shock. I've already started and that means that I can't spend time with you on the case."

He wrapped one arm around her waist while reaching with his other hand and lifting her heavy bag off of her shoulder. Ella leaned against Chris, content to let him lead the way. "We can talk about it at home, but you know I'll help you as much as I can. Knox is waiting for us. He'll drop us at the office and we'll get my car. What do you want for dinner?"

They'd just stepped off of the curb to cross the street to where Knox was parked when a flash of headlights caught Ella's attention. She didn't have a chance to answer Chris's question because those bright beams of light were coming closer at a frightening rate. The powerful roar of an engine filled her ears and her body froze even as her mind raced in a hundred different directions. Like a deer in headlights, she couldn't move to save her own life. She was going to become roadkill, flattened like the proverbial pancake because she sucked at crisis moments. She squeezed her eyes shut and braced for the worst.

A heavy weight slammed into her, shooting the air in her lungs out in a whoosh and sending her flying through air. With a squeal of tires it was over and Ella realized that she was still alive. And the pavement wasn't all that hard underneath her. Frantically, she tried to move her arms and legs. For some reason, they were fine and she wasn't in any pain at all. She should have several broken bones.

"Easy, honey. Just relax for a minute so I can make sure you're okay."

Chris. His voice.

Opening her eyes, she was nose to nose with him. He was lying underneath her.

Looking around, she wasn't under the wheels of a vehicle but safely tucked in between two parked cars. Chris had knocked them both out of the way and now she was lying on top of him.

He'd taken the brunt of the impact with the unforgiving pavement so she wouldn't be hurt. But what about him?

Even more frantic now, she tried to sit up but their arms and legs were tangled together, making it almost impossible. When she'd almost given up, Chris simply stood up taking her with him, his arm still wrapped around her waist. Gently he set her on the ground, but she had to cling to him for support. Her legs were jelly and her pulse racing. The street spun for a moment but then righted itself as she learned to inhale oxygen again.

I'm not dead.

"I'm okay," she finally choked out, her breathing ragged. "What about you?"

She was no dainty flower and her entire weight had landed on top, sandwiching him between her and the concrete.

"I'm fine." He brushed off her concern, his gaze already looking past her and down the street. "Looks like Knox went after him. I'll call Logan and let him know what's going on. Are you sure you're okay? I can call an ambu–"

"No, I'm fine. Honestly."

Chris was listening but with only half an ear. The laidback, relaxed, wise man she'd come to know had suddenly morphed into someone far different. This man's icy stare was intense, a muscle in his jaw working. His entire demeanor had changed, giving off an air of aloofness and…danger. Yes, that was it. *Danger.* Chris was angry…furious…and it radiated from him in waves.

The whole cop and bringing in a murderer thing had become a hell of a lot more real in the past two minutes.

Thank goodness he'd had the wherewithal to save their lives.

And thank goodness she wasn't the person he was hunting. Because she wouldn't want to be the guy behind the wheel when Chris got a hold of him.

IT WAS ALL a blur. The next few hours flew by after Chris's coworker Knox circled back to pick them up. He wasn't any happier than Chris was. He'd lost the guilty vehicle a few miles away. Knox was new to the area and unfamiliar with the roads but he was sure that the driver wasn't.

"I almost didn't go after him," Knox had admitted after he'd bundled them back into the car. "But I saw you both stand up so I figured you were okay. Jesus, he came out of nowhere. There was nothing I could do."

"We're fine," Chris assured him, patting Ella's thigh through the blanket from the trunk that they'd tucked around her. "You did the right thing."

Chris's bosses were called and they'd showed up at the apartment, all wearing identical grim expressions. Ella hadn't really known what to say or do so she'd made herself busy making coffee and keeping their cups refilled while they hashed out some sort of plan that involved her. However, no one was asking her what she wanted. At first she'd been irked but then she'd had to remind herself that she wasn't a professional and that emergency situations weren't her forte.

Eventually it was decided to move Chris and herself to a safe house situation which she'd only heard of in the movies, but apparently it was a real, actual thing. Merc kept circling her feet wanting attention as she'd packed a bag – again – this time a hell of a lot more scared than she'd been last night. This wasn't just an intimate violation. This was more. This was someone who wanted to kill her, or at the very least hurt or maim her. If Chris hadn't been there, she would probably be dead right now.

She didn't say much when they drove through to the safe house either, content to let Chris make the decisions and lead her around. She didn't know what to say or what to do or her mind shutting down for self-protection. She couldn't think about her life at the moment. Instead, she held onto Merc's carrier like a lifeline as she was ushered into a Craftsman style house on the outskirts of the city. The suburban neighborhood was quiet at this time of night, although there were still lights on in most of the houses.

Chris escorted her upstairs to the master bedroom, laying her bag on the dark blue comforter. The house was clean and tidy with a minimum of furniture. No one lived here, she was sure of that.

"You might want to soak in the tub while I talk to the guys. It might help you relax."

Ella doubted that calm and serene were in her future but a hot bath sounded like nirvana right about now. Any sort of small escape would be welcome.

"I'll do that. Will you be long?"

In other words, how long will you be discussing how to keep me alive?

"Not too long," Chris assured her, leaning down to brush his lips with hers. "But if you need me I'll be right downstairs."

She could hear his soft footfalls on the stairs as he left her and that's when the dam broke loose. All the adrenaline that had been coursing through her body and getting her from point A to point B quickly drained away, leaving her pale, sweaty, and shaking like a leaf. It was a really crappy delayed reaction that she couldn't begin to control so she crumpled onto the mattress and curled into ball, Merc meowing through the mesh door of his carrier.

Tears began falling down her cheeks and the blessed numbness that had invaded her bones after the close call was slowly dissolving, leaving her rocking back and forth for comfort. It was all too much. Someone had tried to run her down tonight and they'd almost succeeded.

Someone was determined that she and Chris wouldn't find out the truth.

★ ★ ★

A PHONE PRESSED against his ear, Logan nodded and then ended the call. Chris and Knox were also huddled in the kitchen debating their next steps. So far it had been decided to put Knox and Brew on duty to guard the house – one in front and one in back.

"That was Ryan," Logan said, his voice cutting through their voices. "He swept Chris's place for any sort of surveillance devices and didn't find anything. Whoever it was that tried to run both of you down had to find out your whereabouts another way."

Knox nodded curtly. "Could have been monitoring your cell phone calls, but I'd put money on your movements being watched. You've certainly got someone rattled. You must be getting close."

"That's news to me," Chris said, his teeth clenched so hard his jaw ached. He could still see that vehicle barreling toward them. Toward Ella. "I don't know who killed Kelly Perkins. Not yet, anyway, but I sure as hell am not giving up now."

Logan lifted up an edge of the curtains and looked outside. "I'd imagine it's someone you've already talked to. They're scared and trying to run you off the case."

"They won't succeed."

"Didn't think they would. Now you and Ella are safe here. We're going to watch the house all night but we need another plan for tomorrow."

Chris had already decided what he needed to do. "I'm going to go talk to Steve Adams. All roads seem to lead back to him. A boyfriend or husband is always the most likely suspect. I'd also like to talk to the best friend again. I don't think she was telling me the whole truth about that last night with Kelly."

"What about Ella?" Knox queried. "Are we going to keep her here?"

The idea was absurd. Ella wouldn't stand for it.

"She's supposed to be starting a new story at the station tomorrow. I doubt she'll let us tell her she can't go."

Logan chuckled grimly. "She sounds a little like Ava. It's not a problem. She can go to work. We'll put a protection detail on her. If she leaves the station, someone will go with her."

Chris sat down in a chair, suddenly exhausted. "I hope we're overreacting, but that wasn't an accident. That car was coming for us. No brakes. It was accelerating. Fuck. If it wasn't so dark I could have seen the driver."

"That was the point." Logan reached for the carafe and re-filled his coffee. "They didn't want you to see them. I bet they didn't even use their own car. I'll have one of the guys check for stolen vehicles within the last twenty-four hours. We might get a break there. Maybe he stole it near his home or work."

"That's how they caught Son of Sam," Knox said. "A parking ticket."

Chris rubbed at his forehead where he had a pounding head-ache. Every bone in his body hurt like hell. "I've never been that lucky but I live in hope."

Logan looked out of the window again. "Brew and Reed are here. We're going to install a few cameras around the house and then get out and let you get some rest."

"I doubt I could sleep."

"You need your rest. Ella does, too. If she sees you upset, she's going to be upset so try to control your emotions a little bit. I know you're pissed as hell but you need to rein it in."

"I'm not–"

Chris broke off, knowing he was lying through his teeth. "Okay, I'm mad. Furious. They almost hurt Ella on my watch."

He hadn't known her long but he couldn't imagine his life without her in it.

"You couldn't have foreseen what happened. Cut yourself some slack." Logan gave Chris a meaningful look. "Just make sure you're not caught off guard again."

The bad guy wasn't going to get near Ella. He'd make sure of it.

CHAPTER TWENTY-NINE

ELLA HAD EVENTUALLY stopped crying and shaking. By the end of her sobbing jag, her eyes were red and swollen and her body ached. She practically crawled on her hands and knees into the hot bath but once submerged in the steamy water it was exactly what she'd needed.

The tears had been cleansing to a certain extent and she felt better – lighter – than she had before. Life was still in turmoil and she was still in danger but the world didn't seem as dark as it had a while ago. She had a great deal of emotional work to do regarding her biological parents, her adopted parents, her job, and her future in general. The only thing that wasn't really in question was how she was beginning to feel for Chris. She didn't have a crystal ball and she couldn't read his mind, but her feelings appeared to be returned.

"I brought you a bottle of water. I thought you might be thirsty."

Chris had stuck his head around the door of the bathroom, holding out a plastic bottle. Good thing because after all of that crying there was a decent chance she was dehydrated.

"That sounds perfect. Thank you."

He entered and perched on the edge of the bathtub before twisting open the top and handing her the bottle. His gaze scanned her from head to toe, taking in every detail. His expression was still hard and cold, his anger unabated.

"You've been crying. Are you okay?"

"It was all suddenly just a little too much," she confessed, taking a long swig from the cool bottle. "I had a moment. I'm good now."

"Are you sure?"

"I am, but I'm keeping my options open for another sob-fest later. That one came out of nowhere so I doubt I'll be able to predict the second."

"You don't need to. With everything that's happened, you deserve to have a good cry."

"A good cry," she repeated with amusement. "It's strange when crying is a good thing but I do feel better. What about you, cowboy? That car almost hit you, too."

He shrugged as if it was a daily occurrence. "I'm fine. It's you that I'm worried about."

"You don't need to do that. I'm okay. You and your friends have made sure of that." She looked around the white tiled bathroom. "Your boss has an extra house for occasions like this? That's handy."

Chris didn't even crack a smile, which instantly worried Ella. He wasn't dealing with this well at all, no matter what he said.

"It's a house that Jason bought as an investment. He just

finished renovating it and was planning to sell it. That's why there's a small amount of furniture here. They were working on staging it. Lucky for us. We can stay here until this is all cleared up."

Ella had a million questions rolling around in her brain and he'd brought one of them up.

"How will we know when this is all cleared up? How long will we have to stay here?"

His blue eyes a flinty gray, Chris's jaw tightened. "Until I catch the person that did this. We have to be getting close. That's why they've gone after you...and us. They'll regret that."

"You're angry."

Something flashed across his features and then was gone before she could recognize it. He quickly stood and began to pace the small space, muttering under his breath.

"If anything had happened to you, I don't know what I would have done. I should have been more cautious. I should have expected something like this after your place was broken into but I assumed since it was non-violent the first time that they'd stay that way. Son of a fucking bitch, I'm going to get this guy and he's–"

"Chris."

"When I find him–"

"Chris!"

She had to yell to get his attention. Stopping abruptly, he turned to gaze at her, his brows pinched together.

"What?"

"You're mumbling and threatening to beat the crap out of an unidentified human being. Do you hear yourself?"

He blinked once. Twice. "Of course, I hear myself."

"Then you know that you don't sound quite hinged."

"Hinged?"

"The opposite of *unhinged.*"

"You think I'm crazy?"

"I think you're madder than hell but I'm not sure that's going to be helpful when you try and catch this guy. You didn't make this much progress on the case letting your emotions do your thinking for you."

"I'm not letting my emotions–"

"Yes, you are. You're pacing a path onto these brand new ceramic tiles because you're mad. I think it's cute and kind of wonderful to find out that you're not perfect, thank goodness, but I doubt being pissed off increases your prowess as a cop."

His cheeks had turned red and his hands were on his hips. She'd succeeded in making him even angrier.

Oops.

"Are you giving me advice?"

Am I? Looks like it.

"Yes. I think you need it. Plus, I owed you. You've given me advice. Did you think we were going to have a relationship where only you get to tell me what to do? I don't think so. That's for the birds."

Chris didn't speak for a long moment and for a split second Ella thought she might have gone too far. This man wasn't nearly as affable as the Chris she'd known before this evening. He might not appreciate her strange sense of humor anymore.

Then the corners of his lips quirked up in the first smile she'd seen in over two hours.

"Have I been that pissy?"

"Well–No–It's just that…Yes. Yes, you have. It doesn't bother me because you deserve to be mad or whatever it is that you are, but I was just thinking that you probably don't really want to be that way when it's time to get back to work. You can be mad all you want tonight, if you like. It doesn't bother me. Get it all out of your system if you need to. I had a good cry, maybe you need a good yell. Or you could go down to the nearest convenience store or bar and kick somebody's ass. That might make you feel better."

"My last barfight was a long time ago, honey. I'm done with those." He took a deep breath and his tense shoulders visibly relaxed. "I am wound a little too tight. You're right, I'd rather have a clear head. This guy is pissing me off but that's not going to help me find him."

"I know just the thing to help you relax."

"If it's meditation, forget it. I sucked at that during rehab. I can't turn my mind off."

She ran at hand over the surface of the water, still nice and hot.

"I bet a hot bath would relax you."

And it would distract me, which I need right now.

"Is there room?"

Scooching up against the back of the tub, she pointed to the other end. "I think we could make it work. What do you say?"

"I say yes."

Maybe this was exactly what the both of them needed. A temporary diversion. Then back to the sucky reality.

★   ★   ★

SEX DIDN'T SOLVE anything but it didn't make it worse, either. Ella had needed to feel close to Chris, and she'd accomplished that. When his strong arms were around her things didn't seem so bad. They were still bad...but not quite so much. She certainly couldn't say that about any of the other men she'd dated in the past. Heck, a few of them had made things worse.

Wrapping a robe around her, Ella padded into the kitchen on bare feet, Merc on her heels. Chris's friends had laid in a few supplies and she'd seen the bottle of orange juice being placed in the refrigerator. A small glass sounded just about perfect. Would Chris want one? He was still outside talking to the man named Brew who was watching the front of the house. Another man named Ryan was covering the back. Knox had been called away on another assignment at the last minute.

Ella was perusing the snacks they'd brought – cheese and crackers – when a telephone chimed. Both her and Chris's cells were on the kitchen counter and it was his lighting up and making noise. She swiped the phone to accept the call, mostly out of habit. It was only after she'd done it that she questioned whether it was a wise decision. The screen display said it was

Stacey, his ex-wife.

This might be a huge mistake. Damn.

Too late though. She'd answered. She'd apologize to Chris when he came back inside. He'd mentioned earlier that he'd left his ex a message about not being home for a day or two because of the case he was working on.

"Hello. Chris's phone."

There was a small silence that wasn't all that surprising since Stacey was expecting Chris to answer.

"Hi. Is Chris there?"

"He's just outside right now. He won't be long. Would you like me to go get him?"

"No, that's okay. Can he call Annie when he comes inside? She wants to talk to him."

"Absolutely," Ella promised. "I'll give him the message the minute he comes in the house. I can go get him if you like. It's really no trouble."

"No, it's not important. It's the weekend so Annie gets to stay up later." There was another small silence before Stacey continued. "You're Ella, right? Annie mentioned you."

Okay, here we go.

"Yes, I'm Ella. I hope Annie is feeling better these days."

"Much. In fact, you'd never know she was sick at all. She bounces back so quickly. Kids are lucky." Another pause. "You're Chris's new girlfriend."

It wasn't phrased as a question so Ella didn't feel like she needed to answer but somehow her mouth had a mind of its own.

"Yes, I am."

I mean...I hope I am. We never actually discussed titles and such.

"That's great. Just wonderful. Chris is a great guy and he deserves to have someone in his life."

This call was becoming increasingly awkward. Time to bring it to a whimpering end if possible.

Lesson learned. Don't answer Chris's phone. In fact, don't answer anyone else's phone. Ever.

"He is a great guy. I'll be sure to give him your message."

Ella was trying to close it out but Stacey had other ideas.

"I just think that you should know...well...Chris has a drinking problem."

Shit, shit, shit. I do not want to be having this conversation.

"I am aware. Is there any other message that I can give him?" The front door swung open and to her utter relief Chris walked in. "Wait, he's inside now. I'll hand off the phone."

Blowing out a breath, she quickly handed him his phone before he could even ask who it was. "It's Stacey. I answered it. Sorry."

She'd give a better apology when he was done. Grabbing her own phone, juice and a box of crackers, she exited the kitchen and plopped down on the couch, turning on the television while Merc settled himself on the arm. She didn't care what she watched and she turned on the news as usual. One of her colleagues was discussing some road construction and how it was snarling traffic for some commuters.

After a few minutes, Chris came and joined her on the couch. "That was Stacey. Annie wanted to talk to me since she didn't get to stay with me this weekend."

"That's good that you got to talk to her. How did you explain the situation? I assume you don't want to scare her."

"I told her that I wasn't home because of the case. I think that's enough at her age. She says she understands and I think that she does in her way. She's disappointed but I promised her a big movie night with lots of popcorn. I warn you, though…she's going to want to go see something animated with lots of talking animals and maybe a princess."

He wasn't too mad about her answering his phone if he was planning on Ella being there for that big movie night.

"That's okay. I like animated films with talking animals. And I am sorry that I answered your phone. It was just force of habit. Ringing phone. Answer. It was automatic and I shouldn't have done it."

The last words came out in a rush but that's how it was when Ella was embarrassed.

"It's fine," Chris assured her, wrapping an arm around her shoulders and pulling her closer. "It's no big deal. You can answer my phone anytime. I don't have any deep dark secrets that I'm hiding."

He wouldn't. He was an open book which she adored. She'd been with men that would have been angry as hell for what she'd done.

"I'm still sorry. I shouldn't have done it."

Boy, should I not have done it.

"You worry too much. It's okay. Now are you going to share those crackers?"

The answer to that would be yes. Being stuck in a safe house kind of sucked but being stuck with Chris? That wasn't so bad. She could get used to having him around all the time.

Even after they caught a killer. Whoever he might be.

CHAPTER THIRTY

T HE NEXT MORNING everyone was crammed into the living
room to review the case. Logan and Reed had picked up
breakfast on the way and everyone was digging in as Jason leaned
a large white board against the back of a chair. He'd made a
diagram with Kelly Perkins at the center of a circle, surrounded
by two circles of suspects.

Chris wasn't surprised to see Knox, Ryan, Brew, Logan, and
Reed, but he hadn't been expecting Jason to show up. Jared was
conferenced in on the phone. Even Ella seemed impressed by the
large gathering of support.

Logan tapped the white board, bringing the meeting to order. "It's time to go back to the beginning and review what we
know and what we don't know so we can have a plan as to how
to move forward. Clearly, we've shaken someone up with the
investigation which leads us to believe that the killer is someone
Chris has already spoken to. But who is it? Let's start at the
beginning. Chris, do you want to begin?"

Taking a sip of his coffee, Chris nodded and then stood,
standing by the white board. He pointed to Kelly in the middle.

"We now know that our Jane Doe is Kelly Perkins. We were able to confirm that by matching the clothes that were found at the dump site with the clothes in a photo of Kelly. We also know that Kelly had a substance abuse problem and also had a police record for possession and prostitution."

Chris didn't mention that Ella was Kelly's daughter. That wasn't part of this case and it was no one's business but her own.

"We have several possible suspects," Chris went on. "Some less probable than the others, such as Robert Trask, Connie Chastain, Allen Maxwell, and Sheri Martindale."

"I'm not sure about Trask," Knox interjected. "He found the body and that makes me automatically suspicious of him, even though he doesn't seem to have any connection to Kelly."

"That we can find," Logan replied. "Do we feel like we've really dug into his past?"

Jared's voice piped up from the phone. "I can keep looking but I think I've dug all the skeletons out of his closets, drawers, and cupboards. But just because we can't find a connection doesn't mean there isn't one."

"What about this Sheri Martindale?" Brew asked. "Wasn't she one of the last people to see Kelly alive?"

"She was," Chris confirmed. "So was Kelly's boyfriend, Connie, and Maxwell. But Sheri doesn't have any discernible motive. She also seemed to be unaware of the extent of Kelly's issues."

"The boyfriend said Kelly was playing a role," Ella said. "Do you think Sheri knew? She didn't act like it."

"It's hard to tell," Chris said. "She seemed sincere. But even if she wasn't, I'm not leaning toward a female killer. Whoever did this needed to have a great deal of upper body strength. They moved a dead body and that's not easy. Sheri didn't look like she was capable of that even when she was younger."

"She could have had help," Ella replied.

"That's true, but who? One of our other suspects or someone we don't even know about?"

"That leaves Connie Chastain and Allan Maxwell on the list of low probability suspects," Logan said. "What is your gut telling you about them?"

A question that Chris had been asking himself. He didn't like committing himself but if he had to...

"I don't think either of them are who we're looking for."

Jason pointed to the inner ring on the circle. "Then let's look at the higher probability suspect. Steve Adams. He's got a rap sheet but nothing violent."

Ryan shook his head. "One would think that if he had a murder problem that he'd at least have a battery charge or something."

"He did knock Kelly around," Chris pointed out. "So we know that he can be violent."

Reed, who had been quiet up until now, finally spoke. "Statistics say that the most dangerous person in a woman's life is the man in her life. That would be Steve. We would negligent if we didn't take a much closer look at him. He had the means and opportunity. Did he have the motive?"

"Maybe Kelly wanted to leave him," Chris suggested. "That might have set him off."

"But why?" Ella countered. "She'd left before but always came back. At least that's what Connie Chastain told us. If she was right, why would this time be any different?"

"It could have been an accident. They were arguing, it got a little heated. Maybe she threw something at him or called him a name. He takes a swing and next thing he knows, she's dead. He panics and dumps the body. Pretends that she's left town when somebody asks where she is. Hell, after all these years he might even believe his own story, especially if it all happened when he was high or drunk."

Knox didn't look convinced. "Other people had means and opportunity, not just Steve."

"Okay, what was their motive?" Brew asked. "And would it be any better than the boyfriend's?"

"Motive doesn't have degrees," Jason pointed out. "If the killer thinks their motive is good enough, it doesn't matter what we think of it. People have been murdered over a pack of smokes. But I do agree with the question – what are the motives of these other people? Did any of them have issues with our victim?"

"Not that we know of," Ella answered. "But we only have their stories. Kelly doesn't have a voice here."

"We only know she had issues with Adams," Chris said. "We can only take her friends' word for it."

"She might have had issues with the father of her child,"

Brew pointed out. "She'd pretty much left him holding the bag when it came to parenting. He might not have been too happy with her."

Ryan shook his head. "But if he killed her that's not going to help his situation. He's still going to be a single parent, only now there's never any chance that Kelly is going to step up and be a decent mother."

Chris took a quick glance at Ella but she seemed unfazed by the discussion of her parents. He had a feeling thought that later she might have a reaction when everyone else wasn't around. She'd been holding it all in too long.

"Maybe he was jealous of Steve," Knox suggested. "Maybe he was tired of seeing Steve beat on Kelly."

"Then he would have killed Steve," Chris said. "Once again he doesn't benefit from Kelly's demise."

"So who does benefit from Kelly Perkins' death?" Logan asked. "Who has something to gain?"

"Steve," Knox replied. "And maybe Alan Maxwell. If he tried something on with Kelly and she told him no, he might have been holding a grudge no matter what he says all these years later."

"What about Connie Chastain?" Ryan suggested. "She said they all partied together and that everyone really loved Kelly. There might have been some jealousy there."

Ella was frowning and shaking her head. "Not all women are competitive with each other. That's just what men want to think. We don't have any reason to suspect her other than she was one of the last to see Kelly alive."

"We're just being thorough," Chris said. "We have to consider every angle no matter how far-fetched. I'm leaning toward Steve Adams but his lack of a violent history bugs me. I'm going to talk to him again today, lean on him a little more this time. Maybe he'll slip up and contradict himself."

Ella pointed to the outer circle. "Have we ruled all of them out then?"

The room was quiet, no one willing to speak up. Eventually, Chris had to reply.

"I don't think we can rule anyone out at this point except maybe Wallace Wade, the detective on the case. I'm fairly certain he didn't do it. I do think we need to talk to Sheri Martindale again, though. Her story veered hard from everyone else's. She deserves a second look."

Reed nodded in agreement. "Then we all know what we need to do. Knox and Ryan are going to follow Ella today. Logan and Chris are going to talk to Steve Adams. Jared and I are going to try and dig up some more information regarding the others on the outer circle. Any questions? Then let's get going."

Chris couldn't wait to talk to Steve Adams and get some answers. That man wouldn't fool him twice.

★ ★ ★

STEVE ADAMS GREETED Chris and Logan happily when they showed up at his door, gratefully accepting the box of photos back. He had no idea what Chris was about to ask him about so ignorance was indeed bliss.

They all sat in Steve's living room, their host opening the box and perusing the pictures with a misty smile on his face.

"They're all there," Chris assured him after introducing Logan. "I was very careful when I made copies. Thank you again for letting me borrow those."

"If it helps find who killed Kelly than I'm glad to do it." Steve placed the lid back on the box and set it on the table next to him. "Thank you for bringing them back."

Taking a quick glance at Logan who was content to let Chris lead on this, he plunged into their real purpose for being there.

"Steve, there are a few more questions we'd like to ask you. We talked to your boss Allan Maxwell and also to one of the other waitresses in the bar, Connie Chastain. They both told us that you and Kelly argued a lot and that sometimes it would get physical. Kelly would have bruises the next day. Why don't you tell us about that?"

The color drained from Steve's face and his entire body seemed to curl in on itself, his shoulders hunching and his head hanging low. At least he wasn't proud of his actions.

"It–It wasn't what you think."

"Then tell us how it was."

His voice was so low they could barely hear him. "It was the drugs."

"What?" Logan said, leaning forward. "I'm afraid I didn't hear that."

Steve looked up finally, his eyes shiny with moisture. "It was the drugs."

"They made you do it?" Chris asked, not believing that in the least.

"No." Steve shook his head and took a moment before continuing. "It wasn't like that. It was…It was like the drugs made me a different person. An angry person."

"And when you say drugs, you mean…?"

"Coke," Steve admitted in a small voice. "It made me do things I'm ashamed of now."

Having been in rehab, Chris was well aware of what cocaine could do via the people in his group therapy sessions. Paranoia, anger, and edginess. And that was just for starters. It did make people do things they weren't proud of…but did it make them killers? He didn't know the answer to that question but somehow he doubted it. The rate of murder was a hell of a lot lower than the rate of drug addiction.

"What are some of those things?"

Shrugging, Steve gazed down at his hands, the knuckles white as he wrung them together.

"I'd get mad. Kelly would leave and that would make me even more angry."

"What did you get mad about?"

"Kelly was real pretty and she was always flirting with the customers. And these guys would just eat it all up, you know? That's how she got big tips."

"Let me guess. Sometimes you thought she took it too far?"

"When we would break up, she would go out with them," he

replied defensively, his brow furrowed.

"And she belonged to you, right? She shouldn't be doing that."

A flash of anger crossed Steve's features before he could control it. "I was jealous, man. Really jealous. I loved Kelly."

Revulsion filled Chris's gut but he needed to keep his emotions under control. He was letting his personal feelings show too much.

"When you got jealous, and you argued, is that when you would knock her around? Is that when she would leave for awhile?"

Steve was staring at the floor again, not answering.

"Did you ever get mad enough to kill her, Steve? Did you ever threaten that she would regret leaving you?"

His head shot up and Steve's eyes went round. "Fuck, no. No way. I would never hurt her."

"But you did hurt her," Chris pointed out. "You said you didn't have any control when you were high. So maybe it was all an accident. You were arguing. It got heated. You hit her and maybe she fell. Maybe she hit the back of her head and you panicked. You didn't have any premeditation to kill her. It was just a tragic accident."

The other man was shaking his head, tears spilling down his cheeks now. "No, that's not it at all. I loved Kelly. I wouldn't do that. I would never do that. She was alive the last time I saw her. Things were good then and we weren't fighting or nothing."

"But she was with other guys," Chris pressed. "Whenever she

left you she went out with them."

"Arrogant fucks," Steve muttered under his breath. "A bunch of assholes who thought they were so cool. They'd come into the bar at the end of the day and boast about what they'd done. Hell, half of them didn't do all the shit they said they did."

"What did they do? Were they cops?"

"Journalists. Reporters," Steve said. "And the way they bragged, you would think they were a god or something. They talked about getting the dirt on local politicians or sports stars or maybe they saved a little kid that had fallen down a well. I couldn't stand those guys."

"Journalists," Chris repeated, his mind going a mile a minute but he couldn't quite put his finger on what his brain was trying to tell him. "The bar you worked at…that's where the newspaper guys hung out?"

"Yeah, the newspaper offices were only a block or two away."

"And Kelly flirted with them? Right in front of you? That must have made you mad."

"I told you. I didn't kill her." Steve had his head in his hands, wiping his nose on his sleeve. "I didn't do it. I loved her."

Chris looked at Steve, then at Logan, then back at Steve.

"You know what? I believe you."

But if Steve wasn't guilty, then who was?

CHAPTER THIRTY-ONE

ELLA STUCK HER head into Galen's office. As usual it was a mess – papers, books, and folders piled high on every flat surface. He was currently combing through the files in the cabinet behind his desk.

"Do you have a minute?"

He grunted and then beckoned her to enter. "I can give you three but then I have a meeting. What do you need?"

"I was hoping you could sign off on some of Lujack's time to help me research the case we spoke about."

Her boss was extremely protective of his head researcher's time, especially if it wasn't a priority story. If Galen said no, then Ella was going to have an issue. She didn't want to have to ask Chris to use his job to help her. She wanted to do this on her own.

Barely registering her request, Galen grunted again which was a good sign. If he was going to say no then he would have said it already.

"That's fine. Are you also working on that profile? I'd like that for the Politics Monday segment."

She and Galen had also discussed her doing a personal profile on one of the candidates for mayor.

"Yes, I have a sit down interview with him scheduled for late this afternoon."

"Good," he replied, his head still buried in the drawer.

With any luck, she could duck out of here and he wouldn't even remember she'd visited.

"Thank you," she said hurriedly, turning to exit, but her heel got caught on one of the chair legs and for a moment she was unsteady on her feet. She caught herself at the last minute but somehow her flailing arm had caught a stack of books and they cascaded to the floor with a loud thud.

Shit. Graceful, I am not.

"Sorry," she said, immediately kneeling down to pick them up. "So sorry. I've got them."

This time instead of a grunt, Galen sighed and scraped his fingers through his hair. "Don't worry about it. I really need to clean this place up one of these days."

He'd said that before the last time someone had knocked over a pile on his desk.

She placed a couple of books back on the desk and reached down for a few more, now eye level with the credenza where Galen kept his souvenirs. She had a close up view of his Mickey Mantle autographed baseball and his trophy from when he was captain of another station's bowling team.

That's when she saw it. Hanging from the golden arm of that bowler.

An earring. A long gold earring that looked a hell of a lot like the one Kelly Perkins was wearing the night she went missing. Ella had seen several of the photos. She'd even seen the ones that Chris had blown up to get a detailed look at the earring.

It might not be the same one. What are the chances?

Okay, then why does Galen have an earring among his souvenirs?

Maybe it belongs to him?

He wrote that article all those years ago.

That doesn't mean anything.

But it might…

Ella pasted a smile on her face and chuckled at nothing in particular. She didn't want her boss to know that she'd seen the earring. She needed to get out of this office and call Chris. This might mean nothing but it might mean something. With any luck, Steve Adams had confessed to the murder and this piece of jewelry in Galen's office was simply a strange coincidence.

Chris didn't like coincidences, though.

"Here you go," she said in a sing-song voice. She placed the final two books back on the desk and stood, backing toward the door. Her heart was beating so loudly she was shocked he couldn't heart it. "I better get to work. Thanks again."

Ella exited the office and walked swiftly down the hall, not wanting to run because that would look strange but definitely wanting to put some distance between herself and Galen. Sinking gratefully down into her chair, she breathed a sigh of relief and then reached for her phone to call Chris. She needed to speak with him right away.

Before her fingers closed around it another, larger hand wrapped firmly around her wrist.

"I can't let you do that."

Galen.

Now what?

★　★　★

"I DON'T KNOW why my story doesn't sound like everyone else's, but I'm telling the truth."

Sheri Martindale's cheeks were a bright pink and her brown eyes sparkled with anger. She was defending her version of Kelly's story and was not happy about being questioned about it.

"You're saying that you didn't know about Kelly's substance abuse issues?"

"She dabbled when we'd go out and party. I'd hardly call it abuse."

There were no signs of subterfuge on Sheri. She appeared to truly believe what she was saying. Adams may have hit the nail on the head – Kelly had played a role for her friend.

Chris wasn't thrilled about having to tear down Sheri's memories but he needed to make sure she was telling everything she knew. All of it. Not just the whitewashed parts.

"Did you know that Kelly was arrested for prostitution?"

Clearly no. Sheri's eyes were wide and her mouth hung open in shock before shaking her head vehemently. "No. That's not true. Kelly wouldn't do something like that."

"Are you sure? Because she has an arrest record, Sheri."

"Then it was a mistake," the older woman said, her lips a mutinous line. "Some sort of misunderstanding. Kelly simply wasn't the type."

"Who would be the type?"

"I know what you're trying to do," Sheri said, her finger wagging in front of Chris's nose. "You're trying to trip me up but I'm not going to fall for it. I knew Kelly. She had issues but nothing like that. It was all just a misunderstanding, I'm sure."

"How might that have been a...misunderstanding?"

Sheri shrugged. "She had a lot of boyfriends. Some of them had money. Maybe he thought she was asking him for money but she was asking him to buy her dinner or something."

That was an alternate explanation. Not a good one, but Sheri seemed pleased with it if her expression was anything to go by. She was smiling now, a look of triumph in her eyes.

"That's a possibility, of course. You're not the first that said Kelly had a lot of men in her life."

Sheri snorted. "There were a bunch of men that wanted to be in her life but she wouldn't give them the time of day. She was picky about who she went out with. She turned down plenty of guys, especially at that bar she worked at."

Now they were on to something...

"Did she turn down her boss Allan Maxwell? Did he ask her out?"

"Kelly said that he'd get grabby but he wasn't any sort of threat. She thought he was funny but I don't remember her ever saying that he'd asked her out. It was the customers that were the problem."

"Anyone in particular?"

Once again Sheri shrugged. "I'm not sure. If she mentioned a name I don't remember it. I just remember her saying that she was always turning down the customers that asked her out."

With a nudge from Logan, Chris wrapped up his questions, thanking Sheri Martindale for meeting with them again. When they climbed into their vehicle and drove away, Logan finally spoke.

"There was no point in continuing that. We weren't getting anywhere. If she's lying she sure as hell believes what she's saying."

"I agree but it's damn frustrating. Do you think we should ask Maxwell about any customer that Kelly might have been having trouble with?"

"We could but if we haven't talked to them already then they wouldn't trying to scare you and Ella off of the case."

True. Shit.

Just a minute. Just one damn minute.

His heart pumping faster, Chris slammed on the brakes and pulled into a fast food parking lot. He pulled out his phone to call Ella.

"That's not exactly true. Everyone at the station knows that she's working with me on this case. And they're all journalists. Maybe one of them worked at the newspaper thirty years ago. She could be working with a killer."

"She's got two bodyguards on her, Chris. Relax. She's going to be fine," Logan assured him, his voice encouraging. "We're not going to let anybody hurt her."

Throwing down his phone, Chris put the car in drive and roared out of the parking lot. If he put his foot to the floor and hit all the lights green, he could be at the station in thirty minutes, forty-five if there was traffic.

"She didn't answer," Chris said. "And she always answers. This isn't good."

"Knox is there. I'll call him and Ryan. Tell them to get inside the station right now."

Yes, Knox was there. And Chris was going to have to trust that his former friend had his – and Ella's – back.

CHAPTER THIRTY-TWO

HER ENTIRE LIFE Ella had never been good in a crisis situation. She was, however, in the crisis of her life and she'd better improve fast.

When Galen's hand had wrapped around her wrist her heart had jumped into her throat, making it almost impossible to breathe. Somehow she'd managed to squeak out that she had no idea what he was talking about but clearly he didn't believe her. That's why he was dragging her down the hall back to his office with a gun discreetly pressed into her ribcage, urging her forward.

He'd said they were going to talk, but he didn't need a gun to do that.

Ella desperately hoped that talking was all he was planning to do. She hadn't had a chance to call Chris and although Knox and Ryan were outside, their main goal was to make sure no one dangerous got *into* the building. She'd assured them this morning that the station was secure. No one could get in without an electronic badge. They had, of course, let her know that those little card readers weren't exactly a perfect security system. At no time had she thought that she'd need to be worried about the people *inside* the station.

"Don't make a scene," he hissed into her ear, his hand like steel around her arm. She was going to have a nasty bruise from pulling against his grip. "If we see someone, just act natural."

The great thing about a news station was that there was always someone around twenty-four hours a day. The terrible thing was that most of those people were distracted with their own work and barely paying any attention.

Where is everyone anyway? Did they all go get coffee at the same time?

"If I see someone, I'm going to scream so loudly they'll hear me in Boca Raton."

"I wouldn't do that if I were you."

Or what? What will you do?

She didn't ask the question out loud, however, because she wasn't sure she truly wanted the answer. Her brain had already made up several scenarios and none of them were all that great. She tried to remember what she'd been taught back in college when she and a few friends had taken a self-defense course. Something about kneeing him in the groin... First chance, she was going to try that.

If her brain cooperated. Like when that car was barreling toward them, her mind was saying one thing but her limbs weren't listening. If he dropped her arm now she wasn't even sure she could run for safety.

"I don't want to have to hurt you."

"You don't have to do this," Ella said, sweat beginning to roll down her back, her blouse sticking to her skin. "I don't know anything. Not really."

If she was falling apart, Galen didn't look much better. Beads of moisture had popped out on his forehead and his skin looked ashen and pale. His breathing was fast and his pupils were dilated, maybe from excitement or fear.

"You know enough," he growled. He started to turn left toward his office but he heard voices and quickly pushed her to the right, his head swiveling back and forth trying to see a safe exit. Except that the front and back exits to the building weren't anywhere near here.

Ella opened her mouth to scream but his hand clamped over her face before pushing her through a doorway and into the stairwell.

"Shut the fuck up," he growled, his fingers still covering her mouth. His right hand pushed the gun painfully into her ribs, reminding her that she was a split second from death. Technically, she was free but running was a terrible idea. He'd shoot her in the back while trying to get away. "Don't say a word."

More voices this time from a few flights below them had Galen propelling her up the stairs. Stumbling on her high heels, she swiftly and silently ran through possible escape routes but none seemed like a decent option. If she ran, he'd shoot. If she tried to wrestle the gun away, he'd win as he was much stronger. The third one had the least amount of downside.

Talking to him.

Galen might still kill her but at least she'd go down trying to save her own life. A few tears escaped and ran down her sweaty cheeks as she thought of her parents' grief if she died. She'd never made complete peace with them since finding out they'd lied. Frankly, at this moment what they'd done barely mattered. In the big scheme of life. It was a blip on the screen and it didn't affect her love for them one iota.

And Chris.

If she were honest with herself – and she had no reason to lie when facing death – she'd fallen in love with his old-fashioned manners and laidback attitude. He could be intense when he needed to be but for the most part he was like night and day compared to the other men she'd dated in the past. He was kind, caring, and passionate as hell. He was a good father and a strong man who didn't have to act like a macho jerk to gain respect. Funny how life had brought him to her exactly when she'd needed him.

Wait...I don't want to die.

Galen had dragged her all the way to the roof, pushing the door open with his shoulder so hard the door flew back and slammed into the wall with a loud bang that rang in her ears. Daylight flooded her field of vision and she had to squint as he shoved her forward. She fell to her knees on the hard concrete, the sting of the scrapes on her flesh a sharp reminder that she was still alive. She still had a chance.

Talk to him.

"You don't want to do this, Galen. It's not going to make

anything better."

The gusty wind swirled around her, whipping her hair against her skin and carrying her words far away.

"I can't go to jail. It was an accident."

Ella froze, his statement burrowing a hole into her brain. Galen had *done* it. He'd just admitted it out loud as she lay on the ground, his gun trained on her face. He was an admitted murderer and she was directly in his path to freedom.

This is so very bad. What do I do?

Talk. Delay. Give someone a chance to find out that all is not well.

"Of course, it was an accident. You didn't mean to do it."

"I loved Kelly. She was everything to me."

Galen had loved Kelly? How had he even known her?

"Of course, you loved her," Ella said, her gaze darting to the open door to the stairwell and measuring if she could make it before he caught or shot her. It looked a mile away but was probably less than ten feet. "You wouldn't hurt her on purpose."

"I would never hurt her," Galen replied, his voice thin and weak. His hand shook where he was pointing the gun at her and Ella shrank back slightly, not wanting to be the victim of an accidental discharge. That run for freedom was looking pretty good. She couldn't allow herself to be gunned down like a rabbit in the crosshairs. "We fought and it was an accident."

Keep him talking.

"How did you meet Kelly?"

He frowned as if he didn't understand the question. Finally

he shook his head, wiping his sweaty brow with his free hand. "She was a waitress at the bar we all frequented after work."

"And you fell in love?"

"We loved each other. We argued that day. We were both angry and she hit me. I shoved her away from me and she fell and hit her head. I just panicked. I didn't know what to do."

His voice had risen a full octave by the time he'd finished the story, and that hand was shaking even more. He was falling apart right in front of her. She had to keep calm and think.

Think.

Another gust of wind blew her hair in front of her eyes but she was afraid to even lift her hand to brush it away. Any little movement might set him off. "That's very normal. Panicking is normal. I would have done that, too. People will understand when you explain it. No one will blame you."

She was lying through her teeth but she needed to keep him from going off the deep end and possibly taking her with him.

Galen shook his head, sweat flying into the air. "They will blame me. They'll blame me and put me in jail. I can't go to jail."

Her gaze darted around the roof of the building. He'd effectively cornered himself trying to get away from the others in the station.

"You have to explain it. You can't run anymore. The truth needs to come out."

Apparently, that was the wrong thing to say because he growled and lifted the gun a little higher so it was pointing at her forehead. He glanced over his shoulder and then back at her. "I can run. The station's helicopter is up here."

That was true. It was parked in its usual spot in the middle of a large red circle on the roof. The traffic guy was at lunch.

"Do you even know how to fly a helicopter? You'll get yourself killed. Just talk to Chris. I'm sure he can help them understand what happened. It will all be okay."

She was assuming that Galen couldn't pilot a plane or helicopter. If he could, she had a gut feeling he would have already climbed into it and flown off. What was he delaying for if that was an option?

"It won't be okay. I won't go to jail."

Ever so slowly so as not to spook him, Ella sat up. She didn't try and stand yet... Nope, he wasn't ready for that much movement but it felt better not to be sprawled on the pavement with the wind up her skirt.

She reached out a hand ever so slowly, palm up, and tried to give him her best encouraging smile. Blood roared in her ears and it seemed like the entire world had stopped spinning. Her whole life had come down to this place and time.

"I'll explain everything to them. But you're going to have to give me the gun, Galen. It won't look good if you have a gun pointed at me. They might not understand."

Indecision crossed his features and for a small moment Ella thought he might just hand her the gun but then he took a step back, his grim expression carved in stone.

"I won't go to jail. I'd rather die. I should have died with

Kelly."

With a leap, he jumped on the edge of the building, his swaying body silhouetted against the gray sky. Ella must have cried out because she heard a scream but she wasn't cognizant of actually making the sound. Her hand was still out in offering but he was nowhere near to taking it.

"I'll jump," Galen warned, the gun trained on Ella. "I'll shoot you and then I'll jump."

Fuck. Shit. Dammit.

Ella didn't have the vocabulary for all the curse words she wanted to yell. Her heart was beating madly against her ribs and her breathing was ragged, but that little voice inside of her was saying not to show fear. Be calm and controlled. Keep him talking. The Galen she'd come to know wasn't the type to jump off the top of a building.

"If you shoot me there will be no one to tell your story. And if you jump…well, that's a terrible way to die. You don't want to die that way."

I don't want to die that way, either.

"You look so much like her," he said in an anguished tone. "I thought having you around would make me feel better but it didn't work. You only reminded me of what I'd done. I should have fired you but I couldn't do it."

So he'd ignored her, giving her the worst assignments at the station. It made sense now as much as anything could make sense in this insane situation.

Another gust of wind and Galen wavered, his arms outstretched to balance him, one hand still clutching the gun and brandishing it in front of her.

"You're the one that broke into my apartment. You tried to run me and Chris down last night."

"I was trying to scare you off. You should have left all of this alone. No one cared until that cop came along."

"Galen, please put the gun down. You don't want it to go off accidentally. You don't want another accident."

"I don't want to hurt you. I wanted you to leave it alone."

Pressing a hand to her frantically beating heart, she took a slow breath. He was actually listening to her. A good sign.

"Then please, for the love of God, put the gun down."

It looked like he took a deep breath as well as he turned to stare at the gun, scowling as if he was noticing it for the first time.

He's going to put it down. He's going to do it.

Sirens. Ella could hear them in the distance growing ever closer. Someone in a neighboring building must have seen him on the edge of the roof with a gun and called the police.

She didn't want to die, and she wasn't going to go down without a fight.

As Galen's attention was drawn to the sirens, he turned away from Ella, his arm unconsciously dropping to his side. She only had a moment and for once – when it most counted – her arms and legs obeyed her brain. Pushing up with the palms of her hands, she took off at a dead run for that open doorway, high heels be damned. She'd either make it or be shot in the back but she wasn't going to stay to be shot in the head by a clearly disturbed individual.

It was the longest ten feet of her life and there was no guarantee she was going to make it.

CHAPTER THIRTY-THREE

C HRIS AND LOGAN had leap-frogged the badge reader at the entrance to the station, setting off a chase by the portly security guard but Logan quickly recruited the man to their side, explaining that it was an emergency and that he should call the police. There was a man standing on the edge of the roof brandishing a weapon. Luckily, they hadn't seen Ella.

With Knox and Ryan stationed at the exits, Chris and Logan headed straight for Ella's office, following the guard's directions. She wasn't there which had Chris reminding himself of his training. Don't make this personal. It was an emergency situation and he needed to be in control.

It could also be Ella's life.

"Let's go up and take a look," Logan said, already leading the way to look for the stairwell. "She's probably fine and sitting in a meeting completely unaware of the drama."

Except that both Knox and Ryan said she hadn't left the building. Which meant she was here…somewhere. A crowd was beginning to gather on the sidewalk, all heads turned up to the roof, and she wasn't among them.

Chris didn't know who the man was but it wasn't a good situation. Hopefully, Ella was far away from it all and it was a giant coincidence that it was happening.

I don't really believe in coincidences.

"The cops aren't going to thank us for this," Chris observed as they sprinted up the flights of stairs. Damn, he needed to exercise more. Logan didn't even look winded and he was older. What the fuck?

"You're right," Logan agreed, finally seeming to breathe heavy. "Jason will have to smooth it all out over at city hall. We're just going to take a peek at what is happening on that roof. If Ella isn't there, we'll retreat and leave it to the cops."

But if she was...

Chris was scared. He didn't want to lose this woman he had just found. He was...

Shit...he was in love. Not for the first time but this felt so much different. So much more...more. It was more of every-thing, and it felt like there was even more to come in the future.

That was it... It felt like it had a future. He hadn't planned on Ella and this might not have been the perfect time in his life, but when the perfect woman knocks on the door a smart guy doesn't slam it into her face. He just opens it and lets her in.

Speaking of open doors, the door to the roof was wide open and just as Logan and Chris made it to the top of the stairs, Ella flew through it and straight into Chris's arms. She was visibly shaking, her face pale and tearstained.

"Easy, honey," he said quietly, his heart squeezed painfully in his chest. He wrapped his arms tightly around her, lifting her up and placing her on the top step. He sat down beside her, not able to let her go, needing the feel of her against him. It wasn't a mirage. She was alive. "Easy."

The words were as much for him as Ella. His own hands were trembling with the power of his emotions and suddenly what his own father had gone through with Maddie became all too clear. Chris would have covered her body with his own to protect her. Her pain was his pain. Her fear was his as well.

"We have to talk him down," she finally said, pulling away and looking up at him, her mascara running down her face. She'd never looked more beautiful to him. "We can't let him jump."

Before he could stop her, she pulled out of his arms and crawled back to the doorway. She didn't step through it, simply staying there. Immediately, both Logan and Chris instinctively placed their bodies between her and the man.

"Galen," she called out, elbowing her way between them so she could look out. "Don't do this. Well talk to the police. We'll make them understand."

The man – who Chris now knew was her boss Galen – shook his head, his short hair ruffled by the wind gusts. His position appeared to be rather precarious on that edge and Chris was already eyeing the distance between them, wondering if he could cross and pull the man down before he did something tragic.

"They won't understand." The man looked down to where the crowd and police were gathered. "I won't go to jail."

"He says it was an accident," Ella said softly. "He loved her."

If Chris had a dime for every time some guy had said it was an accident and that he wasn't guilty he wouldn't have to work for the rest of his life. He'd be lying on a beach listening to the waves, but Ella had a soft heart.

Not me. I'm a cynical asshole.

But it might be the truth. Either way, this guy jumping wasn't going to solve anything or answer their questions. He wouldn't face the justice system.

"Tell him we'll hear him out," Chris whispered, keeping his arm around her waist so she couldn't suddenly bolt out from behind him. "That we want to hear the whole story."

"They'll hear you out," Ella said to Galen loudly over the wind. Another gust had come up, making the man sway on his feet and placing Chris's heart into overdrive. "They want to hear what happened. Don't do this, Galen. You have so much to offer people. You've given so much and helped so many."

The man's arm holding the gun dropped to his side, his head hanging down. What Ella was saying was having a visible effect.

"Keep it up. He's hearing you."

"Kelly wouldn't want this," Ella said urgently. "She wouldn't want you to jump. Think about her. Think about the good times between you. Think about how much you loved each other."

The man's shoulders were shaking now, his body wracked with sobs. The gun fell to the concrete as he buried his face in both of his hands. Chris didn't hesitate. Shooting across the roof, he grabbed Ella's boss and pulled him down. The man gave no resistance, simply falling to the ground and crying, his body curled into the fetal position. Chris kicked away the firearm.

"I loved her so much," Galen said, his words barely audible and choked. "She was everything to me."

Chris's gaze went to where Logan was standing with Ella, her own eyes filled with tears. This entire investigation had been hard on her but she'd never given in or up. She was strong and amazing and for some reason she was looking like she might feel the same about him.

"I know exactly what you mean, buddy," Chris said, kneeling down to help the sobbing man to his feet.

Love was a powerful force. It could make a person happy, sad, joyous, or miserable. It could bring a grown man to his knees or make him a king.

It could also make him a murderer. Time to find out what this man had to say for himself. This part was over but the story was only beginning. Did he kill Kelly in cold blood? Would there be justice for her after all of these years?

They were finally one step closer to getting some answers.

JUGGLING THE BAGS of takeout, Ella fiddled with her jangling keys, trying to find the right one. Before she could locate it the door swung open, revealing a smiling Chris with his arms wide open. He relieved her of the bags and carried them inside his apartment, placing them on the counter before turning back to give her a big hug and nicely delicious kiss.

"Not bad, cowboy," Ella teased, pressing her hands to his chest. She could feel the reassuring thud of his heart under her palms. "Are you only glad to see me because I'm bearing food?"

"It does help," he admitted. "I just got out of the shower and was planning to order us something but this is even better. I'm starved."

Ella slung her purse over the back of a chair and gratefully kicked off her shoes. "I am, too. I missed lunch because of that six car pileup on the highway. Luckily no one died."

Merc zigzagged between her legs, wanting attention so she leaned down to give him a scratch on the head. "And hello to you, too. Were you a good boy today?"

"He didn't rip up the couch so I think the answer is yes. He's taking a liking to my recliner, though. He was lying in it when I got home from work."

She shrugged off her jacket while Chris pulled two plates from the cabinet.

"The work on the apartment will be done by the end of next week. Me and Marc will be out of here before you know it."

He leaned down and brushed her lips with his own. "You don't need to be in any hurry. I kind of like having you around. Annie does, too."

Explaining Ella's presence wasn't half as bad for Chris as she'd thought it might be. He'd kept it simple, but it wouldn't have mattered anyway. Annie was thrilled to have another female in the house along with a cat. Chris and Ella had had to make sure she understood the feline was on loan temporarily.

"You like it when I'm here because I help with the dishes."

"That is a plus." He dished up their food before putting their plates on the table. "Logan heard from the prosecuting attorney today."

Her body tensed and she had to force herself to breathe and relax. It had been over a week since that day and there hadn't been much information trickling out of the District Attorney's office. Galen had been arrested, and they were building a case against him.

Sitting down, she picked up her fork but didn't start to eat. "And?"

Chris sat down opposite and reached across to place his hand over hers. If anyone was aware of how difficult all of this was for her, it was him. He'd held her that first night when she'd cried and cried. Once the drama was all over her emotions had been everywhere. He'd encouraged her to see a therapist to deal with it all and she had an appointment next week. This wasn't something that she could cry about and it would all be better. She had a bunch of shit to deal with and it went deep. Her parents were on board with it as well. Of course, they were just glad that she was alive. They would have cheered any decision she made.

"They talked to Allan Maxwell, Steve Adams, and Connie. They both swear that Kelly was never in love or had any sort of relationship with Galen. They did say that he seemed overly fond of her and he only wanted her to wait on him, he'd leave her big tips, and a lot of other semi-creepy stuff like giving her a card on Valentine's Day. They said she had no interest in him but he was persistent. He didn't give up until she disappeared."

"But he said...they loved each other."

He'd sounded so sincere.

"After all of these years he's probably convinced himself that they had a real relationship. But from what the people around her said, she wasn't part of it. He was in it by himself. Him and his obsession."

Ewww. That was...creepy as hell.

"That's disturbing."

"He has admitted to the police that they argued. He said it was because she wouldn't leave Adams and in a way I believe him. He probably did try and convince her to leave him but she wouldn't. He became enraged and they fought physically. He said she fell and the current coroner says that the skull fracture was consistent with that story. She may have fell against a piece of furniture or a curb. They're planning to charge him with manslaughter. They think they can prove that. Of course, he might plead out."

"He told the truth as he knew it."

Chris nodded. "His version of it. Then he panicked, cut off her hands so she couldn't be identified, and dumped her body on the way to work. He was counting on the fact that no one would find her and that no one would go looking for her. He told the detective that he was the only one that truly loved her."

Shuddering, Ella placed her fork next to her plate, her appetite vanished.

"That wasn't true."

"He wanted to believe that it was. He wanted her to be…his and his alone."

It was more a madness than love.

"He never married."

Chris shook his head. "I doubt it was because his love was so true, honey. It was probably because he has an obsessive personality and the women that dated him figured it out before they walked down the aisle. I doubt very much that Kelly is the only woman he's obsessed about in his life. If the cops do some digging, there's probably a long line of them."

Her first thought came tumbling out of her mouth. "But are they alive?"

"Maybe. If it truly was an accident then they hopefully are. Remember what you said before…Kelly isn't here to tell us her side of the story."

That was something that Ella was going to have to come to terms with. Her biological mother would never be able to tell her all her thoughts, dreams, and fears. She'd have to live not knowing any of that.

"And he kept the earring because he missed her?"

"Yes," Chris conceded. "They asked him about that and he said that it kept Kelly in his heart. Then he took the job at the station and he had a daily reminder. He started avoiding you as much as possible but he just couldn't seem to bring himself to fire you."

Sitting back in the chair, Ella slowly blew out a breath. "But he wanted to. That's awesome. Just fantastic. I've been thinking–"

She broke off and picked up her fork, shoving a bite of food in her mouth. This wasn't a subject for now. But Chris wasn't the type to let it go. She should have known that.

"You've been thinking what?" he prompted. "What's going on?"

Sighing, she rubbed at her aching temples. It had been a crappy day. "I've been thinking that maybe being a reporter isn't what I really want to do when I grow up."

"What would you like to do?"

"I don't know," she admitted with another heavy sigh. She'd been sighing too much lately. "It just doesn't feel like how I want to spend my days anymore. I should have gone to law school like my parents suggested."

"Would you be any happier?"

"I don't know," she replied honestly, "I just think I need to shake up my life a little bit. Everything…has changed. I need to change with it."

His expression was serious, his smile vanished. "Do you want to change your mind about me?"

Is that what he thought? Silly man.

Swiftly standing, she shifted so that she was sitting on his lap. "Hell, no. You're the one thing in my life right now that feels solid. And good. Why? Are you thinking that we're moving too fast?"

They had moved kind of quickly. If he was having second thoughts…

"Fuck, no," he said bluntly, his fingers capturing her chin so she had to look into his earnest blue gaze. "I love you, honey. I'm a grown man and I know what I want out of life. I'm not some wishy-washy kid who wants to date around and see what's out there. I know what's out there and that's why I want you. In my life, my bed, my heart, and my future."

She leaned forward and rested her forehead against his and placing her palm on his chest again. She wanted to feel that heartbeat again. There was something about it that centered her and made everything okay.

"For a former cop, you sure sound like a poet."

"I'm a complicated guy."

Giggling, she pressed her lips to his, a tingle running up her spine. "I love you too, by the way."

"I know."

Her brows rose. "Oh, you know, do you? How do you know?"

"Because you wouldn't be here if you didn't."

"You're such a know it all."

"I know that, too."

She ran her finger down his stubbly cheek, rubbing their noses together playfully. "Then you'll know what I want to do after dinner."

His smile was slow and sweet. And a little sexy, too.

"I do, but do we have to wait until after dinner? The food will reheat."

He was right. Food could wait.

She'd been waiting her entire life for that elusive emotion

love, but it was here and she'd grab at it with both hands.

A future with this man sounded pretty damn good.

"I don't want to wait, either. Sweep me off my feet, cow-boy."

Who was she kidding? He already had.

I hope you enjoyed Elusive Identities. Don't miss the next book in the Serials and Stalkers series – Lethal Allure.

Thank you for reading.

Don't miss a thing! Sign up to be notified of Olivia's new releases:

www.oliviajaymes.com/News.html

ABOUT THE AUTHOR

Olivia Jaymes is a wife, mother, lover of sexy romance and cozy mysteries, and caffeine addict. She lives with her husband, son, and two spoiled dogs in central Florida and spends her days typing on her computer with a canine on her lap.

She is currently working on a new cozy mystery series – *A Ravenmist Whodunnit* – in addition to her other ongoing romance series.

Visit Olivia Jaymes at
www.OliviaJaymes.com